SENSELESS

STEEL DEMONS MC BOOK SEVEN

CRYSTAL ASH

To those who never gave up on someone they loved, even if that someone gave up on themselves.

SDMC series playlist

All American Nightmare - Hinder
Notorious - Adelitas Way
Hail to the King - Avenged Sevenfold
O Death - Ashley H
Joan of Arc - In This Moment
Radioactive - Imagine Dragons
Bad Company - Five Finger Death Punch
Love Me to Death - No Resolve
(Don't Fear) The Reaper - HIM
David - Noah Gunderson
Apocalyptic - Halestorm
Blue on Black - Five Finger Death Punch
Machine Gun Blues - Social Distortion
Wanted Dead or Alive - Chris Daughtry
I Get Off - Halestorm
You Shook Me All Night Long - AC/DC
Nobody Praying for Me - Seether
Loyal to No One - Dropkick Murpheys
Crazy in Love - Daniel De Bourg
Be Free - King Dude & Chelsea Wolfe
Raise Hell - Dorothy
Coming Home - Skylar Grey

Listen on Spotify at:
crystalashbooks.com/sdmc-playlist

Prologue

THE BLOOD BAG

NINE YEARS EARLIER

They cut deeply today, so much so that it made me almost grateful that I stopped feeling anything years ago.

Using the corner of my ragged shirt, I wiped at the blood still seeping out of the red line running from my shoulder to halfway down my arm. The cut throbbed, the skin red and angry around it. It would probably get infected, if it wasn't already.

I looked to the far corner of my cage, where my water container sat with a dangerously low amount of liquid. The cut would feel better if I washed it, but that was also my drinking water. It could be another day, maybe more, before they refilled it. This was a predicament I ran into often—drink or wash my blood away.

Cleaning my cuts always seemed like a waste. The concrete floor of my cage was painted with years upon years of my spilled blood. And the cutting would never stop.

The last man who shared the cage with me said I was already dehydrated. Malnourished. Words he had to explain to me because I hadn't encountered them in my reading yet.

He was surprised that I grew so tall after spending my whole life in here. I had no perception of how tall, short, or malnourished I was compared to other people, and didn't know what to tell him.

The man was a doctor, or so he claimed. They were always different, but their occupations and life stories started to blur together after a few years. It was nice to have company in my cage that didn't want to cut me, but it was always brief. The men would spend a couple nights in here with me, a week at the most, before being taken away, never to be seen again.

I used to cry. I had begged, pleaded, and clung to their legs as they dragged the men out. After the first dozen or so, I learned to stop being attached to my temporary companions. The result would always be the same.

"Those women are brainwashed," the doctor had told me, pacing back and forth in our shared cell. "Not mentally ill, most likely, but manipulated. The old woman, the one up in the chair, she's the master manipulator. The cult leader! Now that one's got a whole slew of mental issues, narcissistic personality disorder for damn sure. Oh, and she's a total sociopath, I'd bet my whole practice on it!"

"It doesn't matter," I'd said, watching his pacing feet

scrape a trail through my dried blood on the concrete floor.

"And you." He stabbed a finger in my direction. "You must have a serious case of Stockholm Syndrome, kid. How long have you been in here?"

I'd peered at him from where I sat against the wall. "I've never been anywhere else."

"Oh, Jesus…" He turned back toward the bars, peering around the room beyond the cell as if looking for some way out. "Am I gonna die in here?"

"No." *Not in here, exactly.* I went back to picking the scabs at one of my cuts. "Your stay won't be much longer."

He had been given a hearty meal later that night, a whole roasted chicken with piles of vegetables, rice, and an entire bottle of wine. More food than I ate in a week, usually. I'd learned to stop looking on enviously as they ate their last meal too. It only earned me more bleeding.

"You honor us," the women had told the doctor with their pretty smiles. "Please eat and drink everything. You are our honored guest and will be released tomorrow."

He fell for it. They always did. None of the men placed with me had known hunger and hopelessness for as long as I had. Their lives had given them reasons to hope. They all had something they wanted to return to. Usually a family, children, or some other purpose.

For me, hope was a foreign word. A concept I didn't understand.

The women took him before sunrise the next morning. Hungover, he stumbled out willingly, hesitating only for a moment. "What about him?" he asked with a glance over his shoulder at me.

Sometimes my cellmates asked about me on their way out. Most didn't care.

"He is a prisoner," the woman holding his arm told him. "He hurt one of us, and is being punished for his crimes against us."

I would have laughed if I had known how to.

The doctor was guided out of the dungeon, a woman on each of his arms. All the usual shuffles and thumps as they guided him to the top floor played out like clockwork. The first ray of sunlight poured through the crack in my wall as I passively listened to the monthly ceremony above my cell. Just one more out of so many hundreds of times I heard it before.

"Let me go! What—what's that for?" I heard the doctor ask over the scuffling as he tried to struggle. "Why do you have a knife?"

"You honor us," came the rough, warbling voice of the elder woman, "with your sacrifice."

"*Sacrifice?!* I thought I was being released! Ahhh, fuck!"

"You honor us," she continued, "with your fear."

"What the fuck is wrong with you?! Stay away from me!"

"You honor us with your blood."

Next came the wet, sucking, squelching sounds as she stabbed him. I never saw the ceremony, only heard it. To me, it sounded like she always took deep, long stabbing motions through them. I wondered if she did it to maximize the pain and fear of the victims. Wouldn't surprise me.

"Agh—God! Stop, please!"

The man's blood began dripping through the floor at that point, raining through the roof of my cell like a dark waterfall. I scooted to the corner to stay out from under it. Being covered in my own blood was enough when I had limited water.

"You honor us with your death."

Then a final, wet slicing sound, which could only be across his throat. The doctor only made choked gurgling sounds now as his blood streamed through the cracks in the boards above me.

The doctor's body made a heavy thump as he collapsed on the ground. He flailed a bit, slapping the ground a few times. The flailing gave way to twitching and then, dead stillness. They would leave him there until his blood stopped draining before taking his body to discard it. I never knew what they did with them.

"Because the only good man is a dead one."

Like all the times before, I wondered why they insisted on keeping me alive if that was true. I'd come to my own conclusion years ago, with the help of another man who had shared my cell temporarily.

"You're a training dummy," that man had said. "They get to practice on you before doing the real thing."

It made sense, especially as to why none of my cuts were lethal. Why the ones who cut me were usually the youngest. Some of my earliest memories were staring through the bars of a much smaller cage, my eyes locked onto a girl's roughly the same age as me.

We were both just children, staring wide-eyed at each other, while an older woman pulled my skinny arm through the bars, placed a knife in the girls' hand, and ordered her to cut me until she drew blood.

Sometimes the girls would cry and say no, but they always did eventually. They grew swift and efficient with it, the horror in their eyes morphing into cold hatred as the years passed.

The doctor had been sacrificed last week, so I was surprised to hear more male voices shouting above me as I contemplated my water rationing. The words weren't clear and there seemed to be multiple men, which was odd. Sacrifices were only conducted once a month, the morning of the full moon. My cage was cramped with two people, so the women rarely imprisoned more than one man at a time.

A series of loud pops rang out, and then many voices screaming and shouting. High-pitched feminine ones, and deeper voices rumbling as they shouted things too fast for me to decipher. Dozens of rapid, running footsteps *thump-thump-thumped* over the ceiling of my cage, running back and forth over the popping noises. My ears started to ring, the pops were *that* loud.

Nothing had ever occurred like this in my lifetime and I didn't know what to make of it. I'd never heard the women scream before, and the sound was jarring. Nor had I ever heard running around like everyone was in a mad rush.

Eventually, the footsteps ceased running. The

screaming and the popping faded away to nothing. It became eerily quiet—I'd never heard anything like this either. Not even at night when most were asleep. Someone was always talking, cooking, or doing some other chore that I could hear through the walls. Was this what death sounded like?

At some point I heard voices and footsteps again, and that was a small comfort. But these steps were louder, heavier than I'd ever heard before.

The door to the basement slammed open with a loud crash, the wood bouncing against the wall as the heavy footfalls made their way down the stairs to my dungeon.

"Whoo-wee! Smells worse than the whorehouse your mom came from, Jensen." It was definitely a man, dressed in some kind of tactical uniform with all kinds of items hanging off of the thick vest he wore. He held a long, dark object in both hands as he examined the corner of the basement by the door.

"Shut up, Lopez." The reply came with a crackling sound from a small, black box on the man's shoulder. "Just clear the area so we can get the hell out. This place is fucking creepy."

The man chuckled to himself as he finished rummaging through whatever supplies he'd found and started making his way toward me. I kept still, barely breathing, and at a complete loss as to what I should do.

"Holy...shit!" The man stumbled back at the sight of me, eyes wide as he pointed his long, black stick in my direction. "Who are you?"

"I'm..." I stared back at him, noticing how his

hands shook and how large his eyes became. "I'm the blood bag."

"What?" He brought a slow, shaky hand to the black box on his shoulder. "Jensen, get your ass down to the basement. Someone's in here, a guy. Looks like a prisoner." He repositioned his grip on his weapon. "I'll ask again. Who are you?"

I didn't know how else to answer. I was a man, and therefore unworthy of an identity, or even a name.

"I'm just the blood bag," I repeated.

"You got a name?"

"No."

"How long have you been here?"

"I've always been here." Why did every man assume I had spent time somewhere else?

"Oh…shit. Okay." He started lowering his stick to point away from me. "Fuck me. They really did a number on you, huh?"

I didn't know what that meant, so I said nothing.

"How old are you?" he asked next.

I coughed, my throat hoarse from how infrequently I spoke. "I don't know."

He blinked several times, his blue eyes narrowing. "So you're tellin' me you've always been in this," he waved his stick around, "in this cage?"

"Yes." Every man that came down here always asked a variation of the same question, and it was tiring.

"Well, huh. Guess we're breaking you out of jail then." His lips pulled to the sides, revealing white teeth as he spread his arms wide. "Every one of those cunts up there is dead. You're free."

"Dead?"

That couldn't be true. The women had always said the blood sacrifices would make them live forever, immune to all earthly suffering. The sacrifices of men were a gift to the goddess and she rewarded them with immortality. So how could they all be dead?

And free? I knew the dictionary definition of the word, but like *hope*, it was a completely foreign concept to me.

"Yeah!" His mouth pulled open wider at the sides. Was that what a smile was supposed to be? "We thought these broads were crazy, but damn." He gestured at me. "Guess they really got what was coming to 'em."

"They're really dead? All of them?"

Dead meant they would never come back. She would never see me again. Never yell, spit on me, or try to hurt me as badly as she could without killing me.

I will never see her again. The thought was never one I'd considered before. It made me feel strange. Heavy. Like I was unraveling from the inside.

"Yeah, man! You should be doing a jig right now. Ah, step aside. Allow me."

I moved to the corner as he raised his long stick, pointing it at the padlock holding my cage doors together. The lock broke apart with a loud clang as something was ejected out of his stick. I covered my ears and shut my eyes at the ringing echoing through my skull.

"There you go, man." I peeked one eye at the man spreading his arms wide as my door swung open. "You're free."

I lowered my hands slowly, the uneasy, unraveling sensation in my body only growing heavier at the sight of the open door. She used to leave it open to test me when I was younger. Even years later, those scars were still the most prominent ones on my back.

"Where do I go?" I looked at the man. "Is there another Sisterhood that needs a blood bag?"

"Jesus Christ…" His lips came together again, face making an expression I didn't understand. "They really fucked you up, man."

Again, I didn't know the meaning of what he was saying. "I'm sorry. I just don't know where to go."

The man scrubbed a hand down his face with a sigh. "It's alright. We'll, uh, we'll figure out some place to take you. I'll be right back."

With that, he headed for the stairs, taking two at a time. I still didn't leave my cell, the only home I'd ever known. I leaned against the wall, listening to the hushed voices outside as they decided what to do with me.

ONE

MARIPOSA

PRESENT DAY

"Okay, are you ready?"

The boy nodded, his face serious and determined. I stole a look at his father sitting across the room, and we shared a smile.

"Okay, here goes." I stuck the syringe in his arm where I'd just cleaned with an alcohol wipe and pressed down on the plunger.

The boy hissed at the needle's poke and bit the inside of his cheek against a whimper, shutting his eyes tight.

"All done!" I dropped the syringe in the wastebasket, grabbed the sky-blue band-aid, and laid it carefully over the injection spot. "That's your last vaccine, Jason. You're so brave!"

"It didn't even hurt," he scoffed as he slid off the exam table and returned to his father's side.

The man chuckled as he ruffled his son's hair.

"Thank you for squeezing us in at the end of the day, Mari."

"It's no problem at all." I peeled my gloves and white coat off before heading to the sink to wash my hands.

They hesitated by the exam room door. "Do you want us to wait with you?"

"It's okay." I smiled as I dried my hands. "My husband should be outside. Thank you, though."

"Have a good evening, Mari."

"You guys too!"

The door closed softly after them as I pulled on the large, black hoodie. I didn't have to put my nose to the fabric to know that Shadow's scent was fading from it. Trying to catch a whiff of him would only make me feel worse, so I did my best to find comfort in the heavy weight of the fabric. Over the sweatshirt, I pulled on my leather jacket, adjusting the hoodie so it didn't bunch up underneath.

I said goodnight to Rhonda, Dr. Brooks, and the other medics with a smile, like I did every night. A smile that I hoped didn't betray how numb I felt inside.

The rumble of Jandro's bike filled the chilly air as I stepped outside, and my man was leaning against the machine while he waited for me.

"Hey, *bonita*." He wrapped around me, warm and strong. "Everything okay?"

"Yeah, I just had a last-minute vaccination." I tilted my face up, accepting his kiss.

His lips lingered on mine tonight, one warm hand reaching up to caress my cheek. "You want to drive?"

"Sure."

I threw a leg over the bike and gripped the handlebars, Jandro easing into the seat behind me. Riding felt like second nature to me now that I'd had weeks of practice. These days, being in the driver's seat and with Jandro were the only times I felt remotely alive.

The road led us to the house far too soon—that cheery, cozy facade mocking me as we approached. What was supposed to be my home with my four husbands was actually an empty shell. A place to crash in the evenings after I spent most of my day working at the hospital.

Such a waste of a beautiful house.

So many times I wished to make a different turn at the bridge leading into this development. I fantasized constantly about leaving town, riding off into the sunset to find the man I missed so badly that my chest physically ached.

But Jandro would never let me go. And Horus kept telling me it wasn't time yet.

So every night I kept returning here, to this house that filled me with resentment, and continued to wait for when the time was right.

"What's for dinner?" I asked, removing my helmet. Not that I was *feeling* hungry, I hadn't truly felt hungry in weeks. I just knew that my body needed food.

Jandro scraped the mud off his boots on the mat outside the front door. "Chicken *pozole*."

I narrowed my eyes.

He laughed, cupping my face to kiss me. "Not *our* chickens, don't worry. Joe is thinning out his flock, so he gave me a couple."

I relaxed, making my way inside the house that I knew would be empty. Jandro started up a warm blaze in the fireplace while I quickly showered and changed out of my scrubs. He had two bowls of *pozole* doled out when I made it to the kitchen.

"Thank you, *guapito*." I kissed his cheek before taking a seat in front of my bowl.

"Of course."

I felt his eyes on me as I started to eat. I ate fast, spoonfuls of broth, hominy, and chunks of chicken breast came robotically to my mouth. Food barely tasted like anything to me lately, it was just a resource. A means to an end. So I ate quickly.

"Mari."

I readied myself with a quick swallow of broth. Jandro was going to try this again today.

"Yes?"

"Slow down, *mi amor*," he urged, his voice gentle. "If you wait, if we can all eat together—"

I shut him down quickly. "No, thank you. I'm tired, and I'm just going to go to bed."

Jandro sighed, clearly disappointed, but didn't push the issue.

We ate together in silence, him mostly poking at his food while I consumed my sustenance like a robot. When my bowl was empty, I thanked him again with another kiss on the cheek, and cleaned up after myself.

The distant rumbling of motorcycles had just begun as I set my bowl in the dish drying rack. I dried my hands and immediately headed toward Jandro's room, feeling his eyes on me the whole way.

The growling engines were just outside the window as I got undressed for bed, pulling sheets and blankets over me as I curled up on the mattress.

When the engines cut, and I heard Reaper and Gunner's murmured voices from the garage, a pain slashed hard through my chest.

I missed them. I missed them both so fucking much.

But right on the heels of my longing came a different pain, one heated by anger and betrayal.

How could they?

It was that second pain that kept me from springing up and running to them, no matter how badly I craved Reaper's rough touch and Gunner's bright sweetness.

Jandro's voice mingled with theirs through the closed bedroom door as they came inside. All of their voices were low, murmuring and serious. I could only pick up a few *fuck*s from Reaper. He sounded angry, his tone harsh and biting.

It hurts to go without your wife, doesn't it? I thought cruelly. *Now you know how I feel, losing a husband.*

Shame flooded my senses, making tears well up in my eyes. When did I become so mean and spiteful? I still loved Reaper, so fucking much. I missed him with every cell in my body. But I also had these moments of hating him so intensely, I felt like a completely different person.

A soft weight dipped the bed near my feet, and then a rumbling purr filled the air.

I reached a hand out for Freyja, her furry head bumping into my palm and rubbing against my whole arm affectionately. She kneaded the mattress directly in front of my chest before flopping down and snuggling against me.

I pet her as she soothed me with that purr. I didn't ask her any questions, nor did she speak to me. Maybe she knew exactly where I was in my grief, anger, and heartache, and simply allowed me to be there. Maybe she knew how touch-starved I was for the three husbands I felt like I no longer had. Whatever the case, Freyja seemed to sense that I didn't want advice, just some comfort to dull the now-permanent ache in my chest.

Jandro came in roughly an hour later, his weight dipping the bed behind me as he shucked off his clothes for the night. The heat of his chest kissed my back as he got settled in, broad body wrapping around me protectively.

"I know you're awake." He brushed a kiss along the back of my shoulder.

"Mm-hm."

Jandro sighed deeply, his breath fanning over my hair. "Mari, how long are you going to keep this up?"

"Keep what up?"

"Come on, babe. I'm serious." His head flopped down on the pillow. "I know you're angry, but it's been almost a month. You have to talk to them at some point."

I curled into a tighter ball, pulling my knees up toward my chest. "I'm not ready."

"Mari." His arm came around my waist, lips light on the back of my neck. "I can tell how much this is hurting you. It's hurting them too. Fuck, it's hurting *me* seeing you all like this."

"And Shadow?" I said. "How much do you think he's hurting?"

"Read his letter again," Jandro said after a few moments of silence. "He wanted you to heal, to be loved by your men. He wouldn't—"

"Stop talking about him like he's dead," I snapped. *He's still out there and he's still mine.*

"I'm not even saying you need to forgive Reap now, or anytime soon. But this whole avoidance thing isn't doing anybody good. Just talk to each other, that's all I'm saying."

"And say what?" I scoffed. "That I'm still angry? That I still want Shadow back? He'll just dig his heels in and stand by his actions like he always does."

"You don't know that. Reap would do anything for you." Jandro brushed a small kiss along the back of my shoulder. "It's killing both of them to not talk to you. They want their wife back."

"Oh, great. Now we've reached the guilt-trip stage," I huffed bitterly. "Well, guess fucking what? I want my husband back. The one *he* sent away when he knew I couldn't do anything to stop him."

"I understand, *mi amor*. You're not the only one who wants him back." Jandro squeezed his arm around my waist. "I miss him too. I don't agree with what Reaper did. I don't think it was right."

"But you still support him." The bitterness coiled deep in my gut, turning all the food in my stomach to acid. "Because you're a good, loyal vice president."

"I understand wanting to protect the woman I love from anything that would harm her, even our own club brothers. Especially if I nearly lost her, and I could remove the cause of her harm for good." Jandro's arm slid from my body as he rolled onto his back. "So no, I don't support it. But I get *why* he did it."

"It was an accident." I felt like I was stuck in an endless cycle of repeating myself. We'd had this conversation so many times already. "It wouldn't have happened again. Shadow would never allow it to happen again. He *never* wanted to hurt me."

"I know," Jandro said gently. "I believe that just as much as you do. On some level, I'm sure Reaper knows it too. He reacted emotionally, as he tends to do. His woman, his whole world, was threatened. So he followed his instincts to eliminate that threat as soon as possible."

"And he did so proudly. He thought it all out. He made a plan, which he carried out in several steps. He could have stopped at any point, but he didn't. He could have waited until I was cleared from the hospital to see how I felt about it, *but he didn't.* He was deliberate about the whole thing, and he will stand by his actions until the day he dies. That's just the kind of person he is."

"*Mariposita,* you won't know that unless you talk to him. He's made mistakes. He does have regrets about actions he's taken. He would never want to hurt you, or jeopardize his marriage."

"Maybe he should have thought of that before, you know, doing exactly that."

Jandro sighed heavily behind me, and I knew he was

rubbing his forehead or his eyes. These arguments going in circles were exhausting, and I was sick of them too. At some point, the cycle would have to be broken. I just couldn't bring myself to take that first step. It was easier to be angry, to shut down and wallow in the hurt and bitterness.

His defense of Reaper's actions made sense, and I could see the reasoning behind them too. Really, it was just as I expected from my passionate, protective first husband. But to admit that felt like defeat. It felt like I was excusing his behavior and letting Shadow down. Shadow needed more people on his side, not less. His letter all but told me he would never defend himself in this matter. He accepted Reaper's exile because he believed he deserved it.

If he wouldn't advocate for himself, then I would. I didn't care if I was his victim. I loved him and I knew his heart.

"What do you want to happen, Mari?" Jandro sounded defeated. "How do we fix this?"

"I want Reaper to apologize and admit he was wrong. I want Shadow to come back, and us all to move forward."

"And if that doesn't happen?" he pressed. "We have no way of finding Shadow. For all we know, he could be out of the country now."

"I don't know."

Jandro rolled toward me, resting a hand on my arm. "You have to make a decision, Mari. It's not fair to keep dragging this on."

"What do you mean?" I knew what he was getting

at, but I wanted to hear him say it. I needed to know he was serious.

"You have to decide if…if you want to stay married to them or not." His hand fell away. "And to me too, I guess."

It wasn't a complete surprise to hear. The gods knew I had fleeting thoughts of leaving them over the past few weeks. But it still hurt, hearing it spoken into reality. Panic clamped down in my chest as I flipped over to face Jandro in the dark room.

"I love you." My fingers found his face and those plush lips I adored. His arms came around me and pulled me into a deep, emotionally-charged kiss. "I'm sorry this has been so difficult, and you're caught in the middle. But thank you for being here while I need you."

"I love you too," he whispered, stroking over my back in a soothing pattern. "With my whole heart, Mari."

I believed every word as our mouths found each other again. Our kisses were warm, passionate, and loving, but not escalating into lust. I wanted comfort and love, but I couldn't bring myself to do anything sexual since Shadow. Jandro was more than understanding, content to hold me and kiss me while I spent many nights crying.

"But," he murmured at the end of our last kiss. "You know I'm not the only one who loves you."

There it was, the reminder. The reality I couldn't escape from. I did *not* want Reaper or Gunner like I had Jandro right then. I didn't trust myself to even look at my two other men without screaming out all my rage at them.

But I wasn't anywhere near ready to end things either. The mere thought of losing them, setting them free to love other women, ground my heart into dust.

"I'll make a decision," I promised Jandro as I turned onto my opposite side. "Soon. Just not yet."

He kissed between my neck and shoulder as he settled in for sleep. "Okay. Goodnight, my love."

"Goodnight."

Morning came quickly. I got out of bed before Jandro, our usual early riser. His bedroom was on the first story, just a short walk to the kitchen where I started making coffee and a quick breakfast for us both. If Reaper or Gunner's bedroom doors opened on the second floor, I'd be able to hear them and zip back to Jandro's room before they could corner me.

The two of them tried getting up early to talk to me at first. When I kept retreating to my safe space with Jandro, they eventually stopped. I couldn't decide if I was relieved or disappointed at that.

Avoiding them wasn't the only reason I got up early, though. Horus's perch was in the kitchen, mounted high near the vaulted ceiling to resemble a cliff ledge, where falcons usually made their nests.

The bird preened his feathers, pointedly ignoring my staring up at him while the coffee maker gurgled. My patience wore out when the pot was full. "Well?"

Horus fluffed up his feathers before smoothing them down, peering at me with those razor-sharp eyes.

Today is not the day, daughter. The time is not right.

I grabbed the coffee pot's handle and jerked it toward me, frustration and disappointment bleeding into my movements as I slammed a cup down on the counter. Another fucking day of waiting.

And so the cycle of numbness and heartache started again.

REAPER

My eyes wouldn't stop aching no matter how much I rubbed them. Exhaustion was setting in hard. I probably only got a single night's worth of sleep in three fucking weeks. Next to me, Gunner didn't look much better. The whites of his eyes were red, dark circles underneath them making him look like a raccoon.

The two of us looked, and most likely felt, like ghosts. Haunted and empty.

"What are we gonna do, Reap?" It wasn't the first time he'd asked that question, his voice coming out like a sad whimper.

I gave him the same answer I always did. "I don't know."

"Is this it?" he went on. "We're coming up on a month of this. Is she done with us?"

Two weeks ago, maybe even days ago, I would have told him no fucking way. Mari was angry and just needed time to cool off. She had Jandro firmly in her corner. He'd make her see reason and come around.

Then the days of silence stretched on. Night after night, I went to bed alone. The closest I got to touching my wife was running my finger over the stone on her ring, which rested on my nightstand. Every single attempt to talk to her was met with a door slammed in my face.

I wasn't ready to give up. Not until Mari looked me in the eye and told me to my face that I wasn't her husband anymore. If she wanted to avoid me and slam doors in my face for another year, so be it. I would wait until she gave me an answer.

But fuck if this weird limbo wasn't taking its toll on me. I fucking missed my wife, everything from her hair drifting over my skin as we slept, to her snappy little comebacks when I teased her. All my waking energy was spent being pissed at Jandro because he was the only one she talked to. Just the fact that he had her in his bed every night made me see red. I fucking hated feeling like an outsider in my own marriage.

It wasn't even about sex. My drive had shriveled down to nothing the moment she called me a heartless piece of shit and took her ring off. I wanted only her, and only if she still loved me. Jealousy burned in me knowing she still loved Jandro, and probably even Shadow, for all the fuck I knew.

That was the worst part—that I no longer *knew* if she still loved me or not.

"Reaper," Gunner whined again after I didn't answer him. "I'm near the end of my rope, man. I can't handle this shit, I *need* to know where I stand with her."

"I. Know." The words came out with a biting growl. "You don't think I feel the exact same way you do?"

"You're the pro at this shit, not me." He lifted his hands, elbows resting on the conference room table. "What would your parents do in this situation?"

"No fucking clue." I rolled my head around on my tired, aching neck. "Nothing like this has ever happened between my parents, or anyone in my community."

"I wouldn't wish this on anyone," Gunner groaned, pinching his forehead. "I feel like I'd fall on my knees with relief if she would just look at me."

"Yeah," I agreed. That was how desperate we were. She could throw us scraps, any small acknowledgment of our existence, and we'd eat it up like starving dogs.

The conference room door opened, and I peered through my bleary eyes to see my dad walking in. He came through with something held high above his head, like a victory trophy, then subsequently dropped his arm when he saw our faces.

"You boys look shittier by the day," he remarked, approaching the table with one of his lieutenants behind him.

"You got somethin'?" I nodded at the folder he placed on the table, not caring to hash out my marital problems at work.

Dad nodded, his grin returning. "Andrea has made contact. So she's alive and carrying out her part of the mission." He turned to his lieutenant, a slender south-Asian man who radiated a calm, understated strength.

"This is Anurak. He developed the code and will be translating Andrea's messages. I figured you boys would want to be the first to know what it says."

"Yes, please." Gunner reached over and shook Anurak's hand. "Thank you for working with us on this."

"It's my pleasure." Anurak took a seat and opened the folder, examining the full page of foreign characters while my dad got him a pen and plain sheet of paper.

I leaned over to look at the glyphs Andrea had written, my weary eyes quickly blurring all the symbols together. "Is that a made-up code or a real language?"

"It's based on my native language, which is Thai," Anurak explained. "But it's altered slightly, so that even if a Thai speaker were to find the message, they would not be able to decode it."

"I didn't know Andrea spoke Thai," Gunner mused.

"She doesn't," Anurak said with a polite chuckle. "She's using the phonetic sounds of the characters to compose a message in English. Because Thai and English consonants don't match up exactly, we did have to invent a few."

"She learned it pretty fucking fast," I remarked.

"We gave her a copy of the codex to carry with her," my dad said. "But encouraged her to memorize it and destroy it at the first opportunity, so her messages wouldn't be compromised."

"Here." Anurak dragged his finger across a row of characters. "She says she burned the codex, and this message is composed entirely from memory."

Dad clapped his hands once. "That's our girl."

The three of us waited as the lieutenant transcribed the message onto the piece of paper, capping his pen with a definitive click. "Would you like to do the honor, General?" Anurak slid the translation across the table to my dad.

General Bray accepted the paper, his eyes scanning it before relaying the information. "Everyone here worships General Tash like a god," he read aloud, his brow pinching. "From food and clothing, to weapons and victories in battle, everything is attributed to his greatness. However, no one seems to have direct contact with him. Everyone is a messenger, or a foot-soldier. The only ones who speak to him directly are a small group called the General's Council. They have immense power and influence, and are the ones who relay the general's orders to the rest of the army. I have met several men in saloons who claimed to be General Tash undercover, keeping a watchful eye over his citizens. It's clear, however, that no one knows who the general truly *is*. He stays out of sight and gives commands from on high like a deity."

Dad paused in his reading, noticing as Gunner and I exchanged a look. "You two said you traded goods with this guy?"

"Yeah." Gunner stroked his jaw, his eyes more focused than they had been in weeks. "It was always the same guy, his uniform decorated in medallions and with general's stars. He claimed to be Tash, and his soldiers referred to him as such. But apparently that's not the case, huh?"

"It was probably one of these council members

acting in his stead." I drummed my fingers on the table. "What else does Andrea say?"

"She says, 'I'm getting close to some of the unit leaders, but must tread delicately. I can't dig for intel too aggressively, or else I risk my position. Below are current estimates based on what I've already found out.'" Dad proceeded to list numbers of Jeeps, ground units, sniper units…and other shit my exhausted brain was too tired to catch, before setting the message back down on the table. "Her message ends there."

"Nothing about Big G's fuckery, huh?" Gunner shoved his hair back. "I still can't wrap my mind around that."

"If she's getting close enough to unit leaders to bring us these numbers already," Anurak tapped his fingers on the original coded message, "she's likely not being regarded as a suspicious person. Is it possible Big G may have done what he did to throw suspicion off of her?"

"Maybe," I sighed. "I hope she gets closer to these council people. I need to know how to topple Tash himself."

"It's just the first message, son," Dad reminded me. "This is a long game. Every message will give us a clearer picture of what's going on in there."

"I know, you're right," I sighed. "Anything else?"

Dad's smile wavered. "Yeah, that was the good news. We're also getting reports that Blakeworth units are mobilizing. They're moving toward us, but staying just out of our reach in the neutral territory north of here. It's looking like they want to draw us out for a skirmish."

"Great." I went back to rubbing my eyes. "Just fan-fucking-tastic."

"Gunner, I'm gonna want your input on the best way to engage them," Dad said. "How many units we should send, what kind of artillery to bring. We want to shove them back, but be mindful that we're dealing with conscripts and don't want overkill. Regardless, they won't go away unless we respond. Can you meet with us this afternoon?"

"Yeah," Gunner said blankly. "Sure."

Eying us carefully, Dad turned to Anurak. "Thank you, lieutenant. I'll leave you to bring these numbers to our tactics teams. Can I have a word with my sons?"

"Of course, General." The man swiftly excused himself from the table and Dad turned on us the moment the door closed. "What the hell is going on with you two?"

"Just the same old shit," I grumbled. "Mari's still not talking to us after the whole exiling-Shadow thing."

"And you still haven't done anything to fix it?" He glared at us. "What kind of husbands are you?"

"I'm sorry, what the fuck are we supposed to do?" I spread my hands out, my voice rising. "No one knows where Shadow went, so we can't exactly drag him back here so everyone can kiss and make up."

"You can be a man and quit with the fucking excuses." Finn Daley was the only man in the world who could make me feel small, and I felt like I was under the stare of a giant right then. "You do whatever is in your power to make this right. Camp outside her door. Spend an entire week on your knees begging for forgiveness, I don't care. Your woman is the center of your family and you have wronged her. You caused her this pain, so it's on you to fix."

"But—"

"Ah!" Dad cut Gunner off swiftly with a raised finger and a look that dared him to keep arguing. Smartly, Gunner shrank into his seat and kept his mouth shut. I knew he'd been happy to bond with my dad, but good father figures weren't always warm and loving. Finn was giving us a much-deserved tongue lashing, and I hoped Gun understood that.

"I know you boys know you fucked up," Dad said in a gentler tone. "You've given her space to be angry, and that's good. But enough time has passed now that you need to assert yourselves as men, *her* men. The longer you let her shut you out, the less respect for you she'll have." He leaned back, crossing his arms over his chest. "And no woman wants to fuck, much less be tied down to, a guy she doesn't respect."

"What if..." Gunner hesitated, chewing his lip. "What if she doesn't want us back?"

"She would've kicked your sorry asses out already if that was the case," Dad replied. "I know how much this hurts, boys, I do. But you gotta fight for your marriage and not let all this bitterness drag out and fester. And when you overcome this, your relationships with her *will* be stronger."

"You've been through stuff like this?" Gunner asked, wide-eyed.

"I've never forced out one of my wife's men behind

her back," Dad laughed. "But have I gotten the silent treatment after being an idiot? Oh hell yeah."

"And doing this…worked for you?"

"Every time," Dad nodded. "For smaller things, Lis would come talk to me on her own when she was ready. But when I *really* fucked up, it was on me to *make* her see how much I wanted to set things right. Otherwise, I knew I'd lose her."

"I'm scared of pushing Mari away," Gunner admitted, raking his hands back through his hair. "Like we're already too far gone and there's no coming back." He looked to me for confirmation and I nodded, letting him know I had the exact same fear.

"You want to make that a self-fulfilling prophecy, just keep doing what you're doing." Dad brought his palms to the table as he stood up. "Your marriage is withering away. You can either keep neglecting it and allow it to die, or put some fucking effort in and bring it back to life."

With that sage advice, he left us to make our decision.

THREE

IVAN

"Remove the bandage in a few hours. Wash it thoroughly with soap and water, and moisturize it at least twice a day until it heals." I gave my client's skin another wipe before pressing the bandage to her fresh tattoo, holding it in place with one hand while I peeled strips of tape with the other. "It's going to start itching after a few days and that's normal, but avoid scratching it. The itch means it's healing." I finished taping the bandage in place and sat back to pull my gloves off. "If it becomes red or painful, beyond the usual soreness, see a medic, or an artist with a good reputation, if you can."

"Got it! Thanks, Ivan." My client hopped off the table, stretching her arms over her head when her feet hit the floor. "I left your payment with the bartender, like you said."

"Great. Thank you." I made a half-hearted attempt to smile, but the expression didn't feel natural anymore. "Enjoy the rest of your stay."

The woman went off to find her fiancé, who was most likely appraising some of the vehicles in the junkyard. Like most of my clients, they were just traveling through. Apparently this couple had heard my name from another tattoo client a few towns over. Good tattooists seemed to be a rare find out here, so they came to this service center specifically to seek me out.

That had been happening more often lately. And my one-week stay soon turned into three weeks. But it wasn't just the tattoo work keeping me here.

I glanced at the clock above the bar as I cleaned up my supplies, anxiety gripping my chest at what was to come in the next half-hour.

Once my area was tidied, I parked at my usual spot at the bar and waited for Jen to finish with her current customers.

"Hey big guy, you want your payment?" she asked me.

"Yes, please." I tried not to outwardly bristle at the nicknames she gave me.

"Always so polite," Jen mused as she reached under the bar and set my whiskey in front of me. "Your mother must have taught you well. You want a glass?"

My mother never taught me anything remotely useful, but she didn't need to know that. "Yes, thank you."

"Want me to pour?"

"Thanks, I got it."

"Such a gentleman." Jen smiled, stretching her forearms out on the bartop next to me.

The bar was slow, which meant she'd likely want to

hang out and talk. Her arms were covered in black outlines that I'd started a few days ago, along with small bits of color filled in for her sleeves. In another two weeks, she'd be covered in bright floral designs from shoulder to wrist.

I liked Jen, which was not something I thought I'd ever feel about another woman. She was friendly and talkative, protective of the service girls when men came to stay, and a hardass when it came to cutting off liquor for sloshed bar patrons. I could have done without the nicknames like *big guy, big boy*, and *handsome*, but other than that, she was a good client and bartender.

"You seein' Doc soon?" she asked, her voice lowering.

"Yeah." I swallowed my first mouthful of whiskey and poured another.

"How's that been going?"

I paused to throw back my next drink before answering. "It feels like hell when it's happening but…I think it's actually working." I started pouring my third shot. "So I keep going back."

"That's good!" Jen's arm slid across the bar to nudge against mine. I fought back the urge to pull away from the touch. It would've been rude, or at least that was what some niggling voice in my head told me.

"I give him shit for being a dirty old man, but I swear Doc saved my life," she continued in a near-whisper. "I was having nightmares, panic attacks set off by the littlest shit. Got hooked on booze, pills, anything I could get my hands on to make it go away. Fuck, I wanted to end it all." Jen nudged her elbow into my arm. "What's your flavor of misery?"

"Um." I felt fine to talk to her about mundane things, but absolutely not this. "Nightmares, mostly. Sorry if you've heard me at night."

She raised one shoulder in a shrug. "Hey, I get it. And I haven't heard a peep out of your room in a week, so that's somethin', huh?"

"Yeah." I stared at my bottle and empty glass, debating on one more drink before going to see Doc. It was still early on in my treatment, so I couldn't be sure if it was Doc's bizarre therapy letting me sleep through the night or simply my old habit of drinking myself into oblivion. "Maybe it is."

Jen lifted her chin, her eyes focused on my other arm. "Your nightmares got anything to do with her?"

I followed her gaze to the fresh tattoo inside my left forearm, where a beautiful, dark-haired woman stretched from my elbow to my wrist. I did it in a pin-up style, the woman's large eyes were sultry and inviting with her lips curved into a coy smile. She wore a cropped T-shirt with a horned skull on the front, black jeans with rips in the knees, and motorcycle boots with her feet crossed at the ankles.

"No," I told Jen absently, my gaze fixed on the image embedded in my skin. "She has nothing to do with the nightmares."

I loved her, and then became her *nightmare.*

While I had no regrets about it, the tattoo was done in a moment of weakness. I had been here a full week, drunk in my room at night, my brain unwilling to let me sleep. I was missing her so badly, the ache in my chest made it difficult to breathe. I stared at the drawing I made of her for hours, tracing the pencil lines with my finger over and over, remembering how I'd mapped her body during our last night together.

The more I drank, the more I sank into the memories. Her voice, her laughs, the sounds she made in her climax. The taste of her, the warmth of her lips on my scars. The way she looked at me—without fear.

The paper wore so thin that it ripped.

I flew into a panic, immediately grabbing a pen to copy the drawing onto my forearm. Another empty bottle later, my tattoo machine buzzed late into the night, making the woman I loved in a past life a permanent fixture on my body. I could barely bring myself to think of her name because of how much it hurt, but not even Ivan could fully let go of the woman Shadow had loved.

Looking at the tattoo brought me no joy, no nostalgia of a better time. It only brought me sorrow. All it reminded me of was how much I lost, how badly I fucked up the one good thing I had. How much I deserved to be here, far away from the woman I missed so much.

With a resigned sigh, I stood from the bar. "I better get going. Thanks, Jen."

"Hey." She reached for me, her hand landing softly on top of mine. Again, I fought the urge to snatch my hand away. "If you ever want to talk after the bar's closed, or you know, get something out of your system..." her fingers stroked over mine, "I'm here for you, Ivan."

It took me a moment, but from the way she kept trying to touch me, I could figure out what she was implying. I tried to see her from the perspective of a normal man—the attractive, edgy bartender with her piercings and tattoos, damaged in her own way but not completely unlike me. She was a good friend, and if I was anyone else, maybe I would take her invitation as a way to distract myself.

But there was only one woman whose touch I craved. Maybe that would change in the future, but right then I was content to wallow in my self-flagellation. Torturing myself with the ink on my arm as a constant reminder, and holding on to memories I wasn't ready to let go of.

"Thanks, Jen," I repeated before sliding my hand out from under hers, unsure of what else to say.

Turning away from the bar, I headed for a side door that could have passed for an office or supply closet. In truth, it was a basement.

Ducking my head and squeezing down the narrow staircase, I reached the basement floor to find Doc waiting for me.

"You keep coming back," he stated, leaning against the chair in the center of the room. "That's promising." The frizzy gray hair on the top of his head was illuminated by the long, tungsten light tubes hanging from the ceiling.

"Let's get this over with." I went to the chair and sat

down. The metal frame didn't budge under my weight, due to being bolted down to the concrete floor.

"Had a couple drinks?" Doc asked casually as he wrapped the attached metal cuffs around my arms and legs.

"Yes." I watched him shackle me in, always making sure to slide two fingers between my skin and the cuffs to check my circulation. "Why do you suggest drinking before this, anyway?"

"Alcohol depresses the central nervous system." His matter-of-fact tone reminded me of *her*.

I swallowed the lump in my throat and shoved thoughts of her away. There was no room for her here.

"With the physical senses dulled and inhibitions lowered, it's easier for the patient to go *inward*." Once I was fully restrained, he tapped my forehead with one finger and gave me an unnerving smile. "That's where we go during these treatments, Ivan. Are you ready?"

I was never ready, not really. I hated, dreaded, *loathed* every second of this. But I could feel it changing me. The monster created within me lashed out in full force during these sessions, but I could feel it weakening, like its energy was being spent. The nightmares still came, but they didn't send me on a destructive rampage like they used to.

She had told Shadow something once, that he—I— had to address the root of my fear, the cause of what morphed me into this creature, before I could get better. Taking sleeping pills hadn't protected her from me, so she was probably right. But I couldn't imagine this being what she had in mind.

"Yeah." I lifted my eyes to Doc. "Go ahead."

The man took his glasses off and stuffed them in his shirt pocket. From the same pocket, he pulled a length of string with one end tied through a hole in a coin.

"Take a few deep breaths, Ivan." The coin spun on the string before Doc held it still with his opposite hand.

I pulled deep lungfuls of air through my nose, releasing them through my mouth as he'd instructed me on our first day. After a cycle of ten breaths, Doc released the coin and held it from the top of the string, roughly a foot in front of my face.

"Continue your breaths," he said as the coin began to swing in slow arc from left to right. "Let your eyes follow the coin as you listen to my voice."

Doc stood just outside of my field of vision, letting my eyes focus only on the coin swinging in front of me, and the empty room beyond. Eventually the two began to blur, my focus pulling inward at the lack of stimulation from my surroundings. I wasn't sure how Doc knew, but this was always the spot where he guided me further.

"Good, Ivan. I'm going to count backwards from ten now. With each count, I want you to descend into yourself. Like stepping into an elevator going down. Ten... nine...eight..."

My eyelids grew heavier as he counted, shutting to the point of not fully closed, but where I could barely see through my eyelashes. I didn't strain for sight, knowing now that my eyes wouldn't show me my physical surroundings, but what I shoved away deep in my mind. That was where my internal elevator was descending.

"…Five…four…three…"

All physical sensations fell away until it felt like I was floating. I didn't feel the chair underneath me or the cuffs locking my limbs down. New sensations took over that felt like they were in my body, but I knew they weren't. It was unnerving how *real* things could feel, deep in the recesses of my mind.

"…One."

Doc's voice fell away and the best way I could describe the feeling was coldness. A chill on my skin and also within me, along with a deep, gaping emptiness. I now knew that feeling to be profound loneliness.

"Where are you, Ivan?"

I didn't need to force my eyes open to know exactly where I was.

"I'm here, in my cage." My body felt small in this place, this time, the voice coming out of it sounded too big.

"Is anyone with you?"

"No, I'm alone."

"Can you tell me how old you are at this point in your life?"

I moved my head slowly, taking in the surroundings of the prison embedded deep in my memories. Iron bars covered in dark specks of my blood. Dark stains on the concrete floor—more of my blood. A small pile of bones in the corner of the cage, some animal I'd eaten and picked clean two days before. I was starving again.

"I…don't know."

"Can you read and write?"

I observed my cell some more, noticing a short stack

of books in another corner. Loose papers were tucked between the pages. Oh yes, I remembered now. If I went over there, I'd find a small groove in the floor where I kept a pen. I used it to practice writing, copying sentences from the books. I'd had it for years and it ran out of ink a long time ago, but it was the only one I had, so I kept it. I just pressed hard to make indentations in the paper.

"Yes," I answered Doc. "I'm…teaching myself how. So I must be around thirteen."

"And how do you feel right now?"

"I feel…sad. Hungry. Lonely. I…" I resumed my breathing as he taught me, using it to navigate this other overwhelming need I didn't have words for at the time. "…I *want* something. No, someone."

"Can you tell me more about that? Are you wanting a particular person? Or more of a general wanting someone to keep you company?"

"No…I mean, I wish someone, anyone, was with me. But there is a person I want too."

"Who is that?"

"I don't know…I can't…"

It was just *there*, the person I wanted to see. Like someone was standing on the other side of a thick fog. I knew they were there, but I had to reach. My mind couldn't seem to—

"Fuck!" I jolted away when her face broke through into sharp clarity.

"Ivan, what is it?"

She appeared out of thin air, like a ghost, standing just outside of my cage. I could feel myself shrinking back against the wall, fear riding my system as she casually spun a knife in her hand. But it wasn't just fear, it was immense relief. A feeling so sweet, I wanted to cry. *Finally, she came to see me!*

The past feelings of relief rolled through me alongside the current ones, like oil floating on top of water, existing together but never able to mix. I *hated* her, hated that I had been waiting like a desperate puppy for her attention again, when she always just came to hurt me.

A violent anger simmered, held back on a tight leash by my breathing and this metal chair restraining me. *How could you?* I wanted to say to her. *I never did anything to you. I* needed *you, and you left me to rot down here!*

"Ivan, tell me what you see." Doc's voice grounded me, reminding me of my true location. "You're safe here, son. No one's gonna hurt you. Just tell me what you see."

"I see *her*," I whispered. "She's standing right outside my cage, trying to decide where she'll cut me today."

"Which one is it today?"

"*Her.*" I emphasized the word. "The one who cut my face and tried to take my eye. The one who always cuts me the deepest because she hates me so much."

"And how do you feel seeing her? What's going through your head?"

"I'm scared," I admitted. "I can't feel pain anymore, but I'm going to bleed a lot and that won't be good. But also I...I'm so happy." A shaky laugh escaped. "She hasn't come to see me in weeks. I'm so relieved she came back."

"Why?" Doc couldn't keep the disdain from his voice. "Why would you be happy to see her?"

"Sometimes I think she cuts me so deeply because she loves me. Why else would she keep coming back? She yells and screams that she hates me when no one else does. She's the only woman who talks to me at all. Maybe it's because I'm so alone and going crazy, but I *want* her to love me. I want her to keep coming back. I get so sad when she's gone for weeks."

Another laugh floated up from my chest, this one weak and embarrassed. "I feel stupid and weak for being happy to see her. I hate her. I hate that I want love or anything from her, but she's the only person in the world I have."

Doc was silent for a few moments. "Why do you want her to love you?"

"Because." I stared back at the woman with hollow, hateful eyes. "She's my mother."

FOUR

MARIPOSA

"Alright, you brave little lady." I scooped up a crying, fussing Vivian and turned to place her in Tessa's arms. "Here's your mama."

Tessa shushed and bounced Vivian against her chest while rubbing her back. "It's okay, sweetie, no more poking. Auntie Mari promises to be nice from now on."

I smiled at the familial term while I cleaned up debris from Vivian's shots. "Normally she'd have boosters in a few years, but there's no telling when new vaccines will be made. So you're off the hook for a while, little miss."

Tessa smiled as Vivian started to calm down. "How's everything going?"

"Eh." I shrugged and flung my hand in a noncommittal gesture, not eager to get into the fact that I hadn't spoken to two of my husbands in a month. "How are you holding up?"

"I won't say it's been easy," the young mother

sighed. "But now that Andrea's made contact, it's a little easier."

My eyebrows lifted into my hairline. "Oh, she has? That's great!"

"You didn't know?" Tessa frowned. "They translated her first message yesterday. T-Bone didn't tell me what it said, but she seems to be okay, which is all that matters to me really." She gave me a strange look. "I figured Reaper would have told you."

"Oh yeah, you know." I shoved my hands into the pockets of my white coat, trying to lean casually against the counter. "We've both been really busy."

Tessa wasn't fooled, her stare was as hard as a sledgehammer while I tried desperately to not shatter into pieces on the floor. I could fall apart again tonight in bed, with Jandro holding me. Not here at work.

"Mari, you'd tell me if something was going on, right?"

I pulled in a heavy breath. "Yeah! Yeah, of course. I mean, it's—" My chest shook, my resolve threatening to unravel. "It's just things are still kinda tense since…"

"Shadow?" Tessa guessed.

"Yeah." My chest deflated and I preferred not to elaborate. Word spread quickly after Shadow left. My guys didn't put out to the club the details of what happened, but people speculated and put pieces together on their own. Shadow was gone without a trace, but my injuries didn't fully heal until a week later. They saw the cuts on my nose, the bruising on my forehead and neck, and drew their own conclusions.

I would have loved nothing more than to set the

record straight, but the Steel Demons were Reaper's men, not mine. They would stand with his decision, no matter how I felt about it.

And it didn't feel right to hash it out with Tessa, who I had encouraged to leave her own husband. As shitty a partner as Big G was, he never hurt her in the way Shadow hurt me.

Thankfully, Tessa didn't press me to talk about it. She stood with Vivian in one arm, diaper bag in the other, as she gave me a quick hug. "You've been with me through so much. Remember I'm here for you too, Mrs. President."

"Thanks." I gave her a half-hearted smile. "I'll walk you out. Is T-Bone picking you up?"

"I dunno. One of those crazy bastards is," she laughed with a roll of her eyes.

It was actually Dyno, the sides of his head freshly shaved and topknot of dark hair pulled tight at his crown. He was all decked out in black leather, sitting atop a rumbling, stretched out Fat Boy in front of the hospital.

"There's my baby!" He grinned, reaching gloved hands out toward us as we came outside. It took me a moment to realize he was talking about Vivian, not Tessa.

"You'll hold her when we get home." Tessa smacked his hands away, but allowed him to take her diaper bag and secure it in one of the compartments.

"But Vivi told me she wants to drive." Dyno unwound a black scarf from his neck and proceeded to wrap it around the baby's head.

"I should've known you spoke Babbling Infant," Tessa cracked, helping him secure the scarf around Vivi's ears to muffle the noise of the bike.

It was cute and wholesome watching them, looking established in this routine like they did it all the time. I couldn't tell right off the bat if there was anything romantic between those two or not. It was pretty clear that the three Sons of Odin were all in a relationship with each other. But there was apparently some degree of openness to it, as I found out on the ride back from Blakeworth. Grudge had helped watch over Shadow when I caught Dyno and T-Bone in bed with a service girl.

"I'll see you guys later," I said with a wave.

Tessa and Dyno waved back as they pulled out of the lot, Vivi strapped to her mother's chest and looking stylish with her black head wrap.

"There you are, Mari." Dr. Brooks came up to me just as I returned to the hospital lobby.

"What do you need, Doctor?" I was itching to get back into work mode and stop thinking about relationships, especially mine.

"Just updating you. General Bray is sending a few units north to engage with some activity from Blakeworth. We want to have some field medics within reach just in case—"

"I'll go."

"Uh." The doctor blinked, taken aback. "You don't have to, we have a team ready. The mission is expected to take a few days, maybe a week. So I figured you'd want to stay here with your family."

"Is Rhonda staying?" I asked.

"Yes, she's retired from combat medic duties."

"Then the hospital is in good hands. If anyone on the field team would prefer to stay, I'll swap places with them."

Dr. Brooks' warm gaze turned piercing as he looked at me. "Are you sure, Mari? You've already been pulling a lot of long hours in the past few weeks. I was actually going to suggest you take some time off."

"I don't want time off. I want to work," I insisted. "Put me out in the field, Doctor. It's what I know and what I do best. My family understands."

His narrow-eyed stare continued to probe but he eventually nodded. "The team heads out tomorrow at five a.m. They're setting up ahead of the army, which is due to leave at six."

"I'll be here."

"Thank you, Mari." He gave a friendly squeeze of my shoulder. "Four Corners is in good hands with you. Go on and head home early if you don't have any appointments."

"Thanks, Doctor. See you in the morning."

Going home early was the last thing I wanted to do, so I killed time in the cafeteria with the other hospital staff on breaks until Jandro came to get me.

The evening wrapped up like every other one. I drove us home, washed up, we ate dinner together, and went to bed. I told Jandro where I'd be going tomorrow and while he didn't seem happy, he didn't fight me too much on it. Right before falling asleep, he agreed to let me take the dirt bike and ride to the hospital on my own. He didn't have to be at the garage until three hours later, and I insisted he get some much-needed sleep.

The world was still dark and cold when I crawled out of bed. After getting dressed, I wrote a quick love note for Jandro to find on the nightstand. It was little more than, *Love you. See you in a few days.* I was still half-asleep when I opened the bedroom door and crashed directly into a wall.

A solid wall that was warm, and smelled like cloves and whiskey.

"What…" My brain was slow to make the connection until a hand with strong, callused fingers clasped around my wrist.

"Mari, please." Reaper's voice was hushed. "We need to talk."

Even with how quietly he spoke, his voice was still a shock to my system. My heart jumped into my throat the moment he breathed my name, breath frozen for a moment until I composed myself.

"I don't have time for this." I pulled my arm out of his grip and tried to move around him, but he blocked my path, bracing a hand on each side of the door frame.

"I'm not leaving until you talk to me," Reaper growled. "This has gone on long enough."

"How did you even know I was getting up this early?"

"I didn't. I slept on the couch so I could catch you." He angled his head back, and I could see the pillow and messed up blanket on the long sectional in the living room behind him.

I also saw Hades and Freyja, their animal eyes bright as they watched us like a couple at a sports match.

Great, so our marriage is just as entertaining for gods as it is for humans, I thought bitterly as I went to duck under Reaper's arm. He stopped me, catching me around the waist. My temper spiked as I struggled to get away, but so did something else.

If my skin could talk, it would be crying out in sweet relief. I didn't even realize how much I missed Reaper's touch. The smell of him and the solidness of his body. It all came rushing back to me like a drug high as he pinned me against his chest with one arm, softly closing Jandro's bedroom door with the other.

"Let me go." I hardly dared to make my voice louder than a whisper, not wanting to involve anyone else in this. "You fucking let me go right now, Reaper!"

"No." His breath was hot, voice harsh against my ear. "You are my wife and I'm *never* letting you go." The fight started to drain from my body as I heard the deeper meaning in his words, loud and clear. The more I sagged against him limply, the tighter he held me. "I love you, and I'm never letting you go."

My legs wanted to give out, to let my strong, capable husband support me and make everything better. But just as my longing for him ripped open like a scab on a fresh wound, so did the resentment and the burning anger. He was stubborn enough to make good on his word, but I'd fight him every step of the way if he insisted on holding me captive.

Sometimes he could be reasoned with, and now that he was desperate, I hoped this was one of those times.

"I can talk for a minute, just get off me."

Reaper's arms released me slowly, like he was afraid I would bolt at the first chance. And I wanted to. We stood outside of Jandro's room, tension wrought between both of us in the dark, early morning.

"Do you, uh," Reaper's voice was harsh and raspy like he'd been smoking too much, "want to sit down?"

I sidestepped toward the couch he'd been sleeping on, pulling the blanket over my legs like it would shield me from him. Hades and Freyja, in their front-row seats to our mess, watched him move to sit on the far side of the couch. Looking at Reaper expectantly, I folded my hands on top of the blanket and waited.

"I..."

So eager to talk just a few moments ago, Reaper now seemed at a loss for words. His forearms rested on his knees, eyes flicking up from me and back down to his hands.

"I really have to get going soon," I told him. "And not just because I'm avoiding you."

"I understand. I just, I..." his head tilted back with an exhausted sigh. "I miss you so much, Mari."

I miss you too. So fucking much. My teeth came down hard on the inside of my cheek to prevent the words from coming out.

"I want my wife back." Reaper's hand moved to the couch cushion next to him, a small motion toward closing the distance between us. "I want *us* back." His hand slid a whole inch toward me, stopping as I scooted away. The hurt on his face cut like glass.

"You...*hurt* me." The words came out through

gritted teeth, my nails biting into my palms to remind me of just how much it hurt. "And you might not have killed Shadow, but you *destroyed* him. I loved him, Reaper. I knew it wouldn't be easy, that he would be a work in progress, and that he'd need help, possibly for the rest of his life. And you undid *all* of it."

"I know." His hand returned to his knee, fingers clasped loosely as his head hung low, his throat worked in heavy swallows. "I'm so, so sorry, Mari."

I didn't want to acknowledge that apology. It sounded half-hearted and cheap, so I said nothing. Silence passed between us, no sounds except for our breaths sawing in and out of our chests.

"I thought I was protecting you. I thought sending him away was my duty, as a president and a husband, to do things right." His voice, now heavy with sorrow, cut through the silent air. "That was wrong of me. I should have trusted your word, instead of writing you off to protect my ego." Reaper's head lowered until his hands touched his forehead. "I'm sorry. I never would have done it if I knew it would hurt you so much." His head lifted slightly, eyes turning toward me. "If I knew it would damage us like this, I'd have never let it cross my mind."

I could hear the aching hurt in every one of his words. He sounded sincere and truly pained by his actions. It dulled the edge of my anger a little, but not fully.

"Shadow is the real victim in this," I said. "You, me, Gunner, and Jandro? We all have the same things we started out with—the club, our jobs, this house, the favor of the governor. But *he* has nothing anymore. Do you realize that?"

Reaper nodded tiredly. "Yes, I know."

"I want to believe that you're sorry. I want to believe that you regret what you did and want to make things right. And I…" My breath shook as my chest tightened. "I want our family back together too."

"But?" he prompted me gently.

"But I can't just let this go while Shadow is still out there, suffering for the consequences of *your* actions." I stabbed a finger toward his chest. "At the end of the day, we still have beds to sleep in and food on our table. We still have a community that supports and cares for us. But *he* doesn't. And that," I shook my head, "means I can't go back to being happily married to you and Gunner. Not until I have *all* the men I love back where they need to be."

"I understand, sug—Mari." Reaper sighed deeply, rubbing his eyes. "If I allow him to come back into the club with no questions asked, would that be a step in the right direction?"

"Do you really mean that or are you saying it because it's what I want to hear?"

"I mean it. He can return to his original position, no questions asked. It's just…"

"What?"

"After knowing what he did to you, seeing it with my own eyes…" Reaper swallowed. "It…might be difficult for me to work with him, to trust him like I did before." His fingers clasped tighter together. "But I'll do it anyway. I'll welcome him back and I promise not to make any issues for him. It's just…something personal I have to get past."

"That's a nice sentiment," I said, skepticism coloring my voice. As long as he followed through on his actions, it didn't really matter to me how he felt. "Now, how are you going to let Shadow know he's welcome back in Four Corners with open arms?"

Reaper spread his hands. "I'll put the word out as far as I can. Governor Vance probably has more reach than me. But even *if* the message reaches him, it's gonna be up to Shadow to come home."

"Right." He wasn't wrong about that, but it hurt too much to think that Shadow might not *want* to come back. I pushed the blanket off my lap before I stood up. "Good talk, Reaper."

"Wait!" He jumped to his feet, panic crossing his face. "Is it…can we…" He swallowed again, the pulse in his neck firing rapidly. "Can we just…start talking again? Please?"

I grabbed my backpack by the front door and pulled it on, purposely stalling while trying not to look like I was. My chest ached with the need to scream *yes*, to run at him with the knowledge that he would catch me, take me to bed, and make everything better.

Instead, I fiddled with my straps while he stood there waiting, like I was about to sentence him to death or set him free.

"I'm going to be gone for a few days," I said. "Maybe a week. I'm going with the field medics to support your dad's units engaging with Blakeworth." My weight shifted on my feet. "We can talk more after I get back."

Reaper pulled his lips between his teeth. I saw his fists close at his sides and brow pinch in the start of his signature, disapproving scowl. I already knew what was going through his head—that he wanted to prevent me from going, or at the very least, send one of the guys with me.

But he dragged a hand down his face with a resigned nod. "Okay. When you get back, then." He seemed unsure of what to do with his hands, settling for resting them on his hips. Normally he'd be holding me tightly against him, hands on my ass and his tongue down my throat, making sure I got a goodbye worth remembering. "Be safe out there."

"Thanks. You be safe back here."

"I will. You, uh," Reaper cleared his throat. "You might see Gunner out there," he called after me as I headed for the garage. "Not in the first wave, but he'll head out there if the troops need backup." He ran a hand through his dark hair, rubbing the back of his neck. "I know he'd really love to talk to you too. Just for a moment, if you're up for it."

I didn't answer as I went through the garage door and headed for my dirt bike.

FIVE

MARIPOSA

I rode to the hospital, helped pack supplies for the field medic team into a couple of Jeeps and vans, then rode my little dirt bike north alongside the other vehicles. Being alone on my little bike, with the open road in front of me and the sun slowly rising, only deepened the yearning in my chest.

It wasn't just my men I wanted back, but our old life. I missed seeing them on their roaring bikes riding next to me and whoever I was clinging to. The grins on their faces and their wild yells as we tore across the landscape. Hands holding mine as I wrapped around them, or stroking my leg as we rode. We'd always had enemies, that was no different now. But Reaper was right about how our family had been fractured. A tear ran through us, separating us. We'd never be the same, but maybe we could move forward into something new.

Once *all* of us were back together.

I'd heard nothing new from Horus that morning, just like every morning before it. The more time passed, the more my emotions seemed to shift. I was growing tired of waiting for the right time, impatient and eager to have Shadow back. Something Reaper said this morning unnerved me though.

What if Shadow didn't want to come back?

What if he found a place to stay? A place where he could be safe, maybe even work as a tattoo artist? What if…

My dirt bike jolted forward, a result of my hand closing into a fist around the throttle. I eased my grip and the breath that had been stuck in my chest with where my mind went.

What if Shadow met someone?

I definitely wasn't the only woman in the world who was attracted to him. And he was confident now, expressing himself with ease. And that said nothing of how generous he was in the bedroom.

My pulse sped up, stomach flip-flopping at the memories of how he kissed me, how much sweetness and care he treated me with. A fresh knot formed in my chest at the realization that he might kiss someone else like that, touch another woman and please her using what he learned from me.

It only dawned on me then that he might be happier wherever he was. He might have found a whole new life to give him fulfillment and meaning. And if that were the case, what right did I have to demand that he return to me?

I leaned over my handlebars, refocusing on the road ahead. My plans wouldn't change. I would wait for Horus to tell me when it was time, then head out and find him. If Shadow was truly happier where he was, I'd leave him be and return home. I would find a way to forgive Reaper and move forward with my three husbands, not four.

No matter how wrong it felt to not have Shadow as mine.

I moved on autopilot when we reached the site in neutral territory to set up the field hospital. Having a team and being fully stocked with equipment was a luxury I never encountered while working alone. Four people got the canvas tents set up quickly, while the rest of us unloaded supplies and stored them where they'd be easiest to access in case of an emergency. We set up beds, gurneys, and curtains to divide sections of the tents for privacy. We had just finished when the sun was rising high, and were finally settling into having break-fast and coffee when one of the Four Corners Army Jeeps pulled up.

"Good morning, medics!" The lieutenant in the passenger seat hopped out to greet us. His name tag read GONZALEZ.

"Morning, sir. Coffee?" asked one of the younger medics, a woman named Cynthia.

"No, thank you. General Bray just recommended I stop by and let you all know essentially what to expect." He pulled in a breath and squared his shoulders back. "Blakeworth's scouts have been meeting with ours in the past couple of days and engaging with hostility."

"Meaning what, exactly?" Cynthia asked.

"Their scouts have started shooting at ours," I said.

"Initiating all the firing, even when they're both in neutral territory, from what Jandro has told me."

"Correct." Lieutenant Gonzalez nodded. "Their numbers and hostility have been increasing in the past week. No serious injuries to our men yet, but they're sending a clear message that they want a fight."

"So this war has actually started?" Another medic paled. "Like, this is the first actual battle?"

"We're hoping it's nothing more than a small skirmish," Gonzalez said. "They're showing off their firepower, trying to provoke a reaction from us. Our goal here is to show them we're just as strong, just as organized. We're still open to peaceful negotiations, if Governor Blake is willing."

"I wouldn't hold my breath on that," I muttered. Then, "Lieutenant, may I add something?"

"Of course, ma'am." He brought his hands together behind his back and stepped aside as I turned to face the wide-eyed group of medics.

"My brief time in Blakeworth showed me that their most vulnerable, their most disenfranchised citizens, will likely be the ones our soldiers meet in battle." I looked at Gonzalez, who confirmed my words with a nod. "It's our duty to tend to *all* the wounded, not just our own. If you are treating a Blakeworth soldier, give him the same care you would anyone coming into the hospital. Most of them are not thrown into this conflict because of love or loyalty, but because they have no other option. If you have someone who is conscious, let them know there is possible refuge in Four Corners." I cast one final glance to Gonzalez. "They'll be interviewed and evaluated by the army for citizenship once they're well enough."

I stepped aside and allowed the lieutenant to hold the team's attention once again. "We will engage the enemy just over that ridge." Gonzalez turned and pointed at a hill in the distance. If you see us coming down this side toward you, be ready. It means we've got injured."

"What if they completely overwhelm you guys?" asked another young medic. "And it's them coming over the hill on their way to capture or kill us?"

"Welcome to being a combat medic," I said sharply, turning toward the young man who spoke. "Being captured or killed is a risk that comes with this job. We're basically soldiers, only we try to keep people alive instead of killing them. As for defending yourself against a hostile enemy, you have scalpels, syringes, and lethal amounts of drugs. I've had to use all of them at one point or another, you probably will too. If any of this is too much for you, you're better off being a medic somewhere else."

Everyone was as still as a statue, except for Gonzalez, who was trying hard not to laugh.

"Understood, ma'am." The medic who asked the question lifted his chin and squared his shoulders.

He was *so* young, barely into his twenties, most likely. I saw a flash of myself in him for a moment, the bright-eyed nursing school graduate who left Texas for better opportunities, who wanted to bring some goodness back into the world. Nothing could have prepared me for the horrors I found along the way. My life on the road molded me, hardened me into someone who shut away all emotional responses when faced with battle injuries. It wasn't who I expected to become—the smiling, joyful labor and delivery nurse who would proudly place a newborn baby into its mother's arms.

Still, I preferred embracing the role of the hardened combat medic to the alternative—falling apart at the horrors of war and being unable to help anyone.

Lieutenant Gonzalez leaned toward me, a smile still playing on his lips. "You'd make a good drill sergeant, ma'am. No wonder General Bray likes you so much."

I snorted out a laugh. "He has to, because I'm his daughter-in-law."

The words stung my throat as they left. I hadn't thought about it until now, but I missed my kind, smiling father-in-law too. Shutting Reaper out also meant cutting off other members of my family. My in-laws and I were still only just getting to know each other, so it wasn't exactly the same. Even so, I had to remember my relationships with Reaper and Gunner weren't the only ones affected by our issues anymore.

The lieutenant only smiled as he headed back to his Jeep. "Thank you for supporting us, medics. And hang tight. The action could start in a matter of hours or days."

He drove off, leaving us to stand outside our tent.

"You heard him," I said to the others. "Be ready. Let's double-check the solar chargers and make sure everything's sterilized."

The rest of the day was uneventful. Gonzalez's men rotated patrol shifts every few hours, with the 'off' soldiers still required to stay nearby. Some of them came over the hill to hang out with us, drink coffee, take naps, and just shoot the shit.

It was early the next morning, roughly twenty-four hours later, when the first shot was fired.

We heard the *pop-pop-pops* of rifles over the radio of a soldier having breakfast with us. Then Gonzalez's voice ordering all units to the front line, and everyone sprung into action. The soldiers on break dropped everything and scrambled into their Jeep, tires kicking up mud and slushy ice on their way up the hill.

I yelled at all the medics once again to be ready. We were about to get very busy, very quickly. Returning to an operating table, I sprayed everything down again with an alcohol solution. I had just set the bottle down when a loud *BOOM* crashed through my eardrums and sent the ground shaking under my feet. It had some medics, myself included, falling on their butts.

"What was that?" someone cried.

"Was that the enemy or us?" another medic asked.

"Not us," I said, scrambling to my feet. "General Bray wouldn't be that aggressive right off the bat. It's Blakeworth."

"Bombs?" The young medic sounded panicked. "They're *bombing* us?!"

"Shh! Hey, hey!" I grabbed her shoulders and made her face me. "The soldiers *need* us. Stay with me, medic."

Another blast went off, this one slightly further away, but an ominous plume of black smoke rose up from the other side of the hill.

"They have backup units," I said, more to myself than the others. "If they're in trouble, help will come."

The first truck loaded up with injured soldiers came about fifteen minutes after the first explosion. I winced at the sight of the vehicle coming down the hill at lightning speed, fishtailing precariously through the mud and ice. The driver seemed to hit every boulder and uneven bit of terrain, which was no help to our patients that he carried. He swung around when he reached the flat plain of our camp, backing toward the main tent where we waited.

My worst fears were already confirmed as medics touched fingers to the necks and wrists of unmoving soldiers.

"Take the deceased to the black tent," I ordered quietly, my voice suddenly feeling like it lost all power. "There's nothing we can do for them right now."

Living soldiers were quickly rushed to different areas to assess and treat their most serious injuries. I helped two other medics lift a larger man onto a bed. He seemed dazed, but otherwise uninjured.

"Watch his head," I instructed, my nursing autopilot taking over. "Check for internal bleeding."

Blasts and gunfire raged on for hours. It was a special kind of torture listening to the variety of weapons and shouting voices, but being completely unable to see it. We only saw the effects of it as the injured and casualties swarmed our tents. The first wave of fighting stopped, but our work only carried on.

The medics took catnaps in rotating shifts, catching a few hours of sleep under a blanket or thick coat wherever we could. I couldn't tell how many days had passed, only that it was sometimes night and daytime at other points. My team was reaching their limit, as evident by the dark circles under their eyes and hollowness in their cheeks. They needed time off and rest, and soon, before the fatigue would start affecting their care.

You do too, my brain seemed to remind me in a small whisper. *You need the love of your men to bring life back to the zombie you've become.*

I shook it off, returning my focus to the tasks of my surroundings. If I put too much thought into how much I missed being surrounded by warm bodies when I woke up, having my feet rubbed and a glass of wine placed in my hand after a long day, I just might give in. I might relent to the fantasy that my body and soul craved, rather than remember the cruel reality.

There was a brief lull in the day during one afternoon. All current patients were stabilized and at the moment, there wasn't a truck hauling a bed full of bodies to us. I took a seat on top of a cooler that had stored some of our food, willing my torso not to slump over and crash in the dirt. Some field medics had developed the talent of sleeping while sitting or standing up. I never seemed to acquire the skill.

My eyelids slipped closed and I just as quickly snapped them open. Shit, I thought my two-hour power nap earlier would be enough to sustain me, but that was apparently not the case.

A few more minutes, I pleaded with my exhausted body. *If another truck comes, I need to be able to help.*

Biology wasn't having it. My head dipped low as I

slumped over, forehead nearly coming in contact with my thighs. I couldn't seem to muster the strength to sit up, I was so damn tired. *Just another day in the field.*

Something happened the moment my eyelids slipped fully closed.

I was instantly dreaming that I could fly, soaring high over a vast landscape of rocky terrain. My eyesight was incredible! From up here, I could see rabbits diving into the dense brush, prairie dogs hiding in their burrows. My body felt light but immensely powerful. I was fast enough to catch one of those animals if I was hungry, kill them swiftly with my talons—

And then, bodies.

Lifeless forms were strewn across black, scorched earth. The few that were still alive would be gone soon, bleeding out or broken beyond repair.

"What is this?" I heard myself ask. Was I actually asleep and dreaming, or was this something else?

Look, daughter.

Below me, someone was digging frantically at a mound of dirt and rock where it looked like one of the blasts had made a crater that had caved in. He started using a shovel, then tossed it away to move handfuls of earth away in a panic.

I circled down lower, taking in every detail with my sharp vision, from the scratches on the man's motorcycle helmet to the dirt under his fingernails. His breaths were ragged, labored, and he was alone. When the exhausted, panicked man looked up and met my eyes, I nearly fell out of the sky.

"Gunner!" I tried to cry out, but only a screech left my mouth. "What happened?"

"Horus!" my blue-eyed man rasped. "Get Mari and other medics! The blast caved it in and they're trapped!"

Like a slingshot, I propelled back into my own body. The momentum was so strong, I fell right off the cooler to the ground. But seeing him and hearing those words sprung me to action.

"Get the van and load it up with oxygen tanks, masks, and shovels!" I yelled, starting for my dirt bike. "Every available medic, follow me!"

I got some confused looks in return, but they sprung into action as I kicked the little bike into gear. Rest would have to wait.

Such was the nature of war.

SIX

GUNNER

E verything had been fine until the Blakeworth lieutenant ordered the use of explosives for no good goddamn reason. Horus felt the effects of the blast through his wing feathers, and I swore the sensation echoed through my human body as I came to in the Four Corners conference room.

"You okay, Gun?" General Bray asked me.

Reaper and I had decided to come out with my abilities to his father, considering that we planned to use Horus' sight to our advantage during the war. I was more than okay with this, as Finn was not only my family now, but one of the best tacticians I'd ever seen, and that included the many decorated generals I'd learned from at McAlister.

"Ugh, yeah." I pressed a hand down on the table, closing my eyes for a moment to get my bearings. "It's not good. They're blowing shit up."

"What?" The general paled, his face betraying the fact that I'd said his worst fear.

"We need to send the second wave out now," I said. "Our guys need backup or they're going to get demolished. I can ride out and be there in two hours."

"Go." With that, he turned to Reaper. "Ride out to the hospital. Tell Dr. Brooks they need to send more medics."

"Fuck, Mari's out there." Reaper brought two fists down on the table as he stood, stilling only when his father reached out to touch his forearm.

"Keep your head on straight. If they send more medics out, she'll be able to come home. Dismissed, both of you."

"If Blakeworth wants to be taken seriously as a territory, they won't attack the medics," I said to Reaper as I followed him out of the room. "Targeting medical staff has been a war crime for centuries. No one will want to ally with them if they pull that shit."

"I don't know if they care," he answered with a shake of his head. "None of the rules apply anymore, Gun. If they didn't make that clear when they kidnapped a governor's daughter, they sure as hell did when they brought bombs to a gunfight." Reaper paused next to his bike, releasing a sigh as he pulled riding gloves on. "I'm just worried about her, and even if she is okay, I know things are still gonna be shitty when she gets home."

"You talked to her, though." I sat astride my ride, pulling on my thickest jacket for the long journey to come. "That's getting somewhere."

Reaper shrugged, turning his engine over with a roar that leveled out to a rumbling purr. "Maybe. It didn't feel like much changed. Her being away just makes it feel worse. Like…" His hand slapped his chest pocket in search of a cigarette. "Like she's already left us."

"I know, man."

He wasn't wrong. The house had felt even more empty the last couple of days, knowing she wasn't at the hospital or hiding in Jandro's room. Even the smallest traces of her presence were gone, like her coffee cup in the sink or the damp towel hanging in the bathroom after her shower. Of course I missed actually talking to her, seeing her, hearing my wife's laugh and squeezing her in a hug, more than anything. But it was the absence of those little things that really made all the other stuff hurt.

That was what made it feel like we really lost her. That she was gone, and not ours anymore.

"We'll get her back." I raised my voice over the sound of our engines as we pulled out toward the street. *We have to. Or I'm gonna go ballistic if we don't fix this and she actually walks away.*

"Be safe out there, Gun." Reaper slipped into the flow of traffic and peeled out with a roar toward the hospital.

"Yeah you too, pres." I made a wide left turn and headed in the opposite direction, picking up speed as I raced toward the second wave units' camp. They would be ready to mobilize as soon as they saw me.

Hang on, guys. Hang on, Mari. I accelerated faster. *We'll be there soon. Just hang on for us.*

———

A SENSE of dread settled like concrete in my stomach as we approached the battlefield. I'd seen the black smoke from twenty miles away, now the air was thick with it and tasted like gunpowder.

"Fan out to the north and south!" I yelled to the unit leaders. "Stay on the perimeter and close in from the outside! Alpha unit, with me!"

Jeeps and motorbikes split off to either side at my instructions, while I led my team straight through the middle.

"Don't let me fall off, man," I mumbled, aiming my bike straight ahead while I slipped into Horus's point of view.

Oh…fuck.

So many dead and dying. Blakeworth's ground units moved over the scorched landscape with rifles and daggers. They shot and stabbed anyone clinging to life, but it wasn't mercy killing. One soldier tried to limp away on one good leg while the Blakeworth soldiers threw daggers at him. Another man crawling on the ground screamed as the enemy shot through his hands.

I returned to my own body, and the rage waiting for me there. My teeth ground like stones in my jaw, my grip painful as I accelerated my bike to its limit.

"Orders, sir!" the lieutenant yelled next to me, struggling to keep up with my speed.

I looked over my shoulder at him. "Protect the injured, respect the dead. And kill them all."

An embankment with a steep upward incline loomed up ahead of me. I kept my speed the same, heading straight for it.

"Sir!"

I ignored those around me, riding up the densely packed dirt like a ramp until I reached the crest and launched into the air. The carnage I saw through my falcon was laid out beneath me, the details dulled through my human eyes, but no less horrific.

In midair, I pulled the rifle from the holster across my chest and started spraying bullets at the Blakeworth ground units. Some shots I missed and the foot soldiers took off running. Thankfully, the perimeter units were already in position and started picking them off.

I landed hard on the ground, my bike's shocks protesting, but I managed to stay upright, shoot one Blakeworth coward in the back, and run him over. *Thank you Jandro, for the all-weather tires, even if they are ugly.*

My rear tire spraying up gravel and mud, I circled around and picked off more Blakeworth guys. They clustered together as they retreated, which was great for us. I did a quick check of all units through Horus before I grabbed the small radio clipped to my cut.

"Beta unit, this is Gunner. They're coming toward you," I said into the receiver. "You'll have a visual in about thirty seconds."

"Roger that, Gunner," Lieutenant Fields replied. "Shall we drop them a present?"

I smiled before responding. "Please do."

After the lieutenant confirmed my order, I returned my attention to the state of my surroundings. This area had been blown to bits, and from the looks of it, at least twenty people along with it. Several of my team were already tending to the injured, tying off limbs that were bleeding out or plugging up large wounds with whatever they had on them.

"Where's the field hospital from here?" I asked my lieutenant, a guy named Davis.

"Just over that hill," he pointed behind me. "There's been a truck going back and forth, transporting people."

"Good, so it's on its way back?"

"I think so, it—"

A deafening *BOOM* made my eardrums cry out in pain, Davis and I covered our heads as we fell to the ground. Dirt and gravel rained down on us, the little stones landing hard like mini-projectiles.

"Fuck, I hope that was ours!" I lifted my head carefully to take a peek when the shower ended.

Lieutenant Fields' voice crackled through my radio a moment later. "They were blown away by our gift, sir."

I couldn't help but laugh. "Good man. Keep your eyes peeled and I'll let you know about more clusters when I see 'em."

"Roger that."

"Sir, the truck!" Davis pointed, and I turned to see the white pickup truck coming down hard over the hill.

The driver turned, backing the vehicle up toward us with a bed covered in blood and viscera.

"Damn, wish we could spray that down," I muttered. I wondered how Mari felt about piling people with open wounds on such an unsanitary surface. Or did she even have time to think about stuff while working in a war zone?

"No time, sir. These people are clinging to life."

Davis and I worked quickly, lifting people in all states

of consciousness as carefully as we could into the truck bed. The driver, a sergeant by his insignia, got out to help too.

"Hey, have you seen a woman with the medics?" I asked him. "Long dark hair, really pretty face? She might be the one in charge down there."

"I dunno," he grunted, lifting an unconscious—or dead—soldier and placing him gingerly in the truck bed. "Half of the medics down there are women. I just drop off and pick up."

"Has the field hospital been targeted at all?"

"Nah. The action's all up here."

I nodded. That was a relief, at least.

The sergeant took off once the truck bed was full, and I damn near had to stop myself from jumping in his passenger seat. Even if it was through a bloody, mud-caked windshield, I wanted to see her. Just for a moment.

Two more trips later and no one remained in our area except for the ones who were unmistakably dead.

"We shouldn't leave them here," I said to Davis as I leaned down to close the eyelids of a soldier who looked barely eighteen. "Once this is over, we should have all the bodies recovered and ID'd."

"They deserve a hero's homecoming," he agreed, his voice rough.

I patted his shoulder as I went back to lean against my bike. "Give me a moment, lieutenant."

He stepped away, probably thinking I needed to compose myself, while I slipped into Horus again for a larger aerial view.

Our perimeter teams were doing a good job of ambushing the Blakeworth soldiers from behind. They expected us all to rush into the center, assuming they predicted we'd have backup at all. Without a doubt, the formations and weapons they used showed that they planned to massacre us. So much for this being a small skirmish. Like Reaper said, they had no qualms about fighting ugly. Unfortunately for them, neither did biker gangs.

If they wanted to fight dirty and underhanded, fuck yeah we'd give it to them.

"Keep pressing in on them, perimeter teams," I said into my radio when I came back to my own body. "We'll take no prisoners today."

"Some of Blakeworth's injured got tossed onto the medic truck," Davis said.

"That's fine. We'll give them a chance to recover and see how much better they'd have it if they were loyal to us."

"And if they try anything?"

I smiled. "I'll leave that up to the governor and my president."

Sudden movement caught my eye behind the dirt mound I'd just jumped off of. A head poked out from behind the hill and I pointed my rifle in that direction, but they ducked down and threw something from where they hid.

"Run!" I screamed, realizing immediately what it was. "Everybody move!"

Davis and his soldiers took off, but it was too late.

The grenade bounced once, rolled a few feet, and detonated with an ear splitting boom.

The force sent me flying, and I knew other bodies had been launched in the air too. Ringing filled my head and I landed hard, pain shooting up my shoulder. Grinding my teeth against the pain of the beating I took, I rolled and climbed shakily to my feet. My legs wobbled unsteadily beneath me as I made my way back to my unit.

"Guys," I rasped, nearly falling to my knees. "I got you guys, don't worry."

A shallow crater had formed at the base of the hill I had jumped from. A few members of my unit lay motionless, but Lieutenant Davis and half a dozen others still moved. Some rolling in pain, others screaming. "Don't worry." My hands shook as I reached for the nearest man. "I got you guys."

I was in shock, most likely. Speaking nonsense to myself, as well as the men. It wasn't until a hand clasped my arm that I realized a fine rain of dirt and gravel had continued to fall down on us.

"It's gonna collapse," Davis told me with a strangled cough as he shoved me away weakly. "Run, captain."

"No, no. Come on." I tried to tug him toward me. "I gotta get you guys to the truck. Can you walk?"

"Go, captain! Anyone who can move, go!" He shoved me more forcefully, and I was already so unsteady that I fell back, landing on my ass. "The hillside won't hold any more weight! You have to get away now!"

It dawned on me only then what he was saying, as

pebbles and dirt began falling in earnest, rolling down the hillside in bigger chunks.

"No," I whispered. "No, come on! You'll be trapped!"

"So will you if you come any closer!"

I grabbed my radio receiver with a shaking hand. "Any available units, we need assistance at the south-eastern side—"

"Negate that!" Davis yelled. "More bodies will mean a bigger landslide…"

His voice was drowned out by a low rumbling sound. It reminded me of the avalanches I'd seen at my father's ski resorts when I was young. But this time it was made by an avalanche of mud, loose earth, and rocks.

"No, fuck!" I scrambled forward, trying to get my useless legs underneath me, but it was already too late. They were getting buried faster than I could run, the soft bottom of the crater giving way so they sunk even deeper.

"I need men!" I shouted into my radio. "All available men and shovels! They got buried."

A crackling, heartbreaking reply came over the speaker. "We have our hands tied here, Gunner! Will assist when we can, but we can't spare anyone at the moment."

"Fuck!"

I crawled forward and started shoveling loose dirt away with my hands, my movements feeling heavy and too damn slow. My shoulders and arms cried out with fatigue and probably a few injuries from the blast as I dug like a dog in search of a prized bone. None of it seemed effective, I only found more dirt as I dug. Panic spurred me on. They probably couldn't breathe, couldn't move with the weight of a small hillside on top of them. Fuck, what if I was compacting the dirt and making it worse? But what else could I do, stop?

It was awful and probably hopeless. But no way in hell was I about to just sit on my ass and wait for help to come.

A screech from the air somehow reached through the ringing in my ears and I looked up, spotting my falcon circling overhead.

"Horus!" I cried out. "Get Mari and other medics! The blast caved it in and they're trapped!"

I didn't know if he heard me or if he even could do as I asked, but I was out of options. Help wasn't coming from the other units. I couldn't reach Reaper or General Bray from here. These people were dying, if not already dead. If that turned out to be because I couldn't reach them in time, I'd work that out with myself later. I just had to try, I had to put everything into getting them out.

My ears were so fucked, I didn't notice the arriving vehicles until I saw movement at the corner of my eye. Even then, I didn't stop. My arms were numb, movements clumsy and inefficient, but I could not fucking stop.

People came into the corners of my vision, wearing camo uniforms with red crosses—the medics! They came in from the sides with shovels, tossing huge clods of dirt over their shoulders. Still, I didn't stop.

Not until a small, gloved hand touched my arm, the other hand on my cheek to turn my face gently. My wife's face filled my vision, so beautiful even with the dark circles under her eyes and her brows knitted together.

"We're getting them out." I could barely hear Mari's voice, but watched her lips move slowly so I understood her. "Rest, my love. Let me help them, then I'll check on you."

I nodded, the fatigue settling deep into my joints with painful aches. Leaning away from the cave-in, I fell unceremoniously on my ass again and stayed there.

Cloudy sky filled my vision now, soft, gray, and endless. Before my exhausted eyelids closed, I saw Horus's dark shape as he circled over us.

SEVEN

IVAN

"Keep your knees slightly bent. Elbows too." I didn't stand too close to Jen, but touched my fingers to her elbows as a small reminder. "Don't hold your breath. You want to stand firm, but keep some flexibility. Try not to lock anything."

Jen nodded tightly, her shoulders relaxing a few centimeters away from her ears as she remembered to take a breath. She was still tense, but wasn't shaking anymore at least. Guns made her nervous. Almost as nervous as women used to make me.

Now she could hold one, and I could stand by and observe, teaching her a few things. Even touch her to help fix her stance, without worrying I was doing something wrong.

"Line up the sights like I showed you," I said, taking a few steps away. "And squeeze when you're ready."

She took a few more breaths before pulling the trigger, her eyes squeezing shut and her whole body startling at the noise. But she shot again and again at the rusted metal target we set up in the junkyard, until her magazine clicked empty.

Jen laughed as she set the gun down and removed her ear and eye protection. "I totally suck."

"You're getting better. You just need practice," I said, bringing over the case to put the gun away. "No one becomes a perfect shot overnight."

"How long did it take you?" She watched me remove the mag and return it to the foam placeholder.

"Two nights." She laughed and my chest relaxed, relieved that she understood I was joking. "I did take to weapons and bikes pretty quickly, to be honest. But I suck at plenty of other things."

"Like what?" Jen tilted her head as she peered up at me, chewing at the metal jewelry through her lip.

"Like people."

"I don't think that's true." She placed a hand on my arm, the second time she did that within a week. "Everyone here likes you."

"Because I keep to myself and don't bother anyone." I closed the case and slowly turned to move out of her reach. I liked Jen, but not to the point of touching each other regularly. Still, I didn't want to be abrupt and hurt her feelings.

"Well yeah, but not in the way you think." Her hand fell to her side. "All the girls are comfortable around you, and that's saying a lot for most of them who've escaped abusive men."

"I'm…glad for that. But it doesn't mean I'm great at socializing."

"Oh, stop being so hard on yourself."

Jen reached out to touch me again, and I let her fingers rest on my forearm. Not because I was open to anything from her, but when she said that, it reminded me of someone else.

The one person I *wanted* to touch me.

Jen stepped in closer to me, closer than we'd been even during tattoo sessions, and I followed my gut reaction to step away.

Shit, I thought at the flash of hurt crossing her face.

"Jen," I started, eager to soften the blow. "You've been a good friend to me—"

"It's alright, Ivan," she laughed sheepishly. "I can take a hint. I'll leave you be."

"I...just..." Fuck, this was difficult. I wish I could disappear into a hole in the ground.

"You're not over her." Jen nodded matter-of-factly, gesturing toward my arm. The arm that had the tattoo of *her* on the inside.

"I...guess not." Nor would I ever be. Not entirely. "How'd you know?"

"All the signs are there," she remarked with a shrug. "A man shows up alone, doesn't respond to any attention, though it's clear he's missing something or someone. But he keeps it all wrapped up, only finding comfort in drinking and staying busy."

"I'm that obvious, huh?" I rubbed at my forearm absently.

"I've been a bar wench a long time," she chuckled. "I've seen all kinds. Yours seems like a hell of a story, though." Her smile dropped and she asked quietly, "Are you gonna go back to her?"

If that was an option, I would in a heartbeat. If I had even the faintest sign, a whisper in the breeze or a vague note in one of those folded up cookies that I could be with *her* again, I'd be gone in a cloud of dust.

But it wouldn't happen. Happiness didn't come for people like me.

"No." I shook my head. "I'll move on from this place eventually, but there's no going back for me."

Jen's eyes widened. "Is she…?"

"No, she's alive. She's fine, actually." I forced my hand away from my forearm, to stop petting my tattoo like it could will Mari into real life. "She's much better off without me around."

Jen tilted her head again, giving me a skeptical look this time. "Not sure if I believe that."

"She is," I insisted. "That's not just me being hard on myself."

"If you say so, big guy." She nudged her shoulder into mine as we started walking back toward the service center. I recognized it as a friendly gesture I didn't need to step away from. "You seeing Doc today?"

"Yeah, as soon as I drop this off in my room." I held up the gun case.

"You want a drink before seeing him?"

"No thanks. He said he wanted me sober for this one."

"Ooh, interesting," Jen mused. "Trying something new?"

"I think so." I swallowed, my thoughts turning anxious. I had just started to feel like I was gaining control on these trips through my subconscious. Every time I made progress, Doc pushed me a little more. I'd come to sweating and panting, but my mind felt a little quieter after every session. A little bit less of the poisonous, evil place that I tried to shove down at every opportunity.

"Well, good luck." Jen made her way behind the bar once we got inside. "If you need me, you know where to find me afterward," she added with a wink.

"Thanks. I'll see you later, Jen."

I didn't want to encourage the idea that anything might happen between her and me, but if the tight clamp in my chest was any indication, drinking it away would be a necessity after tonight.

———

"WHERE ARE YOU, IVAN?" Doc's voice permeated my subconscious, true and clear, solid, like an anchor for me to hold onto.

"My cage." The answer was usually the same, but the feeling was different today.

"How old are you at this time?"

I looked down at myself, at my skinny arms and legs covered in dirt and the infected cuts across my thin body. Cuts that *hurt*.

"I'm young," I said, my voice sounding foreign in comparison to the small body it was coming from. "Eight, maybe ten years old?"

"What do you notice about your surroundings?"

"There's...there's not much." My cage was nearly empty, no books or reading material like the ones I taught myself from in later years. A dirty container of water was nearly empty. My threadbare blanket was laid out neatly in the corner. In front of me was a stick, the end sharpened to a point. A crude drawing was made in the patch of dirt just outside my cage—a simple face with eyes, a mouth, a nose, and long hair. A self-portrait of sorts.

"How are you feeling at this moment in time?"

"The cuts hurt," I said. "They're red and swollen. My whole body aches and I feel so tired."

"So you've been cut recently?"

"Yes, I think yesterday. And she…" My throat closed up at the memory, teeth grinding down and tears springing up at the painful memory.

"Who, your mother?"

"Yes."

"Can you tell me what she did?"

"She…" I lifted my hand to my face, feeling the puffy flesh, the tender soreness around my eye and cheekbone. "She started off being so nice. She said she wanted to give me a hug."

"And what did she do?"

"She…hit me." Doc didn't respond, so I continued on. "She said if I was a girl, that she would love me and hug me. She would protect me and never hurt me. But I'm a boy who will turn into a man. If I was free, I would just hurt girls, so I don't get hugs. That's why I have to stay down here."

"Ivan." Doc's voice sounded strained. "Have you ever been hugged by anyone?"

"No…Wait, yes." Another memory came forward,

one from a different, more recent time. I could feel the gentle pressure of a face resting on my chest, and small hands on my back.

"Do you remember how it felt?"

"Yes, it was…nice. It felt good." It was better than good. It felt like the warmth of sunlight on my skin.

"Good. I'd like you to try to visualize this person who hugged you. Imagine they're there with you, in your cage now."

"No." I shook my head. "She doesn't belong here. She shouldn't be in a cage with me. She's too good."

"It's just an exercise I'd like you to try, Ivan."

"No, I don't want her to see me like this."

"Ivan, take a deep breath. You're okay. You're safe."

My breaths were heavy, panicked and ragged as they sawed in and out of my chest. But after several rounds, my racing heart began to slow down. The bite of the metal cuffs on my chair reminded me of where I was.

"Are you with me, son?" Doc's voice pulled me further out of the panic, the fear, and the shame.

"Yes, I'm here."

"Good. If it's alright with you, I'd like to keep trying."

"Okay."

"You're still in your cage, yes?"

"Uh-huh." I could feel the swelling in my face now —my eye was swollen shut from the force of the blow. My face ached with every dull throb.

"Would you like a hug now? No tricks, no hitting. Just a bit of comfort from someone who showed you kindness."

The thought of such a thing made a sob rattle though my child-sized chest. It was *all* I wanted, just for someone to show me they cared.

"Yes," I choked out. "I wish I had that."

"Picture it, Ivan. While you're here, imagine that person wrapping around you. Soothing you. Telling you it'll be okay. Start with one small detail you remember, and then add another."

I thought of Mari, standing in front of me after I completed her back tattoo. She told me she was proud of me, then shyly asked if she could hug me. I said yes and she approached me, turning her head to place her cheek on my chest, and then her hands on my back.

I could feel it again—the light pressure of her body against me, her fingers moving over my back. It was easy to think of, I'd only thought of that moment hundreds of times.

"Is that helping you, Ivan?" Doc's low voice floated in. "Do you feel a bit better? A bit safer?"

In my memory, now morphing into some kind of fantasy, Mari not only hugged me, but treated my wounds. She put ice on my face and cleaned my cuts. Her touch was warm and gentle, and she always asked permission before doing something. Her brows knitted with concern, eyes just as sharp and focused as when she always treated someone.

She healed me—the eight-year-old me, alone, scared, and confused—just as she healed me as a man, with patience, warmth, and kindness. For the first time since beginning these sessions with Doc, I didn't want to leave.

"Ivan, are you still with me?"

"Yes," I answered. "She's making me feel better. So much better."

"Good. How are you feeling now?"

"I feel…safe. Cared for. I…" My breath hitched, like hitting a roadblock in my chest.

"What is it, son? Go ahead."

"I…miss her." Everything started fading away. Mari, the cage, my pain, all of it. And fuck me, I didn't want it to. "I miss her *so* much."

"Okay, Ivan? You're coming out of it on your own. Take it easy, slow. Remember your breaths."

My leg kicked out, a reflex that jolted me out of my hypnosis with a start. Doc, the room, my chair, every-thing came sharply back into focus. And my sweet fantasy was already fading, like a dream I'd just woken up from and started to forget.

Doc knelt in front of me, unshackling the chair restraints as he peered up at me. "You alright?"

My skin had broken out in a cold sweat and my heart pounded furiously in my chest like I'd just ran for miles. I was back and had mixed feelings about it.

"Yeah, I think so." I stretched out my leg once he released it. "What was that?"

"Just a little visualization practice." Doc stood from the floor with a groan and went to unbind my arms. "If you like that technique, we can try it again next time."

"I…didn't want to leave," I admitted, rubbing my forearm once freed. "I'd never felt anything like that before, at that age, and it was all I really wanted."

"That's the power of your mind, son." Doc leaned

back with a small smile. "We absorb things that other people tell us, then we tell ourselves those things, not realizing that not everything we think is true. By replacing the internalized message with something else, we can unlearn what we thought we knew."

I blinked at him, sort of following, but not really. "What was I unlearning just then?"

Doc's face softened even more. "That you were at fault for the abuse you received. You internalized that belief at a young age, Ivan. But have you ever stopped to think it wasn't true?" The older man gave my shoulder a soft pat. "You were just a kid who needed a childhood, needed hugs. And visualizations like this can help shift your thoughts into something less destructive."

I nodded slowly. His words weren't fully sinking in but they made logical sense. Mostly, I was just trying to recapture the feeling of Mari's embrace, grasping for it as it slipped further out of my reach.

"Would you like to try it again next time?" Doc asked.

"Maybe, but…"

"Yes?"

"What if…the person I thought of, visualized…" The words felt stuck in my throat, but I forced them out. "What if thinking about her is also painful? The memory of her hug was comforting to me, but…"

"Has she also harmed you in some way?"

"No, but…" I sucked in a breath. Doc knew about my violent sleepwalking episodes, but not the extent to which I injured Mari. It felt wrong somehow, to use her in my therapy, even if it was our good memories from before I hurt her. I felt like I was taking more from her, keeping her shackled to me when I should have been setting her free.

"She is someone I…had feelings for," I finally said, watching Doc's slow nod. "It's my fault that it didn't work out, but I want the best for her and I'm…trying to move on. I just worry that thinking of her like this isn't actually good for me. Or her."

"Well, thankfully, no one can police your thoughts," Doc said with a warm smile. "You can rely on another visualization if you think it would be better. The power is really in your hands here." He stroked his goatee. "As for moving on from that relationship, I don't believe a positive memory will hinder your progress in that regard." Doc gave me a curious look. "Time and distance seem to do the job best."

I lowered my gaze. The weeks spent away from Mari only seemed to deepen the ache of losing her. Every passing day that she didn't greet me with a 'good morning' felt emptier than the last. My spontaneous tattoo of her certainly didn't help.

"I'm sure you know," Doc continued, "that people from our past never really leave us, even long after they're no longer in our lives."

A derisive snort left me before I could contain it. If I could escape the people from my past, I wouldn't be in this situation right now.

"Every person we meet shapes us into the people we are. Even brief relationships can have a lasting impact on our lives. If this woman made you happy, well, what's so bad about holding on to the good memories? Especially if they can improve your wellbeing."

"I don't know." I stood from the chair, stretching from my cramped sitting position. "It feels like I don't have the right to them."

"But you do, Ivan." Doc approached me and touched his index finger to my forehead, something Mari had also done before. "You have *every* right to good memories because you were there. You experienced them, they're yours." He tapped his finger twice on my forehead before dropping his hand away. "And no one can take them away from you."

EIGHT

MARIPOSA

With quick work and oxygen at the ready, we were able to save everyone in the cave-in who had survived the initial blast, about half of Gunner's unit.

Those with the worst injuries were quickly transported back to the field hospital. Everyone else, we told to sit tight until the van came back. Even with oxygen and rest, they were no longer in fighting shape after what they'd been through.

Gunner too had been rattled. He was covered in dirt from trying to dig them out, had clearly been in shock, and seemed to experience some hearing loss from the blast.

"We shouldn't stay here," Gunner said, his voice a rough rasp. "The perimeter units are holding off Blakeworth, but we're still in the middle of a battlefield."

"We'll get them moving soon," I said, not wanting to argue. "Let me check you over."

He thankfully kept still while I moved my hands and

stethoscope over him. I had to feel under his clothes and tried to remain as clinical as possible, but something passed between us as my gloved hands pressed on his abdomen.

This was my husband, not just any patient in my care. This was a man I hadn't touched in weeks, despite how intensely I craved him. He let out a soft grunt at the pressure from my fingertips and I fought hard to not recall the last time I heard him make such a noise.

"Any pain when I touch you here?"

He snorted, and I knew he was holding back some wisecrack reply. "No, no pain."

"Any ringing in your head?" I moved to his side and shined my penlight into his ear canal.

"Oh yeah. It's pretty much all I hear."

"Yeah, that'll probably last for a few days."

He snorted again. "Great."

I slid my stethoscope dial up his back, under his shirt, resting it over where he wore the tattoo that matched mine. "Breathe deeply for me."

Stepping away after he took a few breaths, I pulled the eartips out while making sure I put some physical space between us. Being close to him, touching him, it was intense, bordering on too much. Like with Reaper, it was annoying how much his close proximity affected me. I resented all the attraction and chemistry with these two men, hating the possibility that it might influence my judgment of their actions.

"You might have inhaled some particulate tossed up in the air from the blast," I explained clinically. "Take it easy for a week or so. You might have a cough for a few days. Let me know if you cough up any blood."

He lowered his blue gaze to his lap, an ironic smile on his face. "Does this mean I'm allowed to talk to you again?"

I released a sigh and crossed my arms over my chest, knowing this conversation would have to happen sooner or later. "You talked to Reaper, I take it?"

"Yeah." He lifted his shoulder as if to shrug, then winced as he lowered it back into place.

"I'll get you an ice pack for that," I said. "So did he tell you what would set this right for me?"

Gunner nodded. "Yeah, he did." He went quiet after that, looking at me as if waiting for me to explain myself. When I didn't and just continued to meet his stare, he lowered his gaze again with a sigh. "Mari, I love you—"

"Stop right there." I raised a hand. "This isn't a negotiation, Gunner. I know you're good at that, but you won't convince me that I'm better off forgetting Shadow. Frankly, it feels manipulative."

"I'm not—"

"I said, *stop*. Let me finish."

A muscle feathered in his jaw as his mouth clamped shut. He looked determined to speak, but thankfully held back.

I lowered my hand, my throat tightening with emotion. "And it…hurts that you took Reaper's side over listening to me." I sniffed, batting my eyes as I willed the tears not to fall. "That hurt a lot, Gun. So can you understand why I don't want to hear you say you love me? Or are you going to ignore that too?"

His mouth dropped open, brow knitting with tension as his hands wrung in his lap like he was fighting the urge to touch me. With a sharp breath, his jaw closed, teeth clicking with how hard his mouth shut.

"I'm sorry, Mari." Gunner blinked and I saw the beginnings of tears welling in his sky-blue eyes. "I'm sorry I didn't listen to you. I should have. I should have spoken up and told Reap it wasn't what you wanted. I hurt you and we," he paused to swallow thickly, "we probably fucked up his life when there was another way."

The air seemed to whoosh out of us both. It was like a small crack had formed in the tension between us over the last several weeks. We weren't out of the woods yet, but it was something.

"I'm not trying to make excuses, just explain," Gunner said with another shaky breath. "We were just…convinced it was the right thing to do. The *only* thing to do. We wanted to protect you, baby gi—Mari. But I understand," he nodded to himself, "the damage was already done and it wouldn't have happened again. Shadow is the type of guy who will go to extreme lengths to protect you from himself." Gunner met my eyes again, the blue depths filled with sadness. "What Reaper did—what we did—was wrong. It was badly thought out, and we should have listened to you."

"Thank you for referring to Shadow in the present tense," I said softly. "But you know this can't stop here. *Anything* that comes up between us, you will have to listen to me. You can't just steamroll over me when you've already decided what to do. When something concerns me, you have to actually listen to what I want."

"I know." Gunner nodded again. "You're absolutely right, Mari. I'm sorry it took such a painful event for me to realize this. I promise I'll do better." He extended a hand, and I held back as long as I could before placing my fingers in his. His hand wrapped around mine, long fingers stroking over my palm. "It's good to talk to you again."

I nodded, but felt like I'd be unable to voice the same sentiment without bursting into tears, and thus letting myself fall against his chest. "I should check on your unit," I said instead, pulling my hand out of his.

He reluctantly let me go, sad eyes watching me as I turned my back. Even without looking at him, I could feel his stare as tangibly as the kisses he used to leave on the back of my neck.

Further away from him, I could focus better as I checked oxygen levels and injuries. When the truck returned, we helped people into the bed carefully and moved out to return to the field hospital.

"You coming with us, or staying?" I called to Gunner as I straddled my dirt bike.

He stood next to his bike, talking into the radio clipped on his cut. "I'll meet you back there in a bit. Maybe, um—" He shoved a dirt-covered hand back through his hair. "The hospital is sending another team of medics so you guys can take your leave soon. If it's okay with you," he pulled his lip between his teeth, "maybe we can ride home together?"

Oh, how I wanted to. I yearned to ride off to some beautiful, secluded place and catch up on all the time I lost with my golden gunman. But the hurt wasn't completely gone, only slightly healed from his apology. I wasn't ready to go back to being a happy family again. Not until our whole family was back together.

"We'll see," I answered noncommittally. "I'll have to give reports to the new head medic when they arrive."

He nodded, reluctantly accepting that answer as he turned to continue listening to his units through the radio.

"Be safe," I told him, turning my bike around. "Don't make me come out here to pull you out next." I saw the hint of his gorgeous smile before I drove off, kicking my bike into gear to catch up with the supply van.

I heard a high-pitched screech rolling through the air, even over my engine, as I spotted Horus dive bombing like a missile for some food. The memory of soaring, of seeing the whole battlefield through a bird's-eye view came to the forefront of my mind.

It wasn't a dream, was it?

No, daughter. You needed to see, so I lent you my eyes.

The answer came clearly through my head as though Horus had been flying right next to my handlebars.

"What's the point?" I demanded, my voice low and barely audible over my bike. "I don't understand any of it. Shadow being exiled, my marriage falling apart. Just why?"

The point is growth, daughter. Just as there is no flying without falling, there is no growth without pain.

He said nothing after that, and I didn't inquire further. The next few hours were a busy hustle-and-bustle of treating new patients. The new medic team showed up just before nightfall, and not a moment too soon. My exhaustion had returned with a vengeance, and I was nearly falling asleep on my feet.

"At ease, Mariposa." The head medic of the second team, a tough woman named Tori, patted my shoulder. "Get some sleep before you head home."

"Has, uh," I forced my eyes to stay open, despite how heavily my lids drooped. "Has my husband come back?"

"He's been radioing updates. The battle is pretty much over. I think he and the remaining units will be heading straight back to deliver intel to General Bray, last I heard."

I nodded as I meandered to a corner of the tent to lay down on a cot with a blanket. A big part of me was disappointed that Gunner didn't come here to ask me again about riding home. Seeing and touching him had reawakened so much *feeling* that had been numbed over the past few weeks. I wanted both of my husbands that I'd pushed away in all of my senses, to consume them like drugs.

The only thing I wanted more were the wrongs committed against Shadow to be reversed, for my beautiful, scarred man to return home to me.

I pulled the blanket over me and curled my legs up to my chest, fluffing the lumpy, cheap pillow under my head into something marginally more supportive. Lying there, settling into my exhaustion, I wondered where Shadow was right then, what he was doing.

Did he still think of me as much as I thought of him? His letter said he would never forget me. I couldn't forget him if I tried, despite him telling me that I should. Did he even have a tent over his head and a blanket like me? Was he hungry or lonely? Or maybe he was just fine, living a life that never would have been possible if he hadn't been freed from the SDMC.

I drifted off to sleep with memories of kissing scars over warm skin and corded muscles, and swore I jolted awake only seconds later to Horus' voice.

Wake up, daughter.

Blinking at the early dawn light coming through the tent, I pulled the blanket tighter around me against the chill. Medics were already up and about, making coffee and breakfast over camping stoves, chatting quietly, and tending to patients.

"Coffee, Mari?"

Someone pushed a steaming cup into my hand before I could answer, and I wrapped my hands around it gratefully. A few careful sips warmed me up enough to get moving, and I was unsurprised to see Horus perched on my bike just outside the tent. He faced east, the same direction as the rising sun.

Make your preparations, daughter, his ancient voice echoed in my head.

"Preparations?" I repeated. "For what?"

For a long journey. The falcon stretched his wings out

to the sides, sunlight illuminating the long, graceful feathers. *Tomorrow is the day.*

"Tomorrow?" I gasped. "You mean…?"

We leave to pull a man from the shadows, he said. *And begin a new stage of growth.*

NINE

JANDRO

I hated empty houses. They always felt fucking weird, like ghosts were lurking, because homes were meant to be filled up with people. With a family.

My house growing up was wild. If me or one of my sisters wasn't causing a ruckus, my aunt and uncle would be yelling at each other across the house from different rooms. It was just how they had a normal conversation.

In Sheol, I didn't spend a ton of time at home until Mari came into our lives. But that place was different. The clubhouse and my bike shop were just as much my home as the place I shared with Shadow. Our club thrived because of the sense of community there.

But here? I didn't know how the fuck we ended up here.

Mari had been gone for going on six days straight to run the field hospital for the Blakeworth skirmish. Four days in, Gunner headed out with the backup units. Back at our so-called home, Reaper and I were just in and out, barely interacting.

I spent most of my days at Dave's garage, tuning up the club's vehicles and helping Dave out with his workload when I had spare time. Coming home to a dark, empty house was the worst. I ate enough to get by, showered and got into bed to start the whole day over. Reaper usually got in later than me, and I didn't care enough to keep tabs on his whereabouts.

Even before Mari left to work out in the field, it was like I could feel the life in our home slowly suffocating. She spent all her free time at the hospital, avoiding the other guys and barely talking to me beyond surface level stuff.

Our new house had been lively and bright the night of our homecoming party, filled with happy people and good cheer. It felt like a turning point for us, a chance to put roots down and become a real family unit. I never expected our sense of home and togetherness to start dying that very same night.

For weeks, I went back and forth between feeling pissed at and sorry for Shadow. We all hated that Mari got hurt, but the big dude never had a say in what happened to him. He didn't have control over how the abuse from his previous life would affect him. Shadow was a victim too, and what happened to Mari was a long-festering symptom of the damage that had been done to him.

But Reaper was president. My bullheaded best friend would have thrown *me* in a damn jail cell if I tried to stop him. I knew him even better than I knew Shadow. The one thing I knew that Reaper would never admit, was how fucking scared he was.

Losing his parents had almost broken him. Losing his brother *did* break him. Finding Mari had helped glue some of those broken pieces back together. If he were to lose her? Nothing would bring him back from that.

He was terrified of losing those who mattered most to him. That kind of fear turned a rational man into a creature who reacted on instinct, relying on past events as a means to protect his future.

Like the parts of a motorcycle, I knew Reaper well enough to fit together all the pieces of his history. The sum of which spurred actions and a mindset that didn't surprise me in the least.

It didn't mean I had to like it. We'd exchanged few words over the past weeks, mostly him asking how Mari was, and me always giving the same answer, "Fine."

I felt like a robot, like those automated machines I heard stories about that used to build cars and computers. My mind was blank, empty and numb as my body went through the motions it was supposed to. Eat, sleep, feed chickens, shower, work.

The emptiness of the house didn't even register when I came inside that evening through the garage door. It would send me on a downward spiral if I let it, and I couldn't. It felt like I was the only one keeping this family together, albeit by fraying threads. Distantly, I knew Mari was due to come home after a week. With six days that had passed now, I'd have to find out if anyone knew if she was on her way back.

I ate a cold dinner, checked the heat lamps in the chicken coop, showered, and got ready for bed. No sooner than my head hit the pillow did I hear the high-pitched rattle of a dirt bike pulling into the garage.

I sprang out of bed and yanked on a pair of shorts, feeling something close to alive for the first time in days. I didn't even notice the cold as I whipped the garage door open.

"*Mariposita!*" I declared with a genuine grin of happiness that felt strange on my face.

"Hey." She turned off her bike and pulled her helmet off, making her long hair stream out like the tail of a comet. "Sorry, did I wake you?"

"Nah, I just went to lie down." I approached her, the concrete floor icy on my bare feet, but I didn't give a shit. "Welcome home. What do you need, *mi amor?*" I rubbed the arms of her jacket, planting a kiss on her forehead. "You hungry?"

"No, I'm okay." She glanced up at me with a weary smile. "I think I'll just shower and go to bed."

"Sounds good to me." I slid my arms around her in a loose hug, dropping another kiss in her hair. I didn't even care that she smelled like dirt and sweat, my girl was home. "I'll keep your side of the bed warm."

"Thanks, love." Mari brushed a soft kiss under my jaw before pulling away. It was nothing like the passion we shared before all of this shit went down, but I would take it.

We got inside and I set out a clean towel for her before slipping back into bed. Her shower was long, probably the first one she had in nearly a week. I nearly fell asleep before hearing the water shut off, but scooted to my side of the bed to make room for her. Mari padded softly across the dark bedroom to her side, lifting the sheets before sliding between them.

"Thank you for warming my side." She scooted to the middle, nestling between my arms for our nightly cuddle.

"*Siempre*," I murmured sleepily before blinking my eyes open, pulling her tighter against my chest. "Do you want to talk about your week?"

"Not really." Mari's lips brushed my chest, her fingertips trailing lightly across my ribs.

"Want to talk about anything else?" I played with the ends of her hair trailing down her back.

"Not tonight. Just…" she trailed off, burrowing into me closer than she had in weeks. "I love you, Jandro."

"*Mariposita*, I love you so much." I reached under her hair to cup the back of her neck. "And I missed you like hell while you were gone."

"I missed you too." She drew in a shaky breath. "I miss…*everyone.*"

"They miss the hell out of you right back." I rubbed into her neck, rolling my fingers over the knots there. "And I'm including Shadow in that."

Mari pulled back to look at me, her gaze finding mine in the darkness. "If he comes back, would you accept him? Into the club, our home, our life again?"

"Yes," I said without hesitation. "I would, if only to see you happy again."

She stiffened slightly. "What about for him?"

"I'd love to have Shadow back in general, but you are my priority." My palms spanned across her back. "Having him around and in…a better mental state would be great, *bonita*, don't get me wrong." I tapped a finger to the tip of her nose. "Just as far as reasons go, you are at the top of that list. Always."

"Jandro..." Mari sighed, her lips landing on my neck when she leaned in again. "When you say that, I actually believe you."

"Good, 'cause it's the truth."

She didn't say anything else, so I shifted into the mattress, pulling the blankets higher over us to settle in for sleep. It was expected to be a cold night, and I silently hoped she'd sleep in late with me after her long, hard week out in the field.

Mari kissed my neck again, lips lingering sensually. Her tongue flicked out against my skin and I let out a soft groan, my body already heating up a few degrees.

"Babe?" I muttered, the hope clear in my voice.

"Mm-hm?" She kept kissing me, her short nails now making trails of heat over my chest.

"Are you seducing me?"

"What do you think?" There was a tone of playfulness in her voice I hadn't heard in so long.

I slid a palm over her hip, taking a handful of her flesh there before pausing. "Has something changed?"

We hadn't done anything sexual in weeks. With how messed up things were, it wasn't like I had an insatiable drive anyway. A couple of half-hearted tugs in the shower was the most action I'd had since the awful night of our housewarming party. Of course I wanted my woman more than anything, but seeing her so heart-broken killed any selfish desire I had.

"I'm just tired of feeling miserable." Mari slid her leg

over mine, resting her thigh on my hip. "I love you and I want you. I want to feel good again."

"Say no more, *mami*."

With a deep kiss, I rolled us to her back. She slid her other leg out and wrapped them both around my hips, already drawing me to her core.

"No, no, not yet." I was already fully hard and aching, my body just as desperate to be with my wife as I was. "I won't last if we go straight to it."

"I don't care, I need you." She pressed up, lining her body flush to mine with another one of those damn neck kisses that never let me think straight. "I just need to feel you, Jandro."

"Mari..." I grunted out a weak protest.

She was so soft and warm. Her need for me sent the primitive part of my brain wild. I wanted to give her what she asked for, to drive deep into her silky heat and just rut until my release.

But I also hadn't touched my wife like this in weeks and I wanted to celebrate it. To spend the whole night savoring and pleasing her. I wanted this to be a new corner we turned, the start of healing our family again and putting the painful weeks behind us.

"Please, Jandro." Her hand grazed down my body to stroke me—fuck—no, to direct me toward her entrance.

"Wait." I grabbed her hand, unwrapping it from my cock. "Let me give you a few orgasms first."

"A few?" Even in the dark, I saw her eyes narrow at me. "How many is 'a few'?"

"Hm." I brought her hand to my lips and kissed her wrist. "Three?"

"No. I want you so bad, I know I'll come when you fuck me."

"Two, then?" I bit lightly on the tip of her finger.

"Jandrooo..." Then she giggled. "I can't believe we're arguing about this."

"Beats fighting over other stuff, right?" I kissed the center of her palm. "So, two it is?"

She smiled wickedly. "One."

"Hmm." I released her hand, running a long caress down the gorgeous curves of her body. "One and a half?"

"A half? What are you—uh, fuck..."

I rolled her clit under my thumb, watching how her hips rose off the bed to meet my hand.

"Fuck yes," I said in a harsh whisper, utterly mesmerized at how she moved. "I want to watch you come like this."

"It's not enough," she whined, fisting the sheets at her sides while her hips chased the pleasure my hand was giving her. "I need more, Jandro."

"I got you, babe. Don't worry." I turned my hand, my fingertips quickly finding her slick entrance.

Her satisfied moan sent my cock twitching as my hand pressed through to the center of her heat. My woman quickly grew needy again as my fingers curled and stroked inside her, my thumb resting next to her clit.

"Jandro..." Oh, how I wanted to hear her say my name like that all fucking night.

"Uh huh, I'm right here." My left hand pressed her thigh to the mattress as I fucked her with my right. My cock twitched again, as if jealous of the other body part that got to touch her.

"Come on, I need you." Mari shifted her hips, an attempt to direct my thumb to move on top of her clit, but my grip on her thigh kept her in place.

"You never said there was a time limit on our orgasm agreement," I informed her with my most charming smile. "What if I don't want you to come until dawn?"

"Ugh." Her head flopped down heavily on the pillow. "I never even agreed to a stupid orgasm deal. I just wanted sex before sleep!"

"And I want to make up for over a month of not pleasing you." I leaned down and drew a pert nipple into my mouth, sucking on the tight bud until she gasped, then releasing it with a pop. "As a husband should."

"I should have known you would," she laughed, scratching lightly over my neck and upper back.

"Trust me, babe." I mouthed my way to her other nipple, bringing that delicious peak under the same treatment of my tongue. "I'm dying to be buried inside you. But it's like I just told you." I scooted up to kiss her lips, our mouths locking for a moment with sweet pulls and tongue caresses. "My priority is you." I kissed her again quickly before making my way back down her body. "Always you."

My fingers dragged along the walls of her channel and her hips shot up from the bed, crashing against my mouth. I took the opportunity to suck a kiss low on her pelvis, a few inches away from her clit that was begging for my attention.

Mari's whines grew guttural, desperate. Her fingers raked over my scalp as my mouth hovered closer to her clit, her thighs already shaking. The reaction was instant when I finally kissed her there, her scream undoubtedly reaching the second story of the house. I secretly hoped Reaper was home, listening to what she wanted with me and no one else.

I heard Mari's panting above me, her pussy starting to close around my two fingers, despite me spreading them wide. Her clit was a small pebble under my tongue, the one hard spot on her supple body that tried to squirm and thrash under my hold.

She came with another beautiful scream, her body going rigid as she convulsed around my fingers. Thighs clasped to my ears, that succulent pussy bucked against my mouth. I sucked at her tender flesh until she pushed my head away and whimpered at me to stop.

Drawing up her body, I lined myself up with her and pressed inside with slow ease. I kissed her mid-gasp as I settled between her thighs, her body so warm and receptive to me.

My first few strokes were long and slow, drawing out all the way before filling her back up. When her thighs squeezed tighter around me, hips tilting up for more friction, I slid my hands under her back and rolled us so she was on top.

"Show me how you were gonna seduce me." I grinned breathlessly, relaxing one arm behind my head while keeping the other glued to her hip.

Mari's breath was still coming in short pants, the

movement of her ribcage and breasts utterly erotic in the dim light. She ripped my hand from her hip, reaching over to pin it next to my other hand behind my head. My woman stared at me with a fiery intensity as she rolled over the length of my cock in a seductive rhythm, while keeping my hands pinned next to my head.

"Is this what you wanted to see?" she asked, lips hovering over mine. "Riding you for myself?"

"Yes," I groaned, lifting my hips to meet her as she crashed down. "Take what you want from me."

The tight buds of her nipples skimmed up and down my chest as she moved. My fingers curled with the need to touch them, to draw them into my mouth and hear her resulting yelps. I could have broken her hold on my wrists easily, but didn't dare. It was so hot being used by her, watching her take her pleasure while I laid back and enjoyed the view.

Mari eventually released my wrists after a few more minutes of vigorous riding, dragging her nails down my chest as she sat upright. Her movements slowed to a more languid, back and forth motion, fluid and hypnotizing.

"You're close again," I rasped, my hands running up her thighs to her waist. I could feel it in how tightly she wrapped around me, the quickness of her breaths and heat in her skin.

"Uh huh." Her hands covered mine. She didn't seem to be chasing the release, but riding the feeling out slowly as she rolled over me. "I just want to keep feeling you."

"Ride me all night if you want to." My touch extended over her ribs, her breasts, and the long curve of her spine. "All I want is to feel you too."

I reveled in every lowering of her hips, her slick heat enveloping me so sweetly. My breath stuttered for control with each long drag out of her pussy, fingers digging into her flesh as I fought to keep the control in her hands. This was for her, after all. This was all about giving her something good, something to start us on the path of healing.

Eventually, Mari's patience wore out and she began rocking back and forth on a vigorous ride again. Her hands braced on my chest as her brow pinched with tension, grinding her body into me with harder crashes and more friction.

"Oh yes, yes," I encouraged her, driving up with hard thrusts to meet her need. "Let me see you come all over my cock."

Her pussy wrung me out with its release and Mari nearly took me with her, crying out and writhing over me. I held back long enough to roll us over once again, pressing her back into the mattress as I pounded into her with everything I had left.

"Fuck! Yes Jandro, more!" She was limp and breathless from her orgasm, soft and pliant for me to pound into, but her hands dug into the backs of my arms, thighs still squeezing my hips.

I crashed into her until my rhythm naturally stuttered, the need too great to ignore as I chased it higher and higher. Lightning zipped up my spine and my heartbeat thundered in my ears. My release pulsed through me into her, rendering me lightheaded and unable to breath for a few moments of pure bliss.

I took in big gulps of air as I rolled off of Mari, weeks worth of pent-up tension now drained from my body. Mari curled into my side, her head on my chest with her cheek over my still-rapid heart beat.

"I love you, Jandro." Her hand slid over my torso and I threaded my fingers with hers, my other arm draping down her side.

"Love you more than anything." I kissed the top of her head and squeezed her hand. "Tomorrow's another day, alright?"

"Yeah," she murmured. "It is."

TEN

MARIPOSA

I knew it would be hard to pull away from Jandro's warm body, his embrace loving even while in sleep. I just didn't think it would be *this* hard. But I had to. Horus said it was time.

Slowly, painstakingly, I peeled away from my lover in the dead of night and dressed silently in the dark. I had already written the note I would leave, carefully pulling it from my jeans pocket and leaving the folded piece of paper on the pillow next to him. It was short and to the point. *I've gone to find him. Don't worry, Horus is my guide. We'll all come home together. I love you. —M.*

I could only say so much to convince him that I *had* to do this, and do so alone. He'd never let me leave if I said anything first, and no one else seemed to get the message from Horus that it was time. This mission was only meant for me.

I had to dig deep to find the old Mari, the woman who'd never met the Steel Demons before and traveled on her own for three years. I had to introduce her to the woman I was now, who knew how to ride and could protect herself with a gun and a dagger. I needed to draw strength from both sides, to combine what I learned to scrape by with what taught me to thrive.

My weapons had come from the remnants of the Steel Demons armory we carried with us. They were the same weapons Gunner had me practice with multiple times, so I'd be better at handling them than anything else. The knife slid easily into my boot while the small .40 caliber handgun fit in a holster under my jacket.

I packed enough food, water, and fuel to last me around three days, plus enough pills to earn my keep somewhere for a month if I had to. It would have felt nostalgic if I didn't keep looking back at Jandro's bedroom door as I packed. How many times had I left one service center with these same items—minus the weapons—without any idea how far away my next stop would be?

Even after everything that happened between Shadow, Reaper, and me, I wouldn't have gone back to my old life for a second. The Steel Demons were my home and my heart. I just had to draw on that old resilience, the tenacity to keep moving, in order to bring our family back together.

Assuming Shadow still wanted to come back.

Horus wouldn't lead me on a wild falcon chase if Shadow didn't want to come home, right?

Who was I kidding? Nothing about this was certain at all. My gut still screamed at me to not be foolish, to tear off all my clothes and weapons and dive back in bed with Jandro. But I couldn't keep living like the past few weeks either. Something had to change, and it would begin by finding Shadow.

Dawn was just starting to lighten up the sky as I walked my dirt bike out of the garage, closing the door by hand as silently as I could. I walked down to the end of our long driveway before throwing my leg over the bike and starting up the engine. The high-pitched growling cut through the early morning silence as I kicked my heels up and sped away, praying the noise hadn't woken up my men and spurred them to come after me.

Because if they did, I might not have the courage to leave again.

———

BY THE SECOND DAY, I realized what a cruel master Horus was.

He pushed me *hard* on the road. Unlike when I was traveling before, I didn't go at my own pace, but at his. I had no compass or map, just the falcon flying ahead of me as my only guide. We were heading east-ish, as far as I could tell.

Every time I wanted to stop to pee or stretch my legs, he just kept flying. I'd hurry back to my bike in fear of losing sight of him and we'd carry on until dark.

At night was the only time I could rest and refuel. Conveniently, Horus always flew down near the end of the day when we were coming up on a service center or some other kind of lodging. To let me know it was time to stop, he'd swoop down at dusk to perch between my handlebars, making soft chirps rather than the loud screeches he threw at me if I got too far behind him.

It got tiring quickly, this journey was feeling aimless.

"Was this the same way and pace that Shadow took?" I wondered aloud early on the third morning, stifling a yawn as the falcon tore apart a squirrel for his breakfast.

He peered at me, beak smothered in blood and squirrel guts, but didn't give me an answer.

We carried on for another grueling four days. The desert landscape turned into flat plains, the air cold and dry as the grasslands stretched on for endless miles. Gradually the plains gave way to humid marshlands full of greenery and thick, heavy air. The sky was covered by clouds and when rain started to fall, I was still warm enough to ride for a full day without my jacket on.

I thought I'd seen abject poverty in the Southwest, but all of the Texas and Arizona territories were lush with riches compared to this area. People lived in tents and broken down trailers next to the road, watching me ride through with empty stares. I saw children with distended bellies and living conditions that were hazardous at best. These people had no one to advocate for them now, which was the worst part of it. Not even a mayor or a congressman to fight on their behalf. These people were the real victims of the Collapse, the ones that everyone forgot about.

My heart squeezed in my chest, the instinct to stop and provide help riding me hard. But Horus was a dark speck in the sky and every rotation of my tires brought me closer to Shadow. I couldn't save everyone, nor could

I let myself get distracted. A spark of determination fired me up, making me bear down hard on the accelerator. The sooner I saw Shadow and convinced him to come home, the faster I could provide help for these people on the way back.

By the sixth day on the road, Horus veered north, the oppressive cold returning to settle deep in my bones. Looking to the east, warm, sandy beaches gave way to a rocky, jagged coastline. The road grew rockier too, and I started to fear all the weathering on my tires from this long journey.

The seventh day was by far the hardest. I was sore and stiff from riding all day for a full week. My bike started to make a grinding noise, the suspension rattling underneath me.

"Come on," I patted the bike's fuel tank as if trying to encourage a living thing. "We made it so far, don't give up on me now."

A few miles later was when my front tire decided to give out. I heard a loud pop, then smelled burning and saw sparks flying near my feet.

"Fuck!" My balance started to wobble, the tire shredding as the rim met the road with an awful grinding sound.

Fortunately I stayed upright long enough to slow down and pull over to a grassy field. I was nowhere near as knowledgeable as Jandro about bike maintenance, but even I could tell it wasn't drivable in this state. I didn't have a spare tire and the metal wheel was already scratched from running along the road at high speed.

The best part of this situation? Horus kept on flying like nothing had happened.

"What the fuck am I supposed to do now?" I called out to the sky, all my frustration and exhaustion leaving my throat in a strangled scream.

Have you forgotten your feet, daughter? The sky god's voice almost seemed to be mocking me.

"What? Walk the rest of the way?" I demanded. "How much farther is there to go?"

Does it matter? Is there any distance you would not go?

No, there wasn't. I knew that answer instantly.

I'd walk the entire journey from Four Corners if it meant I would see Shadow again. I'd cross that freezing-looking ocean on a life raft if that's what I had to do. I shouldered my backpack and started walking, leaving the dirt bike on the side of the road without a second glance. It likely wouldn't be there on the way back, but Shadow and I would find a way home together.

We had to.

It was only another few miles before I started to feel the ache in the soles of my feet, the feeling soon traveling up to my calves and hips. I wished I'd brought my hospital sneakers instead of my riding boots. Even then, running around on flat floors had nothing on this barely maintained road and constant changes in elevation.

I ended up putting on all of my warmest layers, the coldness growing sharper as the sun started to set. I even pulled my shirt over my nose and mouth, the frigid air starting to hurt as I took deep breaths.

Walking was not only slower, but used up all my physical energy. I was more exhausted, hungry, and thirsty than I ever would have been on the bike, and covering far less ground. Moving so much slower also caused me to think more. It made me realize how much I missed my men. My last night with Jandro felt like a distant dream now. I couldn't recall his warm touch anymore, not out here while I shivered in some foreign territory all by myself.

Reaper and Gunner, my heart ached heavily with missing them too, if even more than Jandro. I hated that it felt like so long ago that they were truly my husbands, when we were actually happy. This divide between us seemed to gape even wider with each step I took, every mile of distance I put between us. Even if I did make it back with Shadow, was there any going back with me and my men?

I pulled my arms inside my sleeves, hugging them against my body as I kept walking, although I was so cold, tired, and weak that it was more like shuffling. I tried to draw on memories of warmth, of waking up between multiple bodies pressing into me on all sides. If I shivered at all while in bed with them, someone would always wrap around me, even while dead asleep. Sometimes it got stifling, but I would kill for the heat and company of another person right then.

The sun finally dipped below the horizon, the temperature plunging even lower. I didn't hear wings flapping, but the clicking of talons sinking into wood near me. Horus had settled on a fence post, sharp eyes and beak pointing to a structure up ahead.

Rest here, daughter.

A service center, out in the middle of nowhere, but

with blue and red neon lights in the windows advertising cold beer and spirits. I shuffled forward, any signs of life more inviting than the frigid wasteland out here, even if they were from an old motel attached to a dive bar.

The heat inside was almost suffocating compared to how cold it was outside, even though it probably wasn't any higher than seventy degrees. Laughter and conversations abruptly stopped as I shivered just inside the front door. I looked around, but my eyes seemed unable to focus.

"Holy shit, hun! You okay?" A female voice called out to me. "Doc, go check on her."

"Jen, get a blanket and heat up some water," a male voice answered. Then the weight of a hand rested on my arm with the same voice saying, "There's a chair to your left. Take a seat and we'll take care of you, alright?"

Too weak to argue, I followed his lead and sat down in a large armchair, my feet screaming with relief as I took my weight off them. The man who spoke knelt in front me, his hair and goatee mostly grey. Crows feet lined blue eyes behind thick glasses as he clinically checked me over for injuries, and then my pulse and temperature.

A medic, I realized. *Maybe even a doctor.* The woman had called him Doc after all.

"How long were you wandering out there?" he asked, pulling up on one of my eyelids to check my pupils.

"A w-w-week," I stammered, my teeth still chattering hard.

"Damn," he breathed, rocking back to look at me. "Where'd you come from, the girl's camp?"

"N-no. F-f-four…"

"It's alright, hun. You don't have to explain now. You'll be safe here." His tone was gentle, soothing, something I wanted to trust even though I probably shouldn't yet. I didn't know this man, and plenty of people were good at pretending to be trustworthy.

"I c-c-can p-pay…"

"We'll worry about that later," the man said with a kind smile just as a woman walked up, unfolding a blanket to wrap around me.

"There you are," she said, bundling me tight. "Don't worry about a thing. Believe it or not, we're used to all sorts walking through our doors."

I found myself fixated on her sleeve tattoos. They were beautiful, intricate flower designs decorating her from shoulder to wrist. Parts of them were fresh, still scabbed and healing. The ink fit her overall punk-rock look with her dark burgundy lipstick, ripped stockings under her shorts, and piercings through her lip, nose, and eyebrow.

"Th-thank you," I said, finally allowing myself to relax a little. Horus's screeching be damned, I would need at least two days to recuperate. My body had met its limit on this fucking trek. I hated that it would be even longer until I saw Shadow, but I couldn't keep pushing myself like this.

"Jen." The man with glasses turned to the tattooed woman. "Is Ivan out there?"

"No, he crashed early tonight," she answered. "Otherwise I'm sure he would have swooped this lady up and carried her inside."

"I was wondering why he didn't," the man chuckled. "You got a name, miss?"

"M-Mari," I said, my shivers finally slowing. "M-Mariposa, but call me Mari."

"Alright, miss Mari. I'm Jen and this is Doc." The tattooed woman pressed a glass of room-temperature water into my hands. "We'll get you set up with a room. You should sit tight with us for a couple days. If you see a big, scary-lookin' guy walking around, that's Ivan. He's a gentle giant and will likely be more scared of you than the other way around."

"Huh," I mused, trying to gulp down the water without drinking it too fast. "I'm kind of looking for someone who fits that description."

Jen and Doc seemed to exchange a look, but I was already slipping too far into exhaustion to notice.

ELEVEN

REAPER

T he morning was so bitterly cold, I forced myself to get up early to light multiple fires in the house —one in the potbelly stove in the dining room, and the other in the regular fireplace in the living room.

Electricity was still unpredictable when it came to heat, especially in the winter when we didn't have as much solar power. A good, old-fashioned fire was the best heat source, at least until we had reliable utilities like before the Collapse.

The house was cozy before too long, or as much as it could be with Mari still giving me the cold shoulder. My heartbeat accelerated when I heard Jandro's bedroom door open. It was still early enough for her to be sleeping, and she was supposed to be back from the field mission now. Gunner said she left earlier than him when he got in last night. Her dirt bike had been in the garage and Jandro's door was shut. The same scene we'd become accustomed to.

But that morning it was only my VP padding over to

where I was making coffee in the kitchen, naked except for his boxer shorts, his expression blank like a zombie.

"What?" I grunted at him.

He said nothing, but held a slip of paper out to me. I took it, recognizing Mari's neat handwriting instantly. The momentary excitement of having her back home quickly died as I read the brief note. I looked back up at Jandro, bewildered.

"What the fuck is this?" I demanded. "What does this mean?"

"She's gone." His voice was flat, his disbelief manifesting as numbed shock. "She went to find him."

"How?"

Before I could properly fly off the handle, Gunner came racing down the stairs, dressed only in a pair of flannel pajama pants.

"Hey, have you guys seen Horus?" he asked in a worried tone. "I just tried to see through him, but I can't. It's like he's shutting me out or—."

"Apparently, he's with Mari." I held the note out to him, letting him take it so he could read and join us in our stupor.

"The...fuck?" Gunner kept staring at the slip of paper as if the words might change. "She went to find *him?* Shadow? And my bird is her guide?" His hand fell to his side as he stared at us helplessly. "What the hell do we do?"

"Send the club out to get her back." I stroked my jaw as a plan began to form in my mind. "Let's get the Sons of Odin on it too. We've got to branch out—"

"No."

I whirled on Jandro, his eyes now dark and burning into me. "What did you say?"

"I said no, Reaper." His arms crossed over his chest. "She chose to do this on her own. We're not sending people out to find her because she clearly doesn't want to be found. Not until *she* finds Shadow."

"I don't care—"

"Yeah, that's your fucking problem!" Jandro stepped closer to me, his cool, collected temper now surging. "You don't care. You don't *think*. Someone does something you don't like, and you do everything possible to put them back under your thumb. Fuck the consequences, fuck how other people feel. Am I wrong?"

"Fuck off, I don't want her under my thumb! I want her safe. I want our wife home with us."

"Some fucking home this is," Jandro scoffed, scrubbing a hand down his face. "This isn't a home, it's a mess. It feels like I'm in a fucking nuthouse."

"What are you saying, Jandro?"

"Just fucking think for a minute!" he bellowed. "Think of someone other than yourself, other than what *you* want! Put yourself in *her* place. *Dios mio*, I don't blame her at all for leaving."

I backed up against the kitchen counter, thinking back to my last conversation with Mari, nearly a week ago. Fuck, it felt like an eternity ago, and even longer since I touched her.

She was adamant that nothing would satisfy her except bringing Shadow back, that he was the one who suffered the most in this situation, despite her being the one who was nearly strangled to death.

Even then, she still had us, I remembered. *While Shadow has no one.* A man she loved and wanted to build a life with, was cast out into exile without warning. *I did that.* By hurting him, I hurt her.

And that mattered.

I should have known how much it would matter. I saw how intensely she loved her men, how much work she put into drawing Shadow out of his comfort zone so he could live a full life without fear. Had it been me, Jandro, or Gunner in Shadow's circumstances, she would have done the same for any of us. That was how deep her love went. That was how badly I hurt not only her, but all of us.

My actions told her that her love meant nothing, that it was something meaningless and easily discarded. It hit me right then like a brick to the stomach, just how utterly wrong I had been.

"I…drove her away." The words came out a weak whisper.

"And exiled one of your own men, someone we can never replace." Jandro's gaze bore into me, daring me to argue. "One of your best and most loyal fighters, tossed out on his ass for something he couldn't control."

I could only lift my head up and down in shamed agreement. "Yes, you're right. Shadow was nothing but good to us. Good to *her*, and I threw it all away." I scrubbed a hand down my face, barely able to look at the two of them. "I get it now. *I* did this. I ruined everything, I know."

"We should have listened to her," Gunner added mournfully. "She *told* us she wanted help for Shadow, not punishment. We completely disregarded her wishes, and that's the real reason why everything's fucked."

"I know. I know." A massive sigh left me, my entire body feeling like it was deflating. "So what do we do now, just wait?"

"Don't look at us," Jandro scoffed. "You're still the pres."

"This is pretty fucking bad, actually." Gunner looked at both of us. "We were depending on Horus' sight to plan our battle tactics. Now we're basically blind."

"You can't see through him at all?" I asked.

Gunner shook his head. "It's like he closed a door. He's not letting me in, no matter what."

"That's gonna fuck us," I groaned, pinching my forehead. "We have to tell my dad."

"Keep trying," Jandro told him. "Or I dunno, see if you can look through Foghorn as a backup?"

"This doesn't make any sense." Gunner ignored Jandro's attempt at a joke and frowned at Hades and Freyja, sitting next to each other as they watched. "Why didn't Freyja go with her?"

She does not need love, she has that already. She needs sight, not love.

The answer threw all of us off-balance, grabbing for something like an earthquake had hit.

"Holy shit." Gunner stared wide-eyed at the cat.

"Nice of you to say hello again," I grumbled.

We belong to none of you. Hades' voice cut through our heads next. *We assist at our own discretion, nothing more.*

"I already figured that," I said. "But Gunner has a

point. How are we supposed to win now? We're outnumbered, surrounded, and now blind."

You will find a way. Hades' tone was dismissive. *Humanity is good at that.*

"Fuck me." I turned away, stabbing my fingers through my hair. "Get dressed, Gun. We better tell the general sooner rather than later."

"Need anything from me?" Jandro folded his arms, Mari's note between his fingers like a precious relic. "From the club?"

I thought for a moment, rubbing my jaw. "Get all of our bikes fitted with off-road tires and the biggest fucking mufflers you can find. I want our bikes as silent as you can make 'em. Maybe even camouflage paint, if you have time. With an army this big, we're better off with a divide-and-conquer approach, and we gotta be stealthy."

"You got it." He nodded sharply before a half-smirk pulled at his lips. "That's the fucking president I know."

"Yeah, well." I headed toward my bedroom to get dressed for riding. "Let's hope he's still around when his old lady comes back."

———

"WAIT, WAIT." My dad's eyes pinched shut as he raised a palm. "Say that again."

Gunner swallowed. "I can no longer see through Horus. He's left with Mari to find Shadow."

"And you don't know where they've gone or when they'll come back? *If* they'll come back?"

"There's no *if*," I snapped. "They *will* come back." *They have to, or else there's no fucking reason for me to fight for this place at all.*

General Bray slumped back in his chair, a posture I rarely saw him in, while he rubbed his temple. "I thought I ran through all possible worst-case scenarios, but *this* fucking tops all of them."

"We'll make do." My eyes slid over to Hades, who returned my gaze impassively. "We'll figure something out."

"Son…" my dad sighed, tipping his head back. "We've lost not only our trump card, but our best medic. My daughter-in-law and your wife! How can you be so calm?"

"I'm not calm, I'm…I'm numb." The realization from this morning settled even heavier on me, like boulders pressing in on all sides. "She's gone because of me. This is my fault." My fingers itched for a cigarette but I closed my fist at my side. "So I'm gonna fix it. We'll figure out a way to win, and make this a place Mari wants to come back to."

My father nodded slowly. "I hope to all the gods you hold on to that, son. Because I'll be honest—things look pretty bleak here."

"Jandro's working on stealthing up our vehicles," Gunner chimed in. "I suggest your army mechanics do the same. We're going to need off-road strike teams."

"That *might* help." Dad pushed a manila folder across the conference table to us. "Considering we got this news this morning."

I flipped the cover open and Gunner leaned in to

read with me. The typed words in the memo made logical sense as I read them, forming coherent sentences in my mind, but I couldn't muster up any emotional reaction. I was already too numb.

"They're demanding our surrender?" Gunner voiced angrily, looking up at my dad.

General Bray nodded, his face blank. "Blakeworth, Jerriton, and New Ireland have formed an official alliance. All three of them have pledged to march on Four Corners if we don't surrender by sundown tomorrow."

Gunner shoved the folder away, leaning across the table. "You're not actually considering this?"

"Son." My dad folded his hands on the table and looked at Gunner with a grave expression. "That is a combined army of roughly six thousand troops, to our *one* thousand. A good chunk of which are still recovering from injuries in the skirmish last week."

Gunner sat back, his face despondent.

"If we had eyes in the sky, knew when they were coming and in what formations," Dad continued, "I might say we still had a fighting chance. But like this," he gestured to the message, "even if they don't invade and slaughter us, they could just surround the whole territory and starve us out."

"The alliance doesn't matter," I bit out.

Both of them looked at me. "Reap?" Gunner's voice was tinged with hope.

"General Tash's army is the biggest, best trained, and well-financed," I said. "The other two barely matter."

"Blakeworth is well-financed too—"

"No, they just appear that way because everything goes to their city and elite class."

"You weren't there, Reap." Gunner shook his head. "They came well-stocked with explosives to that skirmish. People got buried, caved in, blown apart. They pulled *no* fucking punches. Whatever we thought of them before doesn't apply. They're serious about taking us out."

"What about Jerriton?" I knew I was grasping at straws, but I had to grasp at fucking something. "Tash has taken over your uncle's army, right? Were those troops loyal to him, your family?"

"I dunno," Gun sighed. "My uncle treated regular citizens like shit, but he kept the army well-supplied I think. Now that it's Tash's, I imagine he's doing the same."

"So what, we just let the three of them come in and divvy this place up to their liking?"

"Rory, just think ahead for a moment," Dad said. "We don't want to risk a bunch of lives for no reason. If we start making a plan now, to strike back at a later date when we've gathered more support—"

"And our wife comes back home to what, exactly?" I demanded. "Tash's soldiers informing her that Four Corners is theirs now? That we just gave it all up while they do fuck-knows-what with her?"

"Son, I love Mari. You know I do," Dad pleaded with one hand raised. "And I know you're heartsick about her, but I'm talking about the whole territory. We have to think 'big picture' here. We're responsible for not just the army, but everyone here."

"I'm with Reap on this one, general." Gunner tilted his head toward me. "You've been telling the governor we need to be ready to fight. Well, we're fuckin' ready. We've always had smaller numbers. The odds have always been stacked against us. We've had losses that hurt really fucking bad, and we still keep going. Sometimes we've gotten out by the skin of our fucking teeth, but we are still here."

"We can't meet them out in the field like a regular army," I added, clarity finally beginning to dawn on me. "We have to fight like an MC."

IVAN

I got up early, following the smell of coffee from my room down to the bar. Jen always made a strong pot first thing in the morning, and Heidi, the cook, made a mean plate of bacon and French toast.

The eggs were okay, but not all that impressive compared to the fresh ones from Jandro's flock. They didn't keep chickens here, but had eggs delivered from some market down south. It wasn't until I tasted the difference that I realized how spoiled I'd been before.

A plate of eggs might do me good today, though. I had a full day ahead of tattoo appointments, and a potential buyer was coming by to look at the Indian motorcycle I had restored in the junkyard.

The pang of missing Jandro flashed through me. I owed a lot to my old friend about what he taught me about eggs, bike repair, and more.

"Morning, Jen," I grunted out, approaching the bar when I hit the bottom of the stairs.

"Morning, Ivan!" she returned with her usual perky chirp. "You want your usual?"

"Yes, with a side of eggs, please."

"Coming right up, big guy."

I glanced down the length of the bar as she set the coffee pot in front of me, then did a double-take when my heart stopped at the recognition of the woman a few seats down.

No...No, it can't be.

I had to be dreaming, but I'd never had a dream this sweet before.

There she was, hunched over a steaming mug with a blanket over her shoulders, hair a tangled mess, and hazel eyes that rooted me to my spot.

The last time I remembered her looking at me, she was falling asleep on my chest and telling me I deserved happiness and healing.

"Good morning, Shadow." Mariposa lifted the steaming cup to her lips and paused. "Or is it Ivan now?"

"Mari..." Stunned didn't begin to cover the state I was in. A feather could have knocked me over. "What...are you doing here?"

"I came to find you."

An answer that was succinct, simple. Too simple for the racing questions in my head.

My mouth was much slower to catch up, to process that she was *here*. "How?"

"Horus led me here."

Jen came out right then, her stance cautious as she

set my breakfast on the bar, watching the exchange between me and Mari.

"You two know each other?" the curious bartender asked.

"Yes," Mari answered quickly. Then to me, "Can we have a word in private?"

Private, what a loaded word. I decided on my first day here that I'd never be alone with a woman again, not after what happened with her.

But she was here, right in front of me. After what I did, she wanted to talk to me. Led by a god that guarded me and renewed my sight, but for what purpose?

I didn't dare hope. I didn't dare dream. I deserved nothing from her, not even the tattoo under my sleeve that started to itch at that very moment.

The hows and whys didn't matter—I had to make her leave.

Jen quickly made herself scarce, but we weren't the only ones in the dining area. I didn't want to embarrass Mari with what I had to tell her, so I grunted out a, "Yes," and made for the side door heading to the junkyard.

Mari's steps sounded odd, a bit of a shuffle, as she followed me, like her feet were hurting her. *Fucking hell, Horus. Don't tell me you made her walk here all the way from Four Corners?* It took all my resolve not to sweep her up and carry her to my room, a much better private place, where I could tell her in a hundred different ways how sorry I was. How much I missed her.

Instead I pushed open the door with a jerk of my shoulder, letting it swing wide so she could walk through.

I walked until we would be out of earshot of anyone at the service center, then turned to face her with my arms crossed.

She pulled the blanket tighter around her shoulders, the drape of the fabric reminding me of how my hoodie had engulfed her when she wore it.

I squeezed my fingers into my own biceps, fighting the overwhelming need to touch her.

"Why did you come here?"

"To bring you back." Mari never was one for beating around the bush, lifting her chin as she looked me squarely in the eye. "To bring you home, where you belong."

I shook my head, looking down at my boots. It was just as I had feared. "I don't belong in Four Corners. I'm not a Steel Demon anymore, Reaper made sure of that."

"Reaper was wrong to do what he did—"

"No, he wasn't." My gaze returned to her. "He was absolutely in the right. I deserved—" I swallowed. "I deserved much worse than this, actually."

My life at the service center wasn't happy by any means, but it was fine for living in exile. I was kept busy, fed, and sheltered. Plus I hadn't sleepwalked in over two weeks, which I most likely owed to Doc's therapy sessions.

"That's not true." Mari started to blink rapidly, her eyes filling with tears. "Shadow, I know it was an accident. I forgive you—"

"Stop." I held out a hand, dropping my gaze. Seeing

the hurt on her face was too fucking much. "Don't say that, please."

"I do, Shadow." She started coming closer, my body was bristling both with panic and yearning. "I...miss you. So much."

"Did you get my letter?" I took a few steps backward to widen the distance between us.

Mari's feet stopped moving, her face crestfallen. "Yes, Jandro gave it to me. I've only read it hundreds of times. And you know what I've realized?" A tear spilled down her cheek. "I can't heal. Not until you're back with the club. With me." She quickly wiped her face. "That is, unless you've truly moved on, and you're happier here. I want you to be happy, to thrive. That's all I really want."

Lie to her. Tell her yes, I've never been happier than in these last six weeks. Let her go home with that peace of mind, so she can be free of you.

But I couldn't lie, not to her. Not when she stood right there, looking so sad, and I was dying to be the one to put a smile on her face again.

"Even if I could...be with you again..." The words came out tight and strangled. "Reaper would never allow me to rejoin the club. He made it abundantly clear I was to stay away from Four Corners and you."

"No, he'll let you come back." Mari spoke with an eager hopefulness as she took another tentative step toward me. "He told me he would, no questions asked."

Puzzled, I stepped away from her again. "Why would he do that?"

Mari's face hardened, a coldness settling over her that

didn't suit her warm personality. "Because I didn't speak to him or Gunner for over three weeks." She looked down at her feet. "I thought so many times about leaving them."

"You...did? Because of exiling me?"

She nodded and I couldn't believe what I was hearing. I injured her to the point of putting her in the hospital, and here she was, tearfully asking me to come back. They locked me away, then exiled me to protect her, and she nearly left them over it. None of it made any sense to me.

"I think they're finally understanding, especially now that I've come here," she went on. "You don't need punishment, Shadow, you need support. All the hard work you've done doesn't need to be thrown away over an accident—"

"Stop." I closed my eyes, the sight of her too much to bear. Another second of looking at her and I'd fall to my knees, begging her to stay. To be mine and no one else's. It would be completely unfair to ask, but that didn't diminish how badly I wanted it.

"I'm sorry, Mariposa." I turned away, intentionally using her full name. "We can't ever go back to how things were before." I started to walk away, pausing only to add, "I'll see about getting you a ride home."

"You said you would never leave."

I stopped in my tracks, her words hitting me like the Blakeworth arrows that once embedded poison into my back.

"You promised to come back if you ever had to leave," Mari called after me.

Turn around, some voice told me. *Turn around and keep your fucking promise to the woman you love.*

I didn't turn around. I clenched my fists and kept walking.

———

I FOUND Doc a few hours later, tinkering with one of the laundry machines that had started leaking.

"Hey, Doc." I approached him, carefully stepping over his tools laid out on the floor.

"Ivan, what can I do for ya?" He barely looked up, elbow-deep in the guts of the machine. "We don't have a session for a couple of days."

"It's not that. I, uh, could use a favor."

He paused in his work, shoving his glasses up the bridge of his nose as he looked at me. "I'm listening."

"Mariposa, the woman who got in last night," I said.

"Uh huh?"

"She could use a lift back home, to Four Corners."

"Clear across the country?" Doc scoffed. "Why don't you take her? Your joints are much younger than mine."

Damn it. I knew he would ask that.

"It...wouldn't be a good idea," I said. "She and I have some...history."

"Uh huh." Doc leaned back, saying nothing else, as if waiting for me to elaborate. When I didn't, he remarked, "She calls you Shadow, I heard."

"Yeah," I sighed. "It doesn't really matter, but maybe you can arrange someone from town to give her a lift?"

"She's who you're running from." Doc clasped his

hands together, a smile pulling at his face from the small epiphany. "Your past has caught up to you, son."

"No," I shook my head. "She has nothing to do with...what I've been seeing you about."

"I never said she did." He continued to observe me in that quiet, curious way that he had since the first night I walked into the service center. "Does she know about it?"

Since talking to her that morning, I felt like I'd been keeping everything bound up tightly with string, and Doc's questions were slowly beginning to unravel it all.

"Not everything," I admitted. "She's a medic and gave me sleeping pills for my nightmares."

Doc nodded sagely as he continued to unravel the thread. "But that's not all, is it?"

I shook my head. "No. We...we got close. Really close." I swallowed. "I hurt her, Doc. Badly."

"I see." A small acknowledgment to the biggest regret of my life.

"She's safest when she's far away from me," I explained. "That's why I left. So please, help me find a way to send her back home."

"You must mean a lot to her," Doc remarked, wiping his hands on a rag. "For her to come all this way."

"Doc," I pleaded, sucking in a breath. "You know my mind better than anyone. You're the only one who knows how fucked up I am to the core. You *must* see that she's not safe here."

"If she's not, then neither are any of the other women." He stroked his goatee. "Are you telling me you're really no better than the camps that Jen and the others escaped from?"

I blinked, taken aback by the comparison he was making. "No, that's different—"

"Listen, son." Doc took his glasses off and wiped the lenses on his shirt. "I've been providing hypnotherapy to trauma victims for over thirty years, and I'll be honest— your case is one of the longest and most extreme I've seen in my whole career."

"Huh, I figured."

"But also." He pointed at me with his glasses. "Your progress has been remarkably fast compared to other patients with such extensive trauma."

"It has?"

"Yes, and that's all due to the work you've done before ever stepping foot into this place. Somewhere along the line, you had a support system. You felt safe and had people you could trust." He placed his glasses back on his face, peering at me over the rims. "Is it fair to say that Mariposa had something to do with that?"

My fists closed at my sides, as did my throat. "Yes," I choked out. "She had everything to do with it."

"Something I try to tell all of my patients," Doc said softly. "You are not your trauma, Ivan. You are not your nightmares, you are not your regressions or your flashbacks."

"But—"

"Are you a man who wants to hurt others? Who enjoys doing such a thing?" Doc's arms crossed over his chest. "Tell me, is that who you are, deep in your soul?"

"No." It was almost shocking how easy that answer was. "I don't want to hurt anyone. I never have."

"Then that is who you are," Doc said. "Everything else is a symptom of what has been done to you." He gave a small smile. "And we're working on that."

"I...think I understand, but," I scrubbed a hand down my face with a groan. "Mari still can't stay here, and I'm still worried about..." The guilt was still as present as ever, choking away any glimmering hope of happiness. "I can't risk hurting her again. I won't, Doc."

"Good. We'll continue with our sessions then." He picked up a wrench and resumed digging into the washing machine. "Mariposa will need a few days to recover from her journey, anyway. Once she does, I'm sure she's perfectly capable of coming to a decision on her own."

I left him to his work, feeling something between reassured and only more confused.

THIRTEEN

MARIPOSA

"You might want to cut back on acidic foods, like tomatoes," I said, handing a glass of water and two antacid tablets to the pregnant mother. "It'll help with the heartburn."

"Oh no, really?" The woman rubbed her belly with a crestfallen face. "But Heidi's tomato soup and grilled cheese is the best! It's all I've been craving during this pregnancy."

I offered a smile. "Cut back doesn't mean giving up for good. I'm just a medic, not the food police."

The woman looked relieved and thanked me as she waddled away with her heartburn tablets. She was the last of the ones who sought my advice this morning, after I had a full day to recuperate and let Shadow's rejection from yesterday sink in.

I didn't know what to make of our conversation, other than the fact that it *hurt*. So fucking much. I would have much rather dealt with another nightmare than hear him crush every hope I had.

What did you expect? I asked myself, wandering the dining room slowly, meandering toward the bar. *He sees himself like Reaper did—an abuser and a monster, even when that couldn't be farther from the truth.*

I slid onto an empty barstool, blankly meeting the eyes of the bartender with piercings and dark lipstick. It took me a moment to remember her name—Jen.

"Want some lunch?" she asked.

I nodded. "Sure, thank you. Anything's fine."

"I'll see what Heidi's got stashed." She disappeared through the swinging doors behind the bar, leaving me to look around the room.

There were a lot of women here. More than I ever imagined Shadow would be comfortable with. Come to think of it, he and Doc were the only men I'd seen since getting in two nights ago.

Small groups of women were spread out through the lobby, mending or knitting clothes as they talked. Some read worn-out paperbacks, painted their nails, put on makeup, or just chatted with each other. I could pick out the service girls pretty easily—they were more primed in their appearance and sat by the windows to look out for potential customers.

Was Shadow ever a customer?

Jen returned right then, pushing open the swinging door with her hip as her arms were full of plates.

My eyes widened at the multiple plates of food she set in front of me, and me alone. "Oh no, this is too much."

"Hey now, don't insult the cook," she cracked with a grin. "Heidi's orders are for you to eat everything you can, and I'm inclined to agree. You keep walkin' up the eastern seaboard, you're gonna need some meat on you." Her tone had a friendly tease to it and I decided that I liked this bartender.

"I think my days of walking around in the middle of winter are over," I said in return.

Jen laughed as she began washing glasses. "Well eat up, anyway. You need the energy."

I helped myself to the first plate she set in front of me, a rich broccoli-cheddar soup. "What territory is this, anyway?"

"They're calling it New Greenland these days. But it was once the great state of *Nawth Carolynah*." She exaggerated the southern accent.

"Wow, is nobody original with coming up with new names?" I remarked between spoonfuls of soup.

"Seriously! If you're gonna run a militia through a town of innocent people and claim it as your own, at least put some thought into what you're naming it."

I laughed, tearing off a chunk of bread to dip in my soup. "So are you from here, Jen?"

"Nah, I'm a Midwestern girl from the mitten." At my blank stare, she clarified, "Michigan."

"Oh, gotcha. Yeah, Texas here."

"Well, giddy-up," she cracked. "Is that where you and Ivan met? I heard they make 'em big down there."

My next laugh was forced, the recent interaction with Shadow still a fresh wound. I couldn't even bear to think of him with another name. This Ivan person was a stranger to me.

"No, we met in Arizona." I tried to keep my tone

light, despite the tightening in my throat. "After nursing school, I traveled west for a while."

"Never been to the southwest," Jen commented, the tattoos on her arms dancing and jumping as she wiped bar glasses. "Dunno about that desert heat."

"Summers can be rough, but it's not so bad," I said distractedly. "Sorry for my staring, I just love your tattoos."

Jen beamed as she propped her arm on the bar to show me. "Aren't those pretty? Ivan did 'em all."

"He...did?" I had suspected, but having it confirmed seemed to suck all the air out of my lungs.

"Yeah, he's the best." Jen turned her arm over to show me the full extent of the design. "Amazing artist and such a sweetheart." Her eyes found mine. "But I'm sure you knew that already."

I did. And I hated this feeling crawling through my body, this twisting anger and jealousy that another woman knew him like I did.

Both of Jen's sleeves matched, so Shadow had clearly worked on both arms. That must have taken hours, over multiple sessions. Which meant many hours of him touching her. Sitting with her. Drawing on her skin and talking to her about the design, among plenty of other things most likely.

I felt ridiculous for being jealous, but compounded with how he rejected me yesterday, and how our relationship had blossomed over his tattoo sessions with me, it was another twist of the knife already deeply embedded in my gut.

Was there more to this? Did their tattoo sessions lead

to anything more intimate? Did he worry about causing her pain like with me? Did they hug afterwards, or do anything else?

I didn't dare ask, afraid of what Jen's answer might be. My once-delicious soup now sat like a brick in my stomach and I lost my appetite for the rest of the food.

"Does Sha-uh, Ivan do a lot of tattoo work here?" I took small sips of tea, hoping it would settle my stomach.

"Oh yeah!" Jen returned to her glass-washing. "He's inked up almost all of the girls."

I nearly choked on my drink. "All of...the...girls?" I thought hearing he had other clients might make me feel better, but it certainly did not.

"Yeah, they made it a little tradition after he got here," Jen went on with a smile, oblivious to my discomfort. "A bunch of them got little matching tattoos to celebrate being freed from the girls' camps. Others were like me," she gestured to her arms with a smile, "and went all-out."

"Oh." I forced a smile. "That's...nice."

"It was a big step for a lot of them," Jen agreed. "Especially trusting a big scary-lookin' man to get it done, but they saw pretty quickly that Ivan's a teddy bear underneath it all." Her voice quieted, hands slowing over the bar glasses. "And it doesn't take a genius to figure out he's been through some shit himself."

"Yeah..."

Jen snorted out a laugh. "I'm sorry! Here I am talking your ear off about him when y'all already have a history. Hey!" Her eyes narrowed. "You look a lot like the girl in *his* tattoo."

I met her gaze, frowning. "What tattoo?" I had seen both of his, and neither of them had resembled a woman.

Jen paled, her brows lifting for a moment before returning to her glasses. "Never mind, I probably should have kept my mouth shut."

I picked at my food, desperate to know more, but also unwilling to ask her those questions. It disturbed me how much she knew about Shadow already.

He's still mine, a feral, possessive part of me whispered. But that voice was becoming diminished, crushed into silence due to his rejection yesterday, and by his apparent ease with making female friends now.

I felt like I wasn't special to him anymore, as juvenile as that sounded. Just him saying good morning to Jen yesterday sparked both pride and a stab of jealousy. He used to say it to me, *only* me. He never would have been able to say it at all if it wasn't for me.

I sat up from my food and began sliding off the stool. Jen and the other girls didn't deserve this vitriol from me. Shadow never believed he would see me again. I had no say over who he talked to, or whatever else he did with other women.

"Want me to box that up and keep it cold for you?" Jen offered, breaking the silence.

"Sure, thanks." I put on a smile, hoping to convey that I wasn't mad at her. "I'm just gonna lie down in my room, I think."

"I gotcha, Mari. Go on and rest."

I left the dining room to the sound of Jen scraping my leftovers into storage containers, and quickly decided I didn't want to stare at the four walls of my room. It was the middle of the day, so it shouldn't be too cold outside for a brisk walk. This was my second full day here and I had yet to properly explore my new surroundings.

I bundled up in all my layers and headed out the side door to the junkyard where Shadow and I talked yesterday. I wasn't exactly *hoping* to run into him again, despite still missing and craving him like mad. Even if I did, I wasn't sure what I would say.

What I really wanted was a reset button. A quick rewind back to the night of the housewarming party. Before drifting off to sleep, I'd remind him to take a pill, and all of this would be avoided.

Or just kicked down the road to deal with later, the more cynical part of me said.

Regardless, Shadow was not in the junkyard, but Doc was. The older man was bent under the propped hood of some ancient sports car in pristine condition, the cherry red paint still glossy, and the whole body of the car lowered close to the ground.

"Afternoon, Doc," I greeted, walking up.

"Ah, hello Mari," he returned. "You're looking much better today." He scratched his forehead as he studied me curiously. "Looking for someone?"

"No, not really," I said, avoiding his gaze to look at the piles of scrap metal surrounding us. "Just out for some fresh air. Exploring a bit."

Doc nodded and gave a polite smile. "You look like a smart cookie. Do you like books?"

"Oh, definitely! I love to read."

He turned and pointed down the main road the service center was on. A weathered brick building, clearly pre-Collapse, stood on the next block.

"We take pride in our library here," he said softly. "About five years ago, me and a bunch of the towns-people prevented an invading army from burning it down. When others invaded to take over, we protected it with guns. It's sacred to us, and one of the few intact libraries left for hundreds of miles."

"That's amazing," I breathed. "You must be so proud to still have something so important."

"Immensely," he nodded. "And there's no use in hoarding knowledge to ourselves, so," he spread his hands, "it's open to you, if your exploration takes you there."

"Don't mind if I do." My feet were already heading in that direction, fingers itching to trail over spines and flip through pages. "Thanks, Doc."

"Enjoy yourself, just put everything back where you found it." With that cheerful quip, he returned to working on his car.

I felt near tears the moment I walked into the library, just from the nostalgia alone.

The smell of books hit me first—there were thou-sands of them here in one place. Paper, glue, and the hushed atmosphere brought me back to long nights studying in nursing school. When my friends and I needed breaks from pouring over anatomy textbooks, we'd head over to the fiction section and devour young adult novels.

I walked through the main aisle now, hardly daring to breathe, as if it would blow away the magic of this place. Other people perused the shelves, though I didn't see a librarian on duty.

In the children's section, I spotted one of the service girls I saw that morning, gently helping a young boy sound out words in a picture book. Down another aisle, two young women giggled and whispered to each other behind books with shirtless men on the covers.

I didn't know where to start looking. When was the last time I read for pleasure? Probably in nursing school, devouring the adventures of a young heroine while I pulled an all-nighter.

I soon reached the back wall of the building and decided to turn down the left aisle. This was a small library, but no less worth treasuring when so many had been burned down in the chaos following the Collapse. Scanning the spines as I walked slowly, this section seemed to be about travel and foreign countries. I paused to flip through a book on the Maya culture through Mexico and Guatemala—something close to my and Jandro's heritage.

Jandro.

My chest squeezed uncomfortably tight at the thought of him. I'd been too exhausted or too focused on my destination to give him much thought since I got here. Now I sank into it, our last night together and how good he felt that I almost didn't leave. Guilt filled me up at how hurt he must have been to find my note in an otherwise empty bed. He was so happy to have been intimate again after weeks of nothing.

Reaper and Gunner were one thing, but Jandro...I hated hurting him most of all. He'd been there for me and Shadow, and didn't deserve to get caught in the crossfire.

Setting the book back on the shelf, I ran a finger down the spine. "I'm coming back to you, *guapito*. Probably sooner rather than later."

I kept making my way down the aisles, passing a row of glass-walled study rooms that people could rent out for meetings or private study groups. Most of the rooms were empty, but two people in one had me looking with absent curiosity, which turned into dread.

Shadow was impossible to miss, organized chaos surrounding him in the form of his open sketchbook, small pots of ink, markers, and his tattoo machine.

But it was the woman with him that made my stomach drop. A pretty—no, beautiful—brunette sitting on the study table, her shirt pulled up past her waist, and her butt perched on the table's edge.

Directly in Shadow's face.

He touched her waist as he leaned over to tattoo her lower back. Their position to each other was close, if even intimate.

The entire wall facing the inside of the library was made of glass, so I quickly slid behind a bookshelf so they couldn't see me. The glass was thick, so I couldn't hear much of their conversation. Those rooms were meant for some privacy after all. Still, I heard the buzz of Shadow's machine and their murmured voices talking to each other.

He said something that made her laugh, looking over her shoulder at him.

My heart drummed a powerful, aching beat in my chest, growing more painful the longer I watched.

I saw Shadow smile at her before his hand returned to her body, resting on the center of her back as he tattooed just above her ass.

It's nothing. It's just tattooing.

But my heart didn't seem to get the memo. It raced painfully, like I was watching something much more nefarious. My eyes only saw one of *my* men touching another woman in a private room.

And I couldn't bring myself to believe anything else as I walked hurriedly out of the library, blinded by tears.

JANDRO

Gravel and small stones crunched under my tires, my body shifting on the bike with the uneven terrain. Sitting behind me, Slick held onto my waist, doing his best to move with me and not throw us off-balance. But it was clear he hadn't done much off-road riding before, and especially not with an arsenal of weapons weighing us down.

We were in neutral territory, roughly two hours northeast of Four Corners, looking like a pair of redneck hunters. The spare bike we rode on was covered in desert camouflage tape, and our borrowed uniforms from General Bray's army had a similar pattern. Even our weapons and gear had been taped and painted to blend in with the landscape. The whole idea was for the opposing army to never see us coming. They had bigger numbers than us, so we had to be smarter.

I wasn't sure about this attempted stealth thing, but me, Slick, and a few other Steel Demons volunteered to scout as close to Blakeworth and Jerriton as we could.

Without Horus' eyes, it was the best chance to gather intel on our enemy. And with us going, we wouldn't put more of General Bray's soldiers at risk needlessly, not until we knew more about what we were dealing with.

We had no orders, except to get as close as we could, find out what we could, and defend ourselves as necessary. That, I could do.

I was a defensive fighter. I didn't have a raging temper like Reaper, the strategic mind of Gunner, or Shadow's innate ability to kill swiftly and efficiently. But I knew how to defend and protect.

As soon as the long city wall came into view on the horizon, I veered sharply to the left, signaling the four other riders spread out behind us to follow my lead.

"Where you going?" Slick asked through the cloth mask covering his face.

"Nothing stealthy about walking up to the front door and ringing the doorbell," I answered. "We're gonna peek through the back door."

This city was once called Grand Junction, Colorado and was technically Jerriton territory, but it straddled the current border between Jerriton and Blakeworth. From our previous intel, we figured that Grand Junction was a hub used to direct troops and goods between Blakeworth, Jerriton, and New Ireland. If Tash was supplying Governor Blake with weapons and soldiers, it was likely through this city. And likewise if Blake was sending payment, it mostly likely came through here too.

The best case scenario would be disrupting a supply chain, maybe blowing up a freight of ammunition or other supplies. Anything to send the army scrambling and buy us some time. The worst case scenario would be getting discovered, probably by their own scouts, and getting captured or killed.

Our odds weren't great, as Gunner emphasized to me while we poured over maps before leaving. It was a risk we felt forced to take at this point, but I was confident in the guys backing me up. Steel Demons were crafty. We fought dirty when necessary. General Bray's men were skilled soldiers, but I didn't have their loyalty and trust as I did with the men behind me right now.

It was another hour of riding to circle around toward the back-end of the city. I took us to a ridge overlooking a sprawling housing development, which might have been a nice suburb at one point, but now looked slummy and for the most part, abandoned. The buildings got taller and more condensed up ahead, with activity bustling through the streets. Mostly people walking or on bicycles, but I noted a few civilian cars among the armored trucks rolling through the streets.

I held up a fist, signaling our team to stop at this lookout point. We'd observe here for now, and get closer if it was safe. Everyone cut their engines and quickly hopped off their camouflaged bikes, eager to stretch their legs.

"Fan out and make sure no one's peeking on us," I ordered. "Slick, stay with me." I crouched at the edge of the ridge, pulled out a small set of binoculars, and spent a whole minute adjusting the damn things to focus. What I would give to have vision like a bird of prey right now.

"See anything interesting?" Slick hovered over my shoulder.

"Maybe." I handed him the binoculars. "That caravan moving through the city center look important to you?"

He watched through the binoculars for several moments before answering. "I dunno, maybe? If it was so important, you think they'd be moving it through the busiest part of the city?"

"It's the fastest route." I shrugged. "Most direct way if it's heading to the Blakeworth capitol. You think they'd be worried about disgruntled civilians?"

"Hm, maybe not." Slick lowered the binoculars and handed them back to me. "Gunner made it sound like his uncle really had the citizens under his boot. I imagine Tash wouldn't be much better once he took over."

"I bet you're right."

A single gunshot popped off just as I lifted the lenses to my eyes. Slick and I dove and flattened ourselves to the ground, both of us reaching for our guns as a few more shots fired.

"You think that's us?" Slick rolled up to his knees and went to crouch behind our bike, weapon close to his chest.

I rolled the opposite way, ducking behind a boulder. "Fuck, I hope so. We could use a win."

Several long seconds passed with no more gunfire, only oppressive silence. Approaching footsteps made me hold my breath, index finger curling around my trigger.

"All clear, it's just us," I heard Brick call out. "Took out a couple of Blakeworth lookie-loos."

"Jesus Christ." I let my hands and gun flop down to my lap, releasing my breath. Slick did the same, relief smoothing out his features. "You scared the shit out of us."

"Sorry, we didn't want to make any noise and signal to others that you were here."

I nodded, coming out from my hiding spot to clap Brick on the shoulder. *This* was why I felt best with Demons at my back. "Good work. Thanks, man."

"How far away could people hear those shots, you think?" Slick looked between the two of us, worry furrowing his brow again.

"Ain't nobody around for miles," Brick said dismissively. "Those Blakeworth fucks must have caught sight of us and started following about an hour ago. Found 'em hiding in the tall grass like a bunch of pussies. None of us heard shit, so we figure they must have left vehicles behind and tracked us to this spot on foot. I got Wells out lookin' for their wheels now. If there's anyone else out there, we'll know."

Two more shots rang out, much further away than the previous ones.

"Ah, guess we found some more," Brick added cheerfully.

"So they are stalking us when we get close," I mused, rubbing the stubble on my chin. "And being stealthy about it."

"It's not *that* stealthy," Brick huffed. "Kinda amateur, really. If Reaper sends his dog out, he could probably sniff out all of 'em hidden in a field before any of us get close."

"Maybe," I offered skeptically. I'd bring it up to Reap, but didn't have high hopes for that plan. Hades was not a dog that he could just send out on a hunt.

"Hey VP," Slick called. "You might wanna see this."

I went to his side, looking out over Grand Junction again. The caravan of armored trucks had left the city center and was moving through the residential area just below us. I didn't need binoculars to see the heavily armed soldiers in the Jeep leading the procession. Another matching Jeep drove slowly behind the pack, the soldier in the passenger seat hanging his arm out the window, casually waving his weapon at frightened families in threadbare clothes.

"That's our target," I declared. "It's headed straight for Blakeworth and we're gonna blow it up."

"It's turning off the main road," Slick observed. "Headed for the single-lane highway winding through the mountains. They're definitely not looking to be out in the open."

"All the better," I said, grabbing the handlebars of my bike and straddling the seat. "We're gonna head 'em off. Brick, you guys hang behind and cover us. Do *not* get close enough for them to hear you. Not unless you can shoot them before they call for backup."

"You got it, VP." The man turned to relay the orders to the other Demons.

Slick climbed on behind me, slow and apprehensive. He took his time settling in while Brick and the others hustled and drove off in seconds.

"Something wrong?" We had to ride fast to get ahead and couldn't afford to dally, but Slick had good instincts and it was clear he had something on his mind.

"I dunno, something just doesn't feel right." He chewed his lip, watching the caravan down below. It was almost out of our line of sight and we'd have to hurry. "You don't think it's weird that this opportunity has just presented itself to us so perfectly?"

"I've learned not to look a gift horse in the mouth." I started up the bike and turned it around, speaking louder over the muffled engine. "But what are you think-ing, a set-up?"

"I dunno, maybe. It's probably nothing." He didn't look convinced by his own words. "Just be careful, VP."

"Always, kid." I tapped his thigh once. "You're my best apprentice. I won't let anything happen to you."

He snorted in response. "Worry about yourself, man."

We drove down the ridge back the way we came, Brick and the others were already out of sight, as they should've been. I headed north, straight for the mountain pass the caravan was heading for. To make decent headway without being seen, we'd have to ride for another hour, maybe two. Then we'd have to set up the explosives and lie in wait to trigger them.

As long as we got there fast enough and no scouts caught us off-guard, it should have been easy.

Maybe too easy.

I accelerated hard, making the landscape whip past us. Grinding my jaw, I pulled my neck gaiter over my face so as to not catch any bugs with my teeth. Slick's words had set me on edge. I didn't have any doubts about this until he said something. Now my stomach clenched with unease.

Damn you, kid. Why'd you have to make me paranoid?

It wasn't uncalled for though, after everything that had been happening. Before Mari took off, I had just regained full mobility of my shoulder and leg after being shot. Reaper was paranoid about me taking her out on the bike then, after just getting stabbed, and he turned out to be right.

We need a break, I thought stubbornly. *Just one small win.* This had to work. It felt easy simply because our people were good at their jobs. We were diligent, and we thought outside the box.

Not a soul could be seen when we reached the mountain pass, a long-abandoned road with train tracks running alongside it. I followed it, heading northbound toward Blakeworth for another ten or so miles. Even though the caravan was moving relatively slowly, putting more distance between them and us just gave us more time to prepare. Plus, if those rich fuckers over in Blakeworth heard the explosion, even better. Maybe they'd heed it as a warning.

I stopped the bike and let it idle, the quietness and lack of any other people around feeling ominous. *Brick and the others are out there,* I reminded myself. *They're watching out for us, lying in wait.*

"Here's as good a place as any." I dismounted the bike and headed for the cargo.

"How long d'you think 'til they'll be here?" Slick

already had his gun drawn, head swiveling in all directions for any threats.

"Half-hour, maybe a little more." I carefully unloaded our explosives, sweat already gathering at my temples. I had to be precise with this shit, just like with an engine.

We couldn't just throw grenades or timed bombs out on the road either. A well-trained military like Tash's would expect that, and mitigate accordingly. No, I had to make sure this puppy was hidden, and detonate it with a remote at the right time. The patrol Jeep in front would be watching for anything suspicious in the road and move it out of the way.

"Start grabbing handfuls of dirt and sand," I instructed Slick. "And little things, like rocks and brush you would just drive over."

He got to work quickly while I set up the device. "What if we put something big in the road that they have to move?" he suggested halfway through pouring sand and swishing it around to make it look natural.

"That way they stop exactly where we want them to," I said, following his train of thought with a grin. "You don't think it'll be obvious?"

"We can make it look like there was a rock slide," he suggested, looking up at one of the embankments. "Shit, I can cause an actual rock slide. It'll look totally normal that way."

"Do it," I said. "Careful, though," I added, watching him scramble up the rocky hill face.

"I wanna yell timber so bad," he laughed, pushing loose rocks of various sizes down the hill.

"That's for trees, dumbass, not rocks. Hey, watch it!" I jumped out of the way just as a head-sized rock came tumbling down the wall to the road below.

"Careful, VP. I can't control where they go."

"Just hurry up with your damn rock slide and be quiet." I looked anxiously to the south. No sign of anyone coming yet.

After making a convincing display of a natural rock slide, Slick and I rolled a larger boulder into place on the road. It was off to the side, not directly in the center, but just enough of an inconvenience that it would need to be pushed out of the way. Roughly three car lengths behind of it, I carefully laid the explosive hidden under one of many smaller rocks littering the road. We dumped more sand and brush to cover the long wire to the remote trigger—which I would hold and press when the time was right.

And then *kaboom*.

Slick kept on covering the wire with sand as it moved off the road while I hid the bike and any other evidence of us being there. We found cover, wedged between two boulders and a tree, and hunkered down. We masked up, trying to blend into the landscape until only our eyes were visible, then sat and waited.

And waited.

It wasn't a half hour like I initially thought, but at least two hours before we saw anything.

"Here they come," Slick said in a tense whisper.

I raised the binoculars, looking south down the length of the road. A speck of black appeared, growing slowly larger.

"They're driving *really* fuckin' slow," I remarked after a few moments. "Like twenty miles-per-hour, max."

"About the same speed they were rolling through the city." Slick squinted at the oncoming vehicles. "You think they're just watching out for obstacles and enemies on the road?"

"Maybe." If that was true, it didn't bode well for us. If they stopped before our supposed rock slide to clear the road of any threats, our bomb would be discovered. I wasn't a fan of any of these people, but I'd rather blow up supplies than a person just trying to clear the road.

If my gut was uneasy about Slick's earlier suspicion, it was screaming at me as I watched the leading Jeep creeping closer up the road, the procession following along behind it. It was like watching toy cars moving along a track—a slow, constant ambling that seemed almost…automated.

I looked through the binoculars again, peering as hard as I could through the windshield of the lead car. It was still too far away to see the driver clearly, plus a black mask covered most of his face. Even so, I could tell there was an eerily un-human stillness to him. No shifting of hands or arms on the steering wheel, nor gentle movement of the head or shoulders that all living people had.

"Fuck!" I threw the binoculars down in frustration, forgetting all about being quiet. "Man, I think we got fucking duped."

"What do you mean?" Slick picked up the lenses and peered through them.

"They got crash-test dummies in the seats. The cars must be locked on some kind of cruise control."

"What? How?"

"I dunno." I rubbed my temples, already dreading having to bring this news to Gun and Reap. "The caravan through the city looked legit, but I bet they switched on us when we lost sight."

Slick lowered the binoculars, looking at me with a harrowed expression. "So they knew we were watching."

I nodded gravely. "Brick must not have gotten all of them."

"Well, shit."

"Yeah."

"What now?"

"Stay put for a sec." Slick looked like he wanted to jump out from our hiding place, so I placed a hand on his shoulder to keep him still. "Let's see how this plays out."

The decoy vehicles looked so obvious as they got closer, and I wanted to kick the shit out of myself for not realizing our mistake. Maybe using decoys was standard procedure on transports to Blakeworth. This road was not easily accessible, but I still should have known they wouldn't have put precious cargo on a direct route. Shit, Blakeworth might have cut a whole network of hidden roads just to transport goods for this alliance. Fucking stupid.

Gravel and dried brush crunched under tires as they approached our fake rock slide area. I wasn't even holding the trigger button anymore, there was no point. Crash-test dummies were indeed outfitted with black uniforms and masks, and placed in the driver seats of the escorting Jeeps. The three armored trucks in the middle had black-tinted windows that were impossible to see through. They might still be worth checking out, but I wasn't about to hold my breath on anything valuable.

"You think it has a sensor for anything blocking the road?" Slick asked as the leading car slowly approached our biggest boulder obstacle.

"We're about to find out."

It did not, as a matter of fact. The Jeep continued on, delayed briefly as the left side of the bumper hit the rock, metal crunching and bending in as the wheels insisted on continuing forward. Whoever set these cars to autopilot did not account for the need to swerve around obstacles. The Jeep continued straight forward, the boulder only nudged to the side slightly. A high-pitched screech echoed throughout the canyon as the boulder drew a deep scratch along the side of the car.

It was like a train wreck happening in slow motion—fascinating and horrifying. The short halt caused by the front car's collision allowed the armored truck behind to catch up, giving a love-tap on the Jeep's rear bumper, and then the second car got scratched to hell by the rock.

Slick and I exchanged a short laugh together. Despite the utter disappointment at the failure of this mission, it was still kind of funny to watch.

"Alright, now can I go check out these cars?" he asked.

"Yeah, go ahead. I gotta make sure I disarm this

thing now." I shifted to the side so Slick could jump out. He approached the road at a jog while I pulled the detonation wires from the trigger. I was preoccupied with insulating the wires so nothing else would set them off when I heard the series of shots.

"Ah, fuck!" Slick shielded his head with his arms, turning abruptly to run back toward me, then he fell.

"SLICK!" I roared, scrambling to get out of my crevice, but more rapid fire popped off and I was forced to duck back between the rocks for cover.

"Jandro—ughh—they're up top!" Slick started pulling himself on his elbows, his legs bloodied and dragging behind him.

"I know, buddy. I'm coming to get you." I barely had the arm space to pull my gun out, but fuck if I was about to leave him out there.

"No, stay covered!"

"Shut *up*, Slick!"

I jumped out, not giving a damn that I was making myself a target. Gunfire rained down around me as I grabbed the back of Slick's cut and dragged him to the bottom of the rocky wall we'd hidden in. Miraculously, nothing seemed to hit me.

"VP, you need to get *out* of there!" I recognized the frantic voice as Brick's, shouting from the top of the ridge.

More gunfire filled the air—some pointed down at us, while other shots exchanged above us. I had to stabilize Slick first but fuck, I prayed Brick and the others weren't overwhelmed.

"You're gonna be fine," I told Slick, taking off my

cut and then my long-sleeved shirt. "Your first time getting shot, huh?" I watched his face, trying to make sure he was still lucid while I wrapped my shirt around his thigh and used the sleeves to tie a knot above his bullet wound.

The kid was squirming and nearly gnawing his lips off in pain, but nodded tightly.

"No one tells you this but *now* you're a real Demon," I said, pulling and tightening the knot. "You know how many times I've been shot? I've lost count at this point. One little slug to the leg ain't gonna do shit to you, man."

I started wracking my brain, trying to remember the major arteries in the leg Mari told me about, when Slick placed a bloody, scraped hand on my shoulder and shoved me hard to the side.

"Dude, what—"

He raised his opposite hand—his shooting hand—and fired three times in rapid succession. The next thing I heard was something heavy tumbling down from the rocks across the road, a body, with his weapon clattering down alongside him.

When another shooter popped his head and weapon out from his cover, I was ready. I fired first at the rock he braced his arms on, then at his chest when he jumped away. He fell dead, stuck in the crevice where he hid.

I looked back at Slick with a shaky smile. "See? You're watching my back like it's just another Tuesday."

He laughed dryly, then immediately winced in pain. "I gotta keep you sharp, VP."

"You're doing a good job." I tapped my palm to his

chest, trying not to show my worry at his face growing paler. "You always have, and will continue to do so when we get back. 'Cause this little scrape ain't no big thing and I need you, okay?"

He nodded, more weakly than before.

"Stay put for a sec. I'm gonna check on Brick." The gunshots above us had ceased and I didn't know whether to dread or feel good about whatever that meant.

No sooner had I started climbing up the ledge than shots sent tiny explosions of dirt and gravel into my eyes. I curled up on instinct, spinning and forcing my eyes open to the coward hiding on the opposite ledge. My shots were wild and panicked, but the shooter slumped limply over a boulder, leaving a red smear.

I looked back down at Slick, making a small noise of disbelief as he shakily lowered his gun and gave me a weak thumbs-up with the other hand.

"Kid needs a promotion," I muttered, finishing my climb to the lookout area.

Staying behind a rock, I quickly reloaded and peeked around cautiously, but soon figured out it was all for naught. I stood, coming out slowly to find several bodies laid out across the ground. Too many. Too still.

"Ugh, Jesus..." I rubbed my mouth, stuck somewhere between wanting to vomit, cry, and scream.

Soldiers clad in black camouflage were lying dead. But Brick was also lying face down. His nephew Wells was a few feet away. I spun around, looking to the ridge across the road, and saw more bodies there too.

Ours and theirs.

Anger and hopelessness hit me like a fist to the chest. Fuck it all. Just…fuck everything.

My knees buckled and I let myself fall, a choked sound escaping my throat. I wasn't crying, I was too stunned, too angry.

Why?

I couldn't stop looking at them, that infernal question on repeat in my head. *Just, why?*

They would need proper burials, but I couldn't carry them all back with me. I needed to get Slick medical attention right away or I'd lose him too, but my knees felt cemented to the ground.

It felt like we had no chance of winning.

I wanted to lie down and give up.

Mari… I wasn't sure why my thoughts turned to her in that moment. *We need you back so bad. We can't do this without you.*

Something answered me.

A warm breeze passed over me like a soft caress on my cheek, and I felt the distinct pressure of something wrapping around me. Supporting me.

Your love will return to you. Freyja's voice seemed to whisper in my mind, while also echoing across the mountains. She spoke gently into my ear and vibrated over my skin. *Your men are at rest. Their sacrifice was not in vain, but you must get the young one home now.*

"I don't know if I can do this," I confessed to the bodies lying in front of me, to the air and mountains surrounding me. "They're just killing us all."

I cannot make you, but you can, Jandro. You must. Dig deep, my son. I promise you, the strength of your love is there and it will not fail you.

I wanted to lean forward and hit the dirt like all the bodies lying facedown. I wanted to scream about the unfairness of it all. I wanted to hold Mari against my chest and hear *her* voice instead of Freyja's.

But I braced one hand against the rock and brought one foot underneath me, then the other. Then I headed back down to the road to get Slick and my bike.

MARIPOSA

I paced back and forth in my room, all but certain that I was wearing new grooves into the floorboards.

My bed was made, and on top of it sat my packed bag. I should have been *in* bed, getting a good night's sleep so I could catch an early ride back to Four Corners in the morning. Because I clearly was not needed, let alone wanted, here.

But I couldn't sleep. Nor could I leave now in the frozen dead of night. And I sure as hell could not ignore the pull to the room down the hall and to the left of mine.

I had come back to my room and packed things up in a hurry after seeing Shadow in the library. I heard his footsteps, more heavy and solid than anyone else's here, make their way to his own room a few hours ago.

I wanted to say goodbye. I wanted to cry and scream and punch at his chest. I wanted to leave without saying anything. So I settled for pacing, back and forth.

Horus had been noticeably absent and silent ever

since I got here. For all his insistence that *now* was the time, and all this growth that was supposed to be happening, the whole trip seemed pretty pointless.

The only point I could see was about hurting myself deeper. To keep my hopes alive, come all this way, only to be completely dashed by Shadow himself. Why would he ever want to leave? He did work he loved and was surrounded by women. He didn't need me anymore. He didn't *want* me anymore.

That last thought slowed my pacing to a halt, the ache in my chest spreading like ice through the rest of my body. Oh, it hurt, and I sucked in a shaky breath.

"Fuck it," I muttered, grabbing my doorknob and turning it with a hard pull.

I forced every step, marching toward Shadow's room, the pain of his earlier rejection thumping with every beat of my racing heart. I had no plan of what to say or do as I raised my fist and knocked at his door. Maybe I'd just put a smile on and say goodbye, that I wished him well. Maybe I'd cry and make an utter fool of myself. With the luck I'd been having, maybe I'd be interrupting him balls-deep inside Jen or that pretty brunette from the library.

Whatever the outcome, I knew it was unlikely to change this all-encompassing ache throughout my whole body. I wasn't really hoping for a different outcome. Mostly, I was just so sad that I'd failed and wanted to see him one last time.

The door pulled open and Shadow stared at me, for a moment looking just as frozen as I felt. His hair was damp like he recently had a shower, the snug, heather grey T-shirt still had a few wet spots on his shoulders. He wore black sweatpants and was barefoot.

"Mari-posa." He forced out my full name with an air of surprise. "Are you okay?"

"I'm..." *No, not okay at all.* "...leaving. In the morning."

The door groaned as Shadow seemed to grip it tighter, swinging it open a few more inches. At least there was no else in his room. "You are?"

I gave a shaky nod, my body hovering in a weird limbo between wanting to flee and feeling nailed to my spot. "There's no point in me staying. I can't force you to go anywhere you don't want to, so." I jerked my shoulders up in a shrug. "I just want the best for you, really. I'm glad you've found some...some contentment here." Now felt like a good time for a smile and an escape, so I plastered one on. "So goodbye, Shadow. Best of luck to you."

"Wait," he bit out as I turned to leave. He was gripping the doorknob so hard I saw veins popping in his forearm.

His *tattooed* forearm.

The sight of the familiar pin-up art clicked into my mind just as he started talking.

"It's not that I don't *want* to go back with you," he began softly. "That I don't want...*us* again. Because I...I do, Mari."

Sudden commotion in the hallway had me jumping, barely able to process what he said. Giggles, whispers, and heavy footsteps traipsed carelessly through the hall of rooms. A service girl, most likely bringing a customer to bed.

"Want to come in?" Shadow asked.

I nodded gratefully and stepped over the threshold, close enough to catch a whiff of his soap, as he closed the door softly.

"You get used to those noises living here," he muttered a bit sheepishly.

Shadow's room was tidy and neat, like all the living spaces I'd seen him in previously. His bed was large, the sheets only turned down on one side. *So he hasn't been sleeping with anyone.*

I brushed the hopeful thought away just as quickly as it came. Cleaning staff made the beds every day. It didn't mean he'd been the only one in his.

I could only awkwardly look around his room for so long before addressing what he'd said.

"You still...want to be with me?"

The only light on in his room was a desk lamp aimed down at his open sketchbook. Deep shadows carved out his imposing form standing across the room from me, and accented the scar cutting through his face.

"Of course I do," he said in a low voice. "You are...simply the best thing that has ever walked into my life."

"Then why—" A hand flew to my chest, a futile effort to stop the sob that wracked through my lungs.

"You know why," he said mournfully.

"Tell me!" I demanded, my teeth clenched and aching.

"Because I *hurt* you. Because you mean too much to me to ever risk that happening again." Shadow's breaths now sawed in and out of his chest, every muscle accentuated in the dim light.

"Is that really why?" I fired back. "You have no problem touching every woman here, but *I'm* the one you want, and you just blow me off?"

"What?" His brow furrowed with confusion. "I'm not—"

"Jen's sleeves are nice work. Those must have taken *hours* to complete." Every pent-up, racing thought came pouring out of my mouth now and I was helpless to stop it. "And matching tattoos for *all* the girls, huh? That must have kept you busy."

"It's just tattoos. What do you think I'm..." Shadow's eyes narrowed at me before widening with clarity. "You think I'm sleeping with all of them?"

"Are you seriously gonna tell me you're not?"

"No! I mean yes, I'm telling you I'm not. Mari—"

"Not even the girl from the library?" I crossed my arms, feeling no triumph in the surprise on his face, only sickening dread. "Yeah, I saw you two looking cozy together in the study room today."

Shadow looked to the ceiling with a sigh. "Telisha is the librarian. She lets me take books in exchange for tattoos. We're friendly, that's all."

"Telisha, huh? That's a pretty name."

"Mari." Shadow returned his gaze to me with a growl of my name. "I'm not fucking her, or anyone else here. I haven't been with anyone since—" He cut himself off abruptly, pausing to swallow deeply. "Since you."

I believed him. I only needed to take one look at him

to know he was telling the truth. For some reason, that knowledge wasn't a relief. It only made it harder to leave.

"I miss you," I blurted out with a pained breath, my stomach and all my emotions feeling like they were hurtling off the edge of a cliff. "I've missed you so fucking much."

"Mari." He was close enough for me to smell again, to feel the heat of his body, to see the scar cutting through his face, so near and kissable. "I have missed you during every moment of being away from you."

Fuck, was this really happening? It couldn't be. But I lifted my hand and found it pressed to a warm chest and a thundering heartbeat underneath my palm.

Shadow's knuckles grazed my cheek to wipe a fallen tear, and I gasped at the contact. His lips hovered inches away, my eyes fixated on them as he spoke again.

"I have never wanted anyone but you."

Our kiss connected with softness, and then with all the power of a storm.

Shadow crushed me against his chest with a powerful arm against my back. His mouth devoured me, tongue surging deep in a passionate war against mine. I clung to his wide shoulders, fists curling and pulling at the thin T-shirt covering his body. My own shirt twisted and lifted from the friction of him holding me closer and closer, despite us being pressed flush together already.

Bare skin slid hot and firm against my navel and I was done for, fumbling down the length of his torso in search of his shirt's hem to pull over his head.

Our kiss broke momentarily as I yanked the fabric up, then reconnected with the same fervent need, even as Shadow was still peeling his shirt down one arm. His skin was scorching hot, almost feverish as my hands ran down the familiar planes I was only just starting to know before he was ripped away from me. I broke away from his mouth to kiss under his jaw, lingering long, drawn-out kisses on his neck as my touch ran up his back.

"Fuck..." he ground out, working the hem of my shirt up past my waist.

Knowing how much he loved it, I kissed his neck for as long as he would allow me, before my own shirt came off. Once it did, I pressed my lips to his chest, kissing scars that I knew I had missed the last time we were together.

Shadow only allowed that for a few seconds before drawing my mouth back up to his, one hand holding my cheek with the other anchoring my hip against his. While no less passionate, his kisses began to slow. His mismatched eyes were partially open, watching me every time our lips locked together and then peeled away. When he didn't lean in to kiss me again, I closed my eyes, unable to take another rejection from him.

"Please don't stop," I begged with a whisper.

I felt the weight of his forehead lean against mine, then his hand on my hip sliding between us to the button on my jeans.

"Not a chance, Mari."

His kiss devoured me again, stealing my breath as he flicked open my jeans and started easing the fabric over my hips and ass. I took off my bra while he did that, enjoying his temporary distraction as his kisses made a path to my breasts, his hands going still below my waist.

"You're still mine," I groaned, voice tinged with a whimper at his careful bites and rough tongue flicks on my nipples.

"I've always been yours." Shadow took a seat at the edge of the bed, his bearded mouth tickling the undersides of my breasts before his kisses moved on to my ribs and waist. "Never anyone else's."

And you'll always be mine. I didn't dare voice the thought, not wanting to bring attention to any point in the future, anything that wasn't happening right now. This could still be a goodbye for all I knew, and I might still be heading home alone tomorrow. But we both needed this—just for once to have what we wanted more than anything else.

I ran my fingers over Shadow's scalp, enjoying the feel of his long, jet-black strands as he resumed peeling my jeans and underwear down my legs. His kisses swept over my waist and belly, trailing lower with every brush of his lips.

"I missed you too, beautiful little scar," he murmured softly, pressing a lingering kiss on my hip while rough fingertips trailed their way up my legs.

Something shifted inside me then, like a dam bursting. And I knew right then I could *never* let this man go.

I pushed hard on his shoulders, sending him flat on his back as I yanked his sweatpants down to his knees. His cock bobbed out, already hard and hitting his stomach with a soft slap. I crawled over him, my knees outside his thighs as I took his thick length in my hand.

"Mari, wait." Shadow pressed up onto his forearms, pupils wide and fixated on where I hovered over him. "You're not—I haven't—"

"Please don't make me wait anymore," I begged in a whimper, stroking him as I touched my sex just over his silky head. "I thought I lost you. I need you, Shadow."

"I need you too, I just...ohh, fuck..." His head dipped back as I lowered onto him, fists clenching the sheets.

The thickness of him stretched me wider than I remembered, a pinching pain making me stop with a gasp. Shadow's gaze immediately returned to me, his hands reaching for my thighs.

"Come here."

"It's okay." I shook my head. "I just need a second to—"

Shadow curled up, wrapping his large hands around the backs of my thighs and dragged me off his cock, pulling me up his torso toward his face as he laid back down.

"Shadow, what—ohh..."

He pulled me up until my knees splayed on either side of his head, his intention clear when he pressed a long, open-mouthed kiss to my sex. I bucked against his mouth with a sharp cry, the pressure so instant and heady I could only move on impulse.

Shadow let out a satisfied groan, his eyelids sliding closed as he devoured me from below. He licked me from bottom to top, tongue teasing my opening before it lashed at my clit. Lips pulled and sucked at my flesh, working with his tongue in a dizzying rhythm to kiss and lick me to bliss.

I quickly got over the shock and rocked against his mouth, my fingers clasping through his hair again. Shadow didn't seem at all worried about suffocating, one hand wandering up to knead my breasts while his mouth devoured me greedily.

His tongue focused on my clit just as he plucked a nipple with his fingers, the combined sensations building almost too fast for me to catch up.

"Fuck, that!" I gasped, grinding hard against his face. "Don't stop, Shadow! Oh God, don't..."

I came apart so hard that I fell forward, my shaking legs unable to keep me upright. Shadow's hands caressing up my spine sent more delightful shivers of pleasure zipping through me. His touch ran over my ass and down my legs as I panted for breath, hanging over him limply, my pussy now seated on his chest. He kissed my belly and waist again, fingers pressing gently on my knees. I took the cue and wearily crawled backwards, down over his torso.

"Now you can ride me if you want." His lips quirked playfully, caressing my cheek when we were face-to-face again.

I huffed out a laugh, still catching my breath. "Is that what you were trying to tell me earlier?"

"Maybe."

Our lips connected in a slow kiss, this one reminiscent of the last time we were in bed together. We spent that night exploring, talking, kissing like we had all the time in the world. Like we'd wake up the next morning and everything would be fine.

I wanted to hold on to this feeling, this sweetness and

warmth of just being with a man I loved. Shadow seemed to be right there with me, his eyes closed and hands moving indulgently, lovingly, over my body.

Never breaking a kiss, I slid a hand down his firm abdomen and swallowed his moan as I took his cock in my fist. Our kiss broke away at the last moment as I settled over him, gripping his waist with my knees as I lowered onto his length.

My body, well foreplayed now, took him easier, but I still had to go slowly and ease into how well he stretched me. Shadow was still as I braced my hands on his chest, letting me set the pace as I raised and lowered my hips, taking more of him every time I sank down. Only when I took him completely did his hips roll underneath me, letting out a choked groan to the ceiling while his fingers dug into my thighs.

"Fuck, you feel so..."

Whatever he was going to say died on another moan as I dragged up his length and slowly sat back down.

"Move with me," I whispered, leaning down to kiss him. "Do what feels good."

His hands slid around my back, holding me to him as his hips surged up, hitting new depths that made me cry out into his mouth.

Shadow broke the kiss abruptly, his brows drawn tight with concern as he pulled nearly all the way out. "I don't want to hurt you."

"You're not," I rasped, earning another moan from him as I sank all the way down again. "Please don't stop. I want you so bad."

Still, he hesitated. "You'll tell me if I'm hurting you?"

"Yes, yes of course! But you're not, you feel so good." I kissed the scar cutting through his eyebrow, then his cheek, then his mouth. "I want you to feel good too."

"Just seeing you feels so good." His mouth skimmed to the edge of my jaw, pausing to kiss me there before moving on to my neck. "Holding you, having you, it feels too good to be true."

Through our kisses, our movements below the waist resumed. Shadow's light, roaming touch found its way to my ass, guiding me on his cock while he rose up to meet me from below. Our breaths and kisses were accented by soft slaps of flesh, his hands on my skin and the steady drag of his cock through me lighting my nerves on fire. I ended a kiss and sat upright, face toward the ceiling as I drove down harder, wanting to take him deeper.

My observant Shadow noticed the instant my pleasure started to build. His hand came between us, giving some extra friction to my clit as I rode him. I rocked hard against his hand, taking my fill of him as his other hand skimmed up my body, running over a breast and teasing my nipple as we crashed together.

"Oh fuck, I can feel you..."

I barely heard Shadow over my pleasure cresting, my pulse thundering in my ears and my scream reaching the rafters. He was so solid and hot inside me, pressing so thickly against my walls, they could barely squeeze around him in my orgasm.

I slumped against his chest, my skin now slick with sweat as my head rested over his heart.

He rubbed my back, brushing a kiss along my forehead. "Again?"

I huffed out a breathless laugh, weakly swatting his chest. "Shut up."

His breath ruffled my hair as he laughed, and he waited all of ten seconds before lazily rolling us over, turning, and scooting us up the mattress to let my head rest on one of the pillows.

"Don't go down on me again," I whined. "My poor clit can't take it."

Shadow laughed lightly, lips tickling my skin as he brushed kisses along my collarbones. "Then where would you like me?"

He was still inside me, so I squeezed my legs around him in reply, bringing his mouth to mine because I couldn't get enough of his kisses. "Right here."

His tongue thrust into my mouth just as his hips rolled forward, filling me with a delicious, sweet ache.

"Yes," I moaned, wrapping my hands around his back. "More."

He answered with a hungry growl, drawing his hips back and snapping them forward, making me see stars with the rough crash of his body into mine.

"Oh fuck, yes!" I clung to the wide muscles of his back, my ragged panting returning. "Like that, Shadow."

"Fuck," he grunted out in return, lips catching mine in a rough kiss as his steady, measured thrusts became frenzied rutting. When he wasn't kissing me, he moaned into the pillow next to my head, finally lost in the plea-sure he took from my body.

"Oh fuck, don't stop," I pleaded over the slaps of our

skin, the headboard thumping against the wall. "Fuck, that's so good, Shadow..."

I was being extra vocal because I didn't want to leave any room for doubts. He was so careful, so worried about hurting me, I didn't want a single whimper or cry to pull him out of this moment, to make him stop and think instead of just feeling good with me.

"Yes...oh, yes..." I dragged my teeth along his neck and shoulder, digging into his back with my nails, knowing he liked some pain with his pleasure.

"Oh fuck, Mari..."

He drove into me harder, the rougher friction and his cock swelling sending me hurtling toward another orgasm.

"Shadow!" I cried weakly, my whole body taut as a wire as he fucked me wildly.

Then sweet, explosive release, Shadow's chasing right after mine with stuttering thrusts and ragged, gasping breaths.

SHADOW

W hen Mari's eyelids started to droop, I rubbed a thumb across her cheek and kissed her forehead to rouse her. "Want me to take you to your room?"

She made a soft grunting noise as she rubbed her eyes. "Why would I go to my room?"

I lowered my forehead until it rested on hers. "Don't make me remind you why."

She blinked at me, eyes more alert than a moment ago. "When was the last time you had a nightmare?"

"Um." I pulled away from her, rolling onto my back as I thought. "Three nights ago. But one where I also sleepwalked?" I scratched my head. "Two and a half, almost three weeks, I think."

"Really?" Mari actually sounded unsurprised as she scooted closer, propping her chin on my chest as she smoothed a hand over me. "What's changed?"

"Doc," I admitted, clasping my hand with hers where it rested on my side. "He's been…working with me."

"I knew it." She grinned triumphantly, letting her cheek fall to my chest.

"How?"

She shrugged. "I know doctors. I can spot 'em in a crowd."

Mari nestled against me with a contented sigh, making no move to leave. My arm wrapped around her back, hand resting on the side of her hip. It felt so good to have her lying here with me, I never wanted this to end.

Just a little longer, I thought, my lips brushing her hairline. *It could be the last moment I have with her.*

That last thought was sobering. She had initially come to my room to tell me she was leaving. Was she still planning to, after what we just did?

Mari's eyelids were drooping closed again, her breaths deepening and blowing warm puffs of air on my chest. Fuck, the last thing I wanted to do was disturb her, but I couldn't let her fall asleep on me. This night would *not* be a repeat of our last one together. If that meant I had to unwrap her body from mine, severing the warmth and peace of this moment, then I would.

"Mari," I murmured against her hair, running a light touch up her arm.

"Hm." She barely opened her eyes at all and just snuggled against me closer, sliding her leg over mine.

"I can't let you sleep here," I said with a frustrated groan.

Her eyes finally batted open, peering up at me. "After two-and-a-half weeks of nothing, you're still worried?"

"It could be two-and-a-half years and I still wouldn't risk it."

She stiffened at that, then the warmth of her body peeled slowly away from me. I watched her long spine straighten up as she turned to sit on the edge of the bed, wordlessly pulling her clothing back on.

I needed a distraction, otherwise I'd tell her to forget it and tug her back into bed with me. So I rolled up and proceeded to get dressed myself. "I'll walk you back to your room."

"No, it's okay." She looked over her shoulder, her smile appearing strained. "It's just down the hall. Get some rest."

My hands gripped the edge of the mattress as I sat frozen, unsure of what to do. Was this it? Was she just...leaving?

"Are you, um..." I pulled in a deep breath like Doc had taught me. Sometimes they helped with the tightening in my chest like I was feeling now. "Are you still leaving in the morning?"

Mari didn't answer for a few long moments as she pulled her shirt back on, then stood and buttoned her jeans closed. She walked around to the side of the bed I was sitting on, regarding me with an expression I couldn't read.

"What do you think I should do, Shadow?" she asked quietly.

Stay with me, my thoughts said in answer. *We'll never be able to sleep in the same bed, but I am getting better. I miss you. I crave you. It's been hell not seeing your face, and I'll strive to be worthy of you every day.*

She'd never agree to it. She had nothing here and a whole life waiting for her back in Four Corners. But the temporary illusion felt nice. Feeling her curled up in bed against me made it seem more real.

"Maybe...stay one more day?" I reached for one of her hands, enveloping her slender fingers in my palm. "So we can sleep on this and maybe...talk it out tomorrow after we've had some time to think."

Even that felt like a long shot. So what if she enjoyed sex with me? She had that and more back home.

But Mari's lips quirked into a small smile, her other hand reaching for my face. "I suppose another day won't hurt."

Temporary as it was, relief finally loosened the tight ache in my chest. I wouldn't have to say goodbye to her yet.

I grabbed her hand that came to rest on my cheek and pressed a kiss to her palm. "Let me walk you to your door."

She sighed and laughed lightly, but otherwise didn't protest as I stood and finished getting dressed. Her room was a mere fifty feet away down the hall, but I couldn't fully relax until I knew she was safe on the other side of that door.

The hall was dark and quiet, all the service girls had finished exhausting their clients hours ago. Mari held onto my arm, trusting my night vision to guide us just like when I showed her the night-blooming Cereus. Fuck, that felt like years ago.

We reached her door too soon, and she spun in front of it to face me. "Thanks for walking me."

Her hands slid up my chest at the same moment my fingers skimmed over her waist. The ease of touching her sent a deep ache rippling through me. Why the fuck did everything have to feel so natural if I was never meant to keep her?

"Sleep well." I bent low, touching my forehead to hers before finding her lips with my own.

I *loved* kissing her. Maybe because it was something I'd only ever done with her, or the simple fact that a kiss was the fastest, easiest way to get my fix of her. I was an addict of many things—alcohol, violence, and misery. But nothing gave me a high like her.

Mari's tongue shoved into my mouth, lips scraping over mine with a need punctuated by her grip around my neck. She was on her tiptoes to reach me and I banded my arms around her back, holding along that sweeping curve of her spine as her body pressed to mine.

I was moments away from pulling her legs around my waist and carrying her back to my room for another round, when her mouth broke away and her palms flattened against my chest to create distance. My hold around her loosened and her shoes found purchase on the floor once again.

Mari pulled away from me slowly, her hand reaching for the doorknob. "Goodnight, Shadow."

"Goodnight, Mari," I returned. "See you tomorrow," I added, almost like a reminder to not leave too soon.

She nodded and started to unlock the door. I had just turned in the hall when she called out, "Shadow?"

I whipped around. "Yes?"

Mari was standing in the middle of her open doorway now, her hand still on the knob. "Will you tell me tomorrow if you sleepwalk tonight or not?"

My teeth ground against each other before I bit out, "Sure."

She disappeared inside and I returned to my room, my elated mood suddenly sour. I would tell her, but didn't see how the information would be useful. It wouldn't change anything.

None of this changed anything.

The realization hit me hard as I fell back into bed, the side where she laid still warm and smelling lightly of her. Now alone, without her voice and her touch allowing me to fantasize about a different life, cold, harsh clarity settled over me. The sex distracted both of us, and only delayed the inevitable.

She would still have to leave.

And I could never be with her.

———

HAVING BARELY SLEPT, I was already at the bar when Mari came down the next morning. My breakfast was cold and untouched in front of me, my mood clearly sour, although Jen was kind enough not to pry this morning.

I could barely bring myself to look up at the sound of Mari's light footsteps. My hand clenched around the coffee cup in front of me, which had also gone cold. If I turned to her, if I allowed myself to relax in her presence, I might end up kissing her again. Getting distracted, and selfishly taking more of what I could never have long-term.

"Good morning, Shadow." She slipped into the barstool next to me, helping herself to the coffee pot Jen left in front of us.

"Morning," I grunted out.

Silence passed over us, with Jen and the others thankfully giving us plenty of space. Did they know how things had changed? Or could they just sense the regret and despair rolling off of me?

"Well?" Mari prompted after a few sips of coffee.

My heart beat painfully in my chest and my throat wanted to close up until I could say nothing. But it had to be done.

I had to let her go.

"Mari, I—"

"Did you sleepwalk?"

We started speaking at the same time and both abruptly stopped. I stole a look at her for the first time, noticing the tiredness under her eyes. It seemed I wasn't the only one who slept poorly.

She returned my gaze but said nothing, waiting for my answer.

"No, I didn't," I admitted, scrubbing a hand down my face. "But that might have more to do with barely sleeping at all."

"What kept you up?" She set her coffee cup down, folding her hands in her lap.

"This." I gestured between her and me. "Us, and...what we did."

"You don't sound all that happy." Fuck, she was starting to sound like Doc.

"I'm always happiest when I'm with you, it's just..." I paused, subtly scanning the room to make sure we had no eavesdroppers. "We both know I can't come back to Four Corners. And you can't stay here, so..."

Her eyes hardened, lips pressing into a thin line that I wanted to kiss away.

"I told you you *could* come back. Reaper told me himself he'd let you back in. He won't go back on his word."

"That's not as simple as it sounds. He would have to rewrite club law and get a vote to have it approved. And even if he did that, Mari..." I ached to touch her, to take one of her hands or just wrap around her in a hug. "I can't be yours."

"You *are* still mine." She dropped a hand to rest on my thigh and I couldn't bring myself to remove it. "You told me yourself last night that you've always been mine."

It was so fucking hard to talk. My heart felt jammed up my throat, but she deserved to know the truth—that I was a lost cause who would never deserve her.

"I loved last night Mari, but," I curled my hand around hers and removed it from my leg, "it shouldn't have happened. It's just making things harder."

The look crossing her face hurt worse than the most painful cut I'd ever received.

"Shadow, why does it have to be like this?" Emotion choked her voice and that sound killed me. "I want to be with you. You want to be with me. Why should anything else matter?"

"Because I've already hurt you," I bit out. "I can't ever forgive myself for that, and now I can't ever trust myself to sleep next to you. I want you more than anything else in my life, but I don't deserve you."

I turned away, closing myself off from her as I faced the bar. Focusing on a random speck of paint on the wall, I took my deep breaths and willed my chest to stop collapsing in on itself. I silently hoped she would slide off the stool and leave, putting both of us out of our misery.

I should have known better when she placed a hand on my arm and leaned in closer, when every nerve in my body screamed at the light touch from her. This was the woman who forced me to say good morning to her after all.

"That's not true, Shadow. You deserve *so* much. You deserve to be loved."

"Mari, please..." I didn't know what I was begging for.

"You've gone nearly three weeks without sleep-walking when it used to happen, what, three, four times a week? Shadow that's *amazing* progress."

"It doesn't mean anything," I argued. "If it happens once a month, or once a year even, it's still putting someone in danger if they're near me."

"We can take precautions. Maybe a combination of Doc's therapy and sleeping pills. We can figure something out, Shadow. It doesn't have to condemn you to a life without any happiness."

"It already has." I stole another look at her. "That happened the moment I hurt you. I can't *ever* take that risk again, do you understand? You mean too much to me."

"Shadow." Mari shook her head with a huff of breath, clearly frustrated, but nothing she said would change my mind. My thoughts had already run in circles about this hundreds of times before. "It was an accident. I *know* you would never hurt me."

I shook my head in response. "Consciously, no, I would never. But my subconscious is a deep, ugly place. I see it with every therapy session and it's...I never want to expose you to that. It'll never go away, Mari." I swallowed deeply. "That violence you experienced at *my* hands is part of me. It's who I am."

"I don't believe that," she said quickly, just as stubborn as me. "It might be part of you, forced on you by what you endured, but that person who hurt me was *not* you." Her voice lowered as she spoke closer to my ear. "Would you let me sit in on a therapy session?"

"No." I forced the word out through gritted teeth. "Absolutely not."

"Shadow, I'm willing to do this." Both of her hands wrapped around my arm now, her cheek nudging my shoulder. "I want and accept all parts of you. Let me prove it. Let me be there for you."

"No, Mari." I forcibly removed her hands from me, sliding off my stool to put distance between us. "It was fucking hard enough letting Doc see what happened. You? No, I could never show you that."

She remained unfazed, crossing her arms in front of

her. "So is it that you don't trust yourself, or you don't trust me?"

"What?" I blinked at her. "What do you mean?"

"Of course, I see it now." Mari tilted her head slightly as she regarded me with some new understanding. Whatever that was eluded me completely.

"What are you talking about?"

"You've set yourself up in a perfect, self-destructive cycle," she said. "You've convinced yourself that you're so undeserving of love, that I'll run away screaming if I get a small glimpse of your trauma, right?"

I bristled, unsure of the point she was trying to make. "Maybe not that exact reaction, but yes. I think it'll change what you think of me and...I don't want to burden you with that knowledge."

Mari held up two fingers. "One of two things needs to be true if that's what you expect to happen. One, you think I'm a fool, that I don't see you for the walking textbook of childhood trauma symptoms that you are, and that I don't understand the weight of what you've been through."

"I don't believe that at all." I stepped toward her, the impulse against my earlier reaction to step away. "You're not a fool, you're brilliant. You and Doc understand me better than anyone else."

Mari put a finger down, her chin wobbling slightly. "Then it's the other thing—that you don't trust me."

"That's not true either!"

"You don't believe that I care about you enough to stick around if I see what's in your past." She blinked away the tears accumulating in her eyes. "You're so convinced that I could never love you, it doesn't matter how many times I tell you. It doesn't matter that I followed a bird across the country *for you*. You'll stand here and tell me I deserve better, because that's what *you* already decided. But your thought patterns affect other people too, Shadow."

She spun on the toe of her boot and headed for the stairs, the reaction I was hoping for just moments ago. But I felt no sense of relief or victory now. I felt gutted, flayed open and exposed. It was like she reached into my mind and laid bare what I had failed to see this whole time.

She'd been trying to tell me I was worth something, worth *wanting*. And to keep rebuffing her like I was, only added insult to injury.

I started after her, my heart pounding in a wild panic. Because I knew after this time, she wouldn't try to convince me again.

"Mari." She was almost to the first landing, ignoring me as she quickened her pace. "Mari, wait!"

The floorboards creaked under our weight. As she neared the top of the stairs, I swore I heard something else among the creaks. Something more like a *click*.

My instincts kicked into overdrive and I lunged up the stairs, grabbing Mari's ankle and pulling her back toward me.

"Get down!" I bellowed.

She fell hard with a scream, knees and forearms hitting the stairs just as bullets sprayed holes in the walls over our heads.

MARIPOSA

In one moment, I was walking away from Shadow for what I was certain was the last time. In the next, I nearly face planted on the stairs to the rapid *pop-pop-pop* of gunshots.

"What's happening?" I cried, arms around my head.

"Traffickers," Shadow grunted out, his voice near my ear. I hadn't even realized he had splayed over me, shielding me with his body. "They come to retrieve runaways from the girls' camps."

"What?" I hissed. "You mean this is a regular occurrence?"

"They didn't get close last time, about three weeks ago. I saw them coming and fired off warning shots from the roof." Shadow's arms tensed on either side of me. "Sounds like they brought bigger guns this time."

Another round of gunfire popped off, forcing us to slide lower down the stairs while making our bodies as flat as possible. This time I heard the panicked screams of the service girls on the main floor and in their rooms.

"Well, fuck! What do we do?" I demanded.

"*You* do nothing," he growled. "Get to your room and wait until it's safe. I have weapons stashed by the bar."

"Do you know how many there are?"

"No, but I bet it's several."

"And who's gonna back you up?"

Shadow's teeth ground in his jaw. "Doc's an okay shot, he's probably loading up now. I know he's scared, though."

I twisted underneath his massive body to the sounds of men shouting outside. "I brought a gun. Let me help."

"No, Mari," he barked. "Just wait for me in your room."

Someone had barricaded the front door and now it buckled under the heavy slams of boots from the outside.

"You know I can shoot," I continued to argue. "Gunner taught me."

"Fine!" he yelled. "Just shoot from your window. I won't let them get past the stairs."

"Okay, be careful."

I didn't know who moved first, but our mouths crashed together in a rushed, clumsy kiss, and then I was crawling up the stairs while Shadow slid down. He was barking at the terrified women to hide and diving behind the bar for his weapons before I fully realized what happened.

The pressure and taste of his mouth still lingered as I finished scrambling up the stairs, crouching low under the hallway windows on the way to my room. I went inside crawling on the floor, trying to stay hidden as I reached for my gun and the holster zipped into my bag on the bed. Wearing it was bulky and cumbersome for me, and I hadn't percieved any danger when I first got here. I was far from making my gun a daily part of my outfit like my men.

I checked to make sure my little .40 caliber was loaded and clicked off the safety, listening hard as I crawled my way around the bed to the window.

I heard shouting and commotion, and what sounded like footsteps running down the hall as more girls surely went to hide. It was impossible to tell if the majority of the male voices were coming from inside or outside the building.

Once I crawled directly under the windowsill, I squeezed my grip on my gun as I dared to take a peek outside.

"Shit," I muttered under my breath. I couldn't see the front door at all from this angle.

It took less than thirty seconds, and more gunshots and screams, for me to make a decision. I slid the window open and popped my head out to see better.

A section of the dining room's roof was directly below my window. It wasn't terribly steep, and the corner of the building would give me enough cover to shoot at the assholes trying to storm through the front door.

I rose to stand, stepping one leg over the windowsill and testing how it held my weight before I brought my other leg to join it. A single loud shot startled me, and I grabbed the windowsill for support.

"You're a fucking Steel Demon," I muttered to myself, pressing my back to the building as I walked carefully along the roof shingles. "Keep your shit together."

Shots volleyed back and forth, likely Shadow and Doc battling the traffickers from inside. With my heart feeling like it was going to beat itself out of my body, I reached the corner and dared to peek around it.

Six men were positioned at the front, the windows already smashed and the door still partially barricaded. They used this to their advantage, using the walls and partially obstructed door for cover as they shot inside. Two of the traffickers lay dead already, bleeding out on the front porch. Shadow's work, mostly likely.

Their vehicle was a pickup truck with a wire cage fitted like a camper shell over the truck bed. A single, dirty blanket was spread out on the bed, with chains attached to the sides of the cage, complete with collars at the end of the chains resting on the blanket. Like they were farmers coming to pick up their livestock.

I thought such a sight would churn my stomach, but an eerie calm settled over me instead.

Mindful to keep out of sight, I raised my gun and braced my arm along the side of the building for stability. The traffickers' backs were turned so they wouldn't see me. Shadow was a great shot even with all the obstacles, but these assholes were clear, open targets for me.

I waited until three of them ducked to reload, the other

three taking aim while I did the same. Lining up my sights, I aimed between the shoulder blades of the closest man to me, who was aiming a rifle through the window, and fired.

"Gahhh!"

"What the fuck?!"

I pulled my arm close and turned out of sight, flattening myself against the wall as I tried to listen over my pulse roaring in my ears.

"Petey, d'you get shot in the fuckin' back—Ahh!"

The man's distraction with his friend's mysterious wound cost him his life as two more shots rang out, and I heard the slump of a body falling on the porch.

"Spread out and head for side doors and windows! Cover your fuckin' heads, someone's tryin' to snipe us."

Fuck, fuck, fuck.

I tried to run back to the window while keeping against the wall and not slipping on shingles. But no amount of roof balancing would make me faster than men running on solid ground, two of which were headed straight toward me.

My body froze while my mind raced. The window was a good fifteen steps away--I'd never reach it before they saw me. They'd see me regardless within seconds, and then I'd be dead, or worse, thrown in that truck and having a collar forced around my neck.

The only advantage I had was if I caught them off-guard. My element of surprise was quickly slipping away, but in these few precious seconds, I still had it.

Forcing a deep breath of air into my lungs, I raised my gun and aimed it at the men running toward my wing of the building. The two of them stuck close to the side of the building for cover, but never bothered to look up at the roof.

When they paused next to a support column almost directly under me, I opened fire.

"Fuck!"

One managed to duck under a small section of overhang. The other guy slapped a hand over the bleeding wounds on his chest and fired back at me with an insurmountable rage in his eyes.

I turned and ran, no longer caring about balance and stealth. His shots were going wide but I was still open and exposed.

"Bitch on the roof!" I heard someone bellow. "Found our sniper!"

I ran for my window, ready to sail through it like an Olympic tumbler. It was only ten steps away, then five, then—

My leg swung out behind me, all my momentum crashing down. I landed hard on my chest and hands, the wind knocked out of me as I realized too late that I'd slipped on a loose shingle.

I couldn't afford to stay still, I had to fucking move even though I could barely breathe.

Pop-pop-pop-pop!

Shots kept whizzing over and all around me. My chest ached so badly when I tried to push up, so my fear and adrenaline-stricken body settled on rolling down the roof.

That was a bad fucking idea.

Holding on to my gun, I started scrambling for a hold with my left hand. My body rolled to the very edge and no amount of kicking and scraping stopped my momentum. I was temporarily in freefall, heading toward the ground, when I somehow managed to grab hold of a gutter.

Now the breaths came, ragged and painful as I dangled by one arm, my boots less than six feet away from solid ground. My relief was short-lived as I heard a gun cock. I swung my free arm wildly in front me, firing off shots at the first sign of motion I saw.

Thankfully it was a trafficker, now dead on the ground.

I released the gutter, collapsing onto the ground, where I fell with an aching left arm. Pulling my arm against my body with a hiss, I rubbed my shoulder that was screaming in pain. It wasn't dislocated, but those connective tissues sure weren't happy.

I only noticed then how quiet it was, and strained to listen. Seconds stretched on without any gunshots. Did that mean it was over?

A nearby door slammed open and I scrambled to my feet, ducking behind a patio chair for cover. I heard the sounds of a struggle, of feet kicking desperately for purchase along the ground. And the most haunting, harrowing cries and screams of protest I'd ever heard in my life.

One of the traffickers had emerged from the front door and headed toward his truck. Behind him, he dragged a wailing, pleading, terrified Jen along the ground.

Her wrists were bound with rope, blood already

running down her tattooed arms from how hard she pulled and tried to get away.

I ran out into the open without a thought, only her tortured screams filling my head as I raised my gun and emptied the rest of my magazine into the man's chest. He fell with barely a sound, only a choked gurgle of blood as life left him swiftly and his hold on Jen's rope went slack.

I went toward her next, unsure if I was running or walking. My body felt too slow, like I was in some kind of daze. It didn't matter.

I never made it to her.

A shot rang out and pain exploded up my leg. Suddenly I was on the ground, my eyes level with Jen's terrified, wide-eyed stare a few feet away. She wasn't looking at me, but past me.

I looked over my shoulder just in time to see the man walking up with his gun pointed at my head.

EIGHTEEN

SHADOW

A shower of splinters rained down on me as I ducked behind the bar to reload. I brushed broken glass out of my hair, barely giving a thought to how the tiny shards cut up my hands.

"Jen!" I barked at the scared-witless bartender, who was curled up in a ball and trembling as she clung to Doc sitting next to me on the floor. He was trying to soothe her as best he could, rubbing her back and making shushing sounds in her ear.

"Jen, get into the kitchen with Heidi." Another round of shots sent splinters and glass falling over us, and Jen let out a pained whimper.

"Sweetheart, do as Ivan says." Doc tried to loosen his hold, but she just clung to him tighter. "Heidi's back there, you two stay together."

"I don't want to go." Jen's lips quivered as she stared at Doc with wide, unseeing eyes, a look I recognized in myself. "I don't want to go, please don't let them take me."

When the firing ceased, I rose up and fired a series of shots just over the bartop. The fuckers were staying outside, using the walls and front door for cover. The window panes had been shot out, and one of them had smashed a head-sized hole in the front door with an axe. I was able to get two head shots through it, but the smarter guys were staying out of my line of sight. If they kept this up, the winner of this fight would be whoever had more ammo stocked.

And my supply was running dangerously low.

My magazine emptied and I'd only managed to graze a guy's shoulder. I ducked behind the bar again, a bullet whizzing past my head and only narrowly missing me as it tore through more glass liquor bottles.

"Jen!" I yelled more insistently. "You could get shot out here. Get back in the kitchen with Heidi *now*."

Her wide, unblinking eyes stared back at me, tears staining her face. I grabbed her arm in a motion I hoped was gentle, but she still recoiled at the touch.

"Doc, go back there with her," I said, releasing her.

The older man nodded, his own hands shaking slightly as he started to crawl across the floor with his arm around Jen. "Come on, sweetheart. My old knees can't do this without you."

Together they shuffled through the swinging kitchen door and I breathed a sigh of relief knowing they were slightly less in harm's way. Maybe it'd let me focus and aim better.

Another shot rang out and I quickened my reloading, but a male curse of pain from the other side of the bar was not what I expected to hear.

"What the fuck?!"

I looked over the bar, seeing two of them in plain sight in front of the window and didn't miss my chance.

"Petey, d'you get shot in the fuckin' back—ahh!"

The guy fell dead over the windowsill with one well-placed shot to his chest. His last observation before death set my teeth on edge. If his friend had been shot in the back, that had to be from Mari's gun.

"Spread out and head for side doors and windows! Cover your fuckin' heads, someone's tryin' to snipe us."

"Shit." I ran along the length of the bar, keeping low as I tried to track the guys, but we still had four of them to deal with and one of me.

Two of us, I reminded myself. *Mari can handle herself.* I needed to believe that she could, at least until I could reach her.

A rattling sound alerted me to one of them running through the junkyard, making a shit-ton of noise. I waited for him by that side door and picked him off easily.

"Bitch on the roof! Found our sniper!" I heard someone yell.

God fucking damn everything, why the fuck was she on the *roof?*

I started to run in that direction, the sound of gunfire just as rapid as my fucking heartbeat.

"Ivan! Oh god, Ivan, *help!*"

The terrified cry had my feet skidding to a stop, quickly pivoting to head back toward the bar. I jumped it and slammed my shoulder into the swinging kitchen door.

It didn't budge.

I heard Jen's screaming on the other side, and Doc pleading with someone to let her go.

"You shut the fuck up," the trafficker answered and a single shot was fired.

Fuck! I pushed harder on the door, using all of my body weight, but the fucker must have shoved the refrigerator in front of it. I ran again, my mind set on the back door they used to receive food deliveries. It was the only other way inside.

Going that way wasted precious time, but I could only hope he didn't intend to kill Jen or Doc. Jen was precious cargo to them, at least. Doc was more expendable. By that same logic, Mari should be able to buy herself some time until I made it back out front.

I reached the backdoor to find it open and swinging. Doc was inside, on the ground with a bleeding cut on his forehead. He seemed otherwise unharmed, but he was alone.

"Where's Jen?" I demanded, my eyes darting around the kitchen that was now in ruins.

A scream across the kitchen answered me, sounding like it was coming from the back of the bar.

"He took her through the swinging door as soon as he saw you leave," Doc said with a pained groan.

I ran through without another word, jumping and climbing over counters and machinery that had clearly been pulled out to slow me down. Fuck, I hated that I fell for such a simple trick, and now Jen would be the one to pay for my mistake.

When I burst through the door, he was already

across the dining room, dragging Jen across the floor with a length of rope that bound her wrists together.

"Ivan!" she cried with body-wracking sobs as she struggled and kicked for her life.

"Stop!" I fired a single shot that would have hit if he hadn't suddenly crouched low, wrapping one arm around Jen's middle as he hauled her up to use her as a shield.

"Shoot again and she dies, Tonto."

I raised both hands, holding my finger away from the trigger. The fucker kept his eyes on me, walking backwards as he dragged Jen out the front door, but my gaze was rooted on her. I recognized the stricken fear in them and hoped she understood that I wasn't surrendering, just buying another opportunity.

He shut the mangled front door and I didn't wait a second longer, crossing the room as fast my legs could carry me. I heard a thump and another cry of pain as he dropped Jen and proceeded to drag her again. When I touched the doorknob, four shots fired in rapid succession, each of them filling me with cold dread.

Fuck, Jen!

I pulled the front door open, weapon raised, to find Jen's abductor dead on the ground.

And Mari standing a few feet away, her gun pointing at the bleeding man on the ground. She didn't see the guy running up behind her.

"*Mari!*" I bellowed.

He fired, the shot low and clumsy, but it hit.

Shock and then pain spread across Mari's face as she went down, blood quickly spreading up her pant leg.

He shot her.

She got hit.

She was hurt.

Someone hurt *her*.

I didn't know when I lost control. The whole event seemed to play out in slow motion, and then fast-forward in a senseless blur, to the point where I was looking down at a misshapen mass of flesh and blood. I blinked several times, realizing I was sitting on top of an unmoving body. The bloody, fleshy blob in front of me had once been a man's face. My fist was bleeding and clenched tight, a few teeth embedded in my knuckles.

I scraped them away with my other hand and took a careful look at my surroundings.

"Mari!"

"Shadow," she whimpered, still on the ground a few feet away, pale and clutching at her bloodsoaked leg.

It was impossible to tell, but my disassociation must have only lasted seconds. I scrambled over in a panic and went to hold her, but immediately froze. I didn't know what to do here.

"I…I need to wrap something tight around my leg," she explained through pained, wheezing breaths. "I'm… I'm bleeding a lot."

"Okay, just tell me where." I tried to keep my voice calm as I shrugged off my holsters and pulled off my shirt. But my hands shook as I tore down the middle of the garment to make it a longer piece of fabric.

"Around my thigh," she told me. "It's—ah! It's…just above my knee."

She ground her teeth and did her best to sit still as I

wrapped my shirt around her leg, but every whimper and wince cut through me worse than any blade.

"I'm so sorry. Am I hurting you?"

"No, tighter," she hissed. "Make it tighter, you have to cut off circulation."

Doc finally stumbled out the front door, followed by a few of the service girls who quickly rushed to Jen's aid. She was still tied up on the ground, but otherwise uninjured.

"Doc, please tell me you have actual medical knowledge," I growled at him, pulling tighter on the knot around Mari's leg.

He took one look at the state of Mari's leg and gulped, running a bloodied hand over his goatee. "It's been about five years since I pulled a bullet out of someone, but I *have* done it before."

"My kit's in a duffel bag in my room," Mari gasped. "I'll walk you through it."

Doc nodded sharply and went to retrieve what she needed. The others were helping Jen inside, leaving us momentarily alone.

"Should I move you?" My hands went to Mari's waist, ready to lift her up if needed.

"Ugh, maybe," she grunted out. "A sanitized surface would be much safer."

"Okay, I got you." I'd only lifted her a few inches off the ground when her howls of pain nearly pierced my eardrums, and I set her right back down. "We're not going anywhere," I decided right then.

"Fuck! Oh fuck!" She shook like a leaf in my arms,

forehead rolling across my chest as she writhed from the pain.

"It's okay." I wrapped around her, squeezing tight. Before I knew it, I was rocking her in my arms and kissing her forehead. "I'm right here. Doc's going to fix you."

"Ugh, it *hurts*…" Mari was hunched over and small, her brows drawn tight over her delicate features. "And he's gonna dig in there and I know it's gonna be worse."

"I'm sorry, love." The word slipped out, the same term of endearment she used for me. "I'm so sorry. I wish I could feel it instead of you." I stroked her hair back, holding her face against my chest. "But Doc's going to make it better. Just hold on with me."

He returned moments later and set to work efficiently with Mari's instructions. First, he cut away her pant leg without issue. When he started to clean around her wound with alcohol, that's when things got difficult.

She screamed and thrashed hard, nails digging into my arm as I tried to restrain her against my chest.

"Mari." I touched my lips to her ear. "You didn't bring any local anesthesia with you?"

Her head shook back and forth, her face in a grimace of pain that I couldn't even fathom, and it broke my heart.

"I can't get it out if she keeps kicking," Doc said with a worried frown. "I hate to even suggest it but… should we knock her out?"

"No," I bit out, holding her with one arm while the other worked to pull apart my belt buckle. "The pain could wake her up, anyway."

Doc watched with a puzzled expression as I pulled my belt through my belt loops and folded it in half with my free hand. "What the hell are you…"

He got his answer when I held the folded strip of leather in front of Mari's mouth. "Bite down on this for me."

She understood, taking the belt eagerly between her teeth.

I returned to holding her with both arms, petting her hair and stroking down her back. "Listen to my voice and breathe deeply for me."

Her breaths came out harsh and ragged, but I felt her body calm slightly. I continued the same pattern of stroking her hair, rocking her upper body gently as I continued to talk to her.

"You're safe with us. You'll get through this, Mari." I pressed my lips to her forehead again. "You're so brave. You know what to do. Let Doc get the bullet out, okay?"

I felt her head nod against my chest, the rest of her body still except for her tremors. Taking a deep breath for myself, I nodded at Doc for him to proceed.

Mari whimpered and bit down on my belt as he finished cleaning her wound, but otherwise remained still enough for him to work.

"Might not wanna look, sweetheart," he said, quickly sanitizing her forceps with more alcohol.

Mari pressed her forehead into my chest, aided by my hand on the back of her head. "You're doing great," I told her, dropping another kiss to her hair. Doc finished cleaning the instrument and started poking around the entry wound, prompting more whimpers and sobs from Mari. "Shh, you're okay, love." I lowered one hand to her ankle, trying to be comforting as well as helping keep her leg still. "You're okay, I'm here. I'm not leaving you."

It felt like hours dragged by. I hated every minute of Mari's sounds of pain, the sweat and shivers erupting on her skin. She burrowed in my chest, blunt nails clawing at my skin and teeth grinding down on my belt. But I'd hold on and keep her steady for as long as she needed me.

After what seemed like an eternity, Doc victoriously held up a metal slug in his forceps. "Got it!"

I stroked Mari's cheek, but didn't loosen my hold on her. "Bullet's out. We're so close to done. Just let Doc close you up, okay?"

She nodded slowly, cheek dragging on my chest. The pulse on her neck beat steadily under my hand, though I was worried it might have been weaker than normal.

Doc finished quickly, placing a thick wad of gauze over her wound and winding tape around her leg tightly to hold it in place. He wiped his brow and looked at us tiredly. "Not as nice of a job as you, sweetheart. But we're not losing you yet."

Mari slackened her jaw, releasing my belt, which now had deep grooves in the leather from her teeth. "Thank you," she said in a barely audible whisper, her eyelids fluttering closed.

"What now?" I looked between her and Doc. She still looked pale and was clearly exhausted.

"She needs rest and that wound needs to stay dry for a few days." He closed her kit and kept the tools he used in his other hand. "I'll sterilize your stuff, Mari. Don't worry."

I still had plenty of worry. She was slumped against me and looked close to death. "What about food? Water?" I asked Doc. "Should she eat?"

"If she's up for it, yes." He climbed to his feet. "But rest is most important. Her heart's gonna work overtime to replenish the blood she lost."

"Mari." I leaned down, touching my forehead to hers. "We're getting up, and I'm carrying you to my room, okay? Tell me if I hurt you."

"Shadow…" Her lips brushed my collarbone as she mumbled my name. "Don't…don't leave me…"

"Never." I slid my arm under her thighs and lifted her carefully from the ground. "Never again. I promise."

Mari made no pained sounds as I carried her through the battered front door and trashed dining room. The others had already started cleaning up, but I barely took notice. I watched every step as I took the stairs, not wanting to jostle her body.

When we reached my room, I was about to lay her down on my bed when her fingertips curled into my chest. "Wait."

"What?" I froze, hovering her a foot above the mattress. "Are you okay?"

"I'm…I'm all bloody." Her tongue flicked out to wet her dry, peeling lips. "Do you…think I can…clean up?"

"I don't care about the sheets getting dirty," I told her. "Doc said you need to rest, and your wound can't get wet."

"I know, but if…if you have a tub…and can…help

me." Her eyelashes batted slowly. "I just want to wash it off."

"Okay," I relented, returning her to my chest and walking around the bed to the attached bathroom. I did have a tub, and a detachable shower head at that.

I paused, still holding her just over the empty bathtub. "How, uh." I cleared my throat. "How do you want to, uh…"

"I'll need your help undressing." Mari's arms went around my neck. "Let…let my good leg down. I'm gonna lean on you."

Slowly, painstakingly, I allowed her uninjured leg to touch the floor. She kept one hand on me for support as she started unbuttoning her pants. Right away, I could see how weak and uncoordinated she was, and went to help her.

Once her clothes were off, I made sure she was stable as I bent to turn the water on. I lifted her around her waist and placed her in the tub as it started to fill. She kept her injured leg bent and hanging over the lip of the tub as she carefully sat down.

"Comfortable?" I took the shower head and ran the warm water over her skin, carefully rinsing away the dirt and blood that coated her.

"As much as I'm gonna be." She gave a weak smile as she leaned against the edge. Relaxation—or just pure exhaustion—began to settle into her limbs.

I drained the tub once to clear the dirty water when she finished rinsing off, then refilled it so she could soak for a while.

"Do you want something to eat?" The thought of

leaving her side punched up my anxiety, but I wanted her in the best shape to heal, to have the best possible chances of recovery.

I needed her healthy and well again. Fuck, I just needed her, period.

"I probably should." Mari nodded tiredly. "Something light…I dunno. Just bread or…something."

"I'll be right back." I squeezed her arm resting on the tub's edge, then kissed her shoulder before reluctantly climbing to my feet.

In the cleaning and repairing madness downstairs, I was able to find part of a sourdough baguette, clean water, and some grapes. I was barely gone five minutes, but still breathed a sigh of relief to find Mari in the exact same position I left her. It almost would have been funny if I hadn't nearly lost her—seeing her slouched low in the tub with her leg dangling over the edge. Jandro would have thought of some funny comment to make.

"Here." I handed her the bottle of water first, then sat on the floor next to the bathtub.

"Are you going to feed me?" There was some brightness in her expression after all, humor in her exhausted smile that made my chest ache.

"Yes," I decided, tearing off a chunk of the baguette and holding it in front of her lips. She ate it all, as well as the grapes I fed her.

When she started sliding down lower in the tub, I cupped the back of her head, making sure her face stayed above the surface. "Ready to get out?" At her tired nod, I got a large towel ready and helped her stand.

Mari leaned on me again, her good leg shaking with effort as I dried her off. "Here we go," I said, scooping her up into my arms again.

It was a short trip to the edge of my bed, where I sat her down and dug out a clean shirt and pair of my shorts for her to wear. When she finally laid down to rest, scooting gingerly toward my pillow, I was at a loss for what to do next.

"Come here, Shadow," she murmured, more asleep than awake.

"Just for a little bit," I relented, moving to lay on my side behind her. At first I made sure not to touch her, then she rolled back toward me slightly, her shoulder colliding softly with my chest. Her hand found mine, then our fingers intertwined, and my arm found its way around her waist.

I let out a breath and closed my eyes, her hair tickling my lips. If only I could stay here, continue to be someone she needed even during sleep. But here was where my usefulness ended. The last place she needed me was asleep in a bed next to her.

When her breathing became deep and steady, I lifted away from the mattress and carefully worked to unlace my fingers from hers. I'd take a nap in her room, or find any empty spot to crash for a few hours before checking on her again.

The moment our hands separated though, she snapped awake.

"Shadow." She looked over her shoulder at me, eyes

wide and fearful as her hand scrambled for mine again. "Where are you going? Don't leave me."

"I'm not, love. I'm just—" My other palm found her cheek, mouth trailing over hers in a ghost of a kiss. "I'll be close. You need to rest."

Mari's grip wound tightly around my forearm, all the fear from the day's events seeming to hit her hard now that the adrenaline wore off. "Please don't leave me. I don't want to be alone."

"I can get someone—"

"No, I want you." She turned over, a pained groan escaping her with the movement of her injured leg. But she was kissing me before I could tell her to be careful.

"Mari," I sighed, sinking into the soft presses of her lips more than I should have. "I can't stay. It's not safe for you."

"You've kept me safe all day," she whispered, hands trailing over my neck and face. "Please, Shadow. I only want you here."

"Mari, please understand—"

"Please don't leave me."

Even if I moved to leave, her grip around my hand threatened to hold on anyway. With a heavy swallow, I lowered back to the mattress and let her nestle into me. Her eyelids fell closed and her body relaxed again, but I kept my eyes open, focusing on the falcon staring at us from the tree outside the window.

I would not close my eyes. I wouldn't fall asleep.

I'd never sleep another day if it meant keeping her out of danger.

NINETEEN

REAPER

I stuck a cigarette in my mouth only to have it immediately yanked away by my mother. She just glared at my disapproving grunt. "Not in the house. You want to be a chimney, do it outside."

"Fine."

I started to roll up from my parents' couch when my dad's palm smacked my shoulder, shoving me back down to the cushions. "What are you, eighteen? You don't speak to your mother that way." His glare was murderous.

My impulse was to shove him right back, make him get the fuck out of my face so I could go smoke in peace. But if the last miserable several weeks had taught me anything, it was that I shouldn't give in to my impulses. All it ever did was hurt the people around me. So I clenched my hands against the desire to lash out, and looked at my mother.

"I'm sorry, ma. I'll be outside."

My parents' stares felt like the tips of knives on my

back, another weight to balance precariously on top of everything else. First the alliance, then the losses at the skirmish, then Mari leaving without a word, and now, more of my own men dead.

I feared the worst when I saw Jandro riding back into town alone, with only a bloodied, limp Slick on the back of his bike. Gunner and I zipped through town, clearing the way for Slick to get rushed to the hospital. The medics told us he might not have lasted another hour, but they were able to stabilize him. That was the only silver lining to that dark cloud.

When Jandro told me about the decoy caravan and the ambush, I couldn't even muster up the strength to react. Those guys were among our best, and they got slaughtered. It was just one blow after another, and I couldn't help but wonder if this was some kind of divine punishment for what I did to Shadow.

Hades, of course, provided zero insight.

After Jandro got back, my dad, his lieutenants, Gunner, and I tried to re-think our tactics *again*. For days we'd been going around in circles nonstop. Without Horus' eyes, we just had no efficient ways to track the enemy. The skirmish had hurt our army's numbers, which were already small by comparison. If I kept sending my men out, the Steel Demons MC would dwindle down to nothing.

And I still had no fucking idea where Mari was, or if she'd ever come back.

My throat was raw from all the stress-smoking. My sleep was fucked, only catching moments of rest here or there. I was a snapping, irritable prick to everyone I ran into, even my own mother. Gunner and I went at each other's throats a few times, and needed to be physically separated by my dad and Jandro. None of us were doing well in the slightest.

There *had* to be something. Had to be a way our little territory could stand a chance against the giant threatening to crush us. But I didn't know what else we could do. Gunner had put forth several formations, but we still only had guesses as to the enemy's numbers and locations. Andrea hadn't yet made contact with more information and I was starting to lose hope in her too.

I thought the despair was bad when Mari wouldn't talk to me. Now, it was crushing. This weight had slowly grown heavier over the weeks and I had finally reached my breaking point.

A door swung open, and I heard both paws and booted feet approaching. My dad stood a few feet away from me in the small patio garden, Hades at his side. *Even my dog has abandoned me.* The melodramatic thought bubbled up from some nonsensical place in my exhausted brain.

"Sucks, doesn't it?" Dad remarked casually, like he was commenting on the weather.

"What?" I grunted.

"Everything. You're lost and not finding a way out. You're exhausted. You're fighting with your loved ones at every turn. You're heartbroken and feeling alone."

"So what, you came to rub it in?" I shot back.

"Nah, son." He shook his head, eyes never leaving me. "Just empathizing."

"Yeah, I know you've been through shit too. Being

taken away to that labor camp, losing Carter, escaping with Mom. I get it. You've had it bad, if not worse than this. Doesn't change dick about where we are now."

"No, it doesn't," he agreed. "But the lesson is the same." He came close enough to touch a finger to my chest. "You have *got* to keep fighting, son." I snorted and he growled. "No, listen to me. It's easy to fight when you're winning. It's easy to have hope when you feel good. But right now?" He tapped his finger to my chest a few times. "Now is when you need to fight the most. I can see that dark cloud in your eyes, Rory. I know you're sick of it all, and it feels like it'll never end. But it will. You've gotta dig deep and find it in you. For Mari, for your family. Fuck, for *yourself!*" He backed away, turning quickly as he wiped his eyes. "I'm not losing another son. Don't give a fuck if it's on a battlefield or by his own depression. I need you around, Rory."

"Dad…" My cigarette had long since turned to ash and I dropped the butt in a tray on the patio table. "I just don't see how we can win."

"We can," he insisted. "You have gods with you."

At first, we only told him about Gunner's ability. After Jandro came back and we had nothing left to lose, I ended up spilling *everything*. From the moment I found Hades and started hearing his voice, to the accelerated healing that seemed to be powered by Mari and Freyja's bond. I even told him about when Shadow and I looked up the gods in books to try to make sense of it all. All this time later, I didn't feel any closer to understanding why they were here, or what they were really doing for us.

"We have gods who only step in when it suits them," I argued. "Maybe this shit is fun for them, I dunno." I gestured a hand to Hades. "He tells me who to kill, big fucking whoop. I don't need him to tell me we have to kill three-thousand troops, to our sub-one-thousand."

"There must be more to it," Dad said, sounding a lot like me back when I actually had hope. "Why can't you see through him like Gunner does with Horus?"

"I don't fucking know, Dad!"

You've never tried, my reaper.

My head jerked to stare at the dog, sitting calmly on his haunches. He stared back with that unsettling human gaze, and then I was somewhere else.

———

WHAT THE FUCK? *Where am I?*

I tried to yell but my jaw was rigid, like it was wired shut. No part of my body could move, as if I was paralyzed. In the next few moments, I realized I wasn't breathing. I went to suck in a breath, but my lungs didn't expand. My heart wasn't pumping. There was no activity going on in my body at all. It was utterly strange to feel panicked with zero physical responses.

What the fuck, am I dead? Hades, what did you do?!

Look.

It was the only answer I got.

I was lying on the ground, not in my parents' yard, but some place I didn't recognize. Someone's boots were inches from my face. I heard gunshots and felt the *instinct* to duck for cover and reach for my holster, but it felt like I was encased in cement.

The boots in front of my face stepped away, the soles tacky with the blood that I realized had pooled around me. *What the fuck is going on?*

More gunshots fired off somewhere further away, like a shootout was going down behind me. In front of me, I saw a pickup truck with a wire cage fixed over the bed. It still had a pre-Collapse license plate that I didn't recognize. I couldn't squint, but tried my best to read it. Did it say West Virginia?

A woman's scream gradually became louder, and I couldn't even grit my teeth at how harshly the sound hit me. A door slammed and booted feet stomped down the porch I was facedown on. Some guy was dragging a woman along the ground by a rope tied around her wrists.

I couldn't see well from my angle, but she was clearly terrified and fought like hell. Her wrists were already chafed and bleeding, red lines dripping down her tattooed arms. The guy was dragging her straight to the truck with a cage on it, and apparently no one was stopping him.

Hades, what the fuck is happening? Do something!

His life is hers to take.

What?!

Someone ran up, arms outstretched toward the man, with a well-trained shooting stance. If I didn't already feel cold and dead, my heart would have stopped at the sight of the woman with long brown hair billowing around her.

Mari?!

The man dragging the other woman paused, but Mari didn't give him an opportunity to draw a weapon. She pulled her trigger and emptied the gun into him— six shots with no hesitation, her expression calm, if even cold.

That's my girl.

My pride was short-lived as I saw movement behind her, and then a shot rang out that wasn't hers. Mari fell, shock and pain on her face as she reached her palms out to break her fall. A dark stain began coloring her pant leg.

Hades! I cried out mentally as loud as I could. *Let me move! She's fucking hurt!*

No movement came, no matter how much I begged and pleaded. It dawned on me too late that I was watching this scene through someone else's dead body, likely one of these fuckwads who had gotten shot.

The man who shot Mari walked up to where she lay on the ground, trying to drag herself to the tattooed woman, his gun pointed toward her head. I'd never felt worse or lower in my life than at that exact moment. What kind of cruel joke was this, being forced to watch the woman I loved die?

HADES, PLEASE! PLEASE DO SOMETHING!

Her life is not yours to take. The ancient god's voice reverberated through my mind, angry and protective.

Footsteps crashed near my head, nearly kicking me. A shot fired and Mari's attacker went down, clutching his stomach. Then a giant of a man crossed the distance with nearly inhuman speed until he crashed into the shooter. From there, the huge man sat on him, punching and crashing the man's skull against the ground.

It went on and on. I saw blood and brain matter flying from the force of the blows. I quickly put together that it was Shadow, turning Mari's attacker into ground meat with a barbaric violence that I had never seen before. Shadow had always been a clean killer, nothing like this.

He finally stopped, pausing to stare at his hands as if coming out of a trance. When he finally went over to cradle Mari in his arms, putting pressure on her wound while his blood-speckled face frowned with worry, it was all I needed to see.

So she found him. And he really does love her.

The dead are your vessels, my reaper, Hades said to me. *Use them to see what you must.*

In a sudden jolting sensation, I was back.

"Rory?"

Both of my parents were staring down at me, concern on Mom's face and curiosity on Dad's. I blinked. I could fucking move again! I sat up with a groan, my head aching slightly.

"You alright, son?" Dad asked. "You went down like a sack of potatoes."

I nodded, smiling genuinely for the first time at the sight of Hades, looking regal with his belly on the ground and front paws stretched out.

"I think…I know how we can win," I said in an excited whisper.

MARIPOSA

The excruciating, burning pain in my leg had dulled to a pulsing ache when I awoke. My whole body was stiff as I attempted to stretch and move. A quick glance out the window told me little—it was cloudy and gray.

I turned over in bed to see Shadow reclined on the opposite end. He was on his side facing away from me, at first looking like he was wearing some kind of jumpsuit. It took a few moments for the realization to dawn on me.

He was wearing a straitjacket?

"Shadow," I croaked out hoarsely. My voice quickly became a whispered cough, and I searched the nightstand for my water bottle.

Shadow stirred and turned toward me as I took a few greedy gulps. He was indeed strapped into a full-body suit, arms bound in front of him, and even his legs were encased.

"Good morning," he said.

I burst out laughing, spitting water all over the sheets, but cracking up too hard to care.

"What's so funny?" Shadow stared at me. "Careful, your leg."

"You…look…like," I took desperate gasps of air between peals of laughter, "a *mummy*!"

He frowned, looking down at himself and then at me. "It's funny to you that I look like an ancient Egyptian corpse?"

"Yes!" I shrieked, falling back down to the mattress. "Why on earth are you wearing that?"

"You wouldn't let me leave." A smile finally curved his lips. "And I didn't want…you know, anything to happen if I fell asleep. So Doc found this thing and strapped me in."

I laughed into the pillow. "What an ingenious idea."

"I figured I'd fall on the floor, squirming around like a caterpillar, and by then you'd be awake."

Grinning at him from across the bed, I propped my head up in my hand. "So how long have I been out?"

"Almost two full days. You were kind of in and out the first day, but you never had a fever or anything, so Doc said to just ride it out." Shadow swallowed deeply as his eyes trailed from my leg back up to my face. "You look much better today."

"I feel better." I stretched long again, mindful of the dull throbbing above my right knee. "How are the others? Is Jen okay?"

"Shaken up, but she'll be fine."

Shadow's arms pulled against the restraints holding his arms to his chest. He wiggled from side to side in an effort to sit up higher, which prompted another laughing fit from me.

"Would you like to be freed from that?"

His lips quirked again. "As much as I love hearing you laugh, yes please."

I crawled across the bed toward him, keeping most of my weight on my left leg. Even then, after everything that had happened and how ridiculous the straitjacket solution was, it was oddly erotic pulling apart the straps of the garment. He even let out a pleasured groan when his arms came loose from the sleeves. When I helped pull the top part of the jacket down to his waist, I saw that he was shirtless underneath, still wearing the red marks on his chest from where I gripped him so hard during the bullet extraction.

"Shadow, I'm sor—"

He grabbed my hand on its way to his chest. "Don't be."

"I was so…" He flattened my palm to his skin as the disjointed memories returned to me in a rush. Most of them sensations rather than images. "It feels like I wasn't even really there. I just get flashes of pain and feeling so scared."

"It's okay." His fingers stroked over the back of my palm. "Whatever you're feeling is okay." He looked a bit sheepish at my evident surprise at hearing such a thing coming from him. "It's something that Doc tells me a lot. To just…*be* with whatever you're feeling rather than try to fight it." Shadow's warm caress over my hand continued. "Fighting just makes it worse."

"Shadow…"

My lips fell to his in a desperate, needy kiss, one he returned with equal fervor and a moan that almost sounded pained. His large hands came to my arms, pulling me closer while my fingers dove through his hair. I remembered how he held me, soothed me as Doc dug the bullet out of my leg. How he helped to undress, bathe, and feed me, thinking only of my comfort and care.

"Shadow." His name escaped my lips again when we parted for a breath. "Shadow, I love you."

"Mari, no."

Rather than meeting me for another kiss, he tore away, holding me back by my shoulders. He looked so sad, sorrowful, and pain sliced through me like another onslaught of bullets.

"Shadow, why? What's wrong?" I held his face, making him look at me. "I've loved you even since before—"

"No." He shook his head, his jaw clenched hard. "Don't tell me that. Don't…feel that way for me, please."

"Too late," I whispered. "I already do." He just kept shaking his head, the hurt and rejection making me blurt out, "You don't feel the same for me."

That caused him to stop and look at me. "No, that's not it at all." He looked at my hands like he wanted to grab them again. "I do…I do feel the same way."

"Then what is it?"

He looked to be struggling so much, like he was fighting against something that was clawing to come out of him.

"You don't...know me." Shadow's voice was small, hesitant. "You don't know what led to the me you see now, all of this." He rubbed a hand over his arm, scars running over scars. "And I'm scared to death of you knowing that part of me."

I scooted closer in small movements, his eyes watching me like a wary animal backed into a corner. "If I told you nothing will change how I feel, would you believe me?"

"I want to." He pulled in a deep breath. "More than anything, I want to believe that."

"Then trust me." I placed a hand on top of his, threading through his scarred fingers. "If you feel the same way about me, please take this chance. Trust that I would never hold your past against you."

He stared straight ahead, his hand passive in mine as he spent a few long moments thinking. Finally, his fingers curled around mine in a light squeeze. "I'll tell Doc to meet us in the basement."

I STOOD off to the side as Doc methodically shackled Shadow into the metal chair, like they'd done this dozens of times before.

"Are the restraints really necessary?" I asked.

"I don't think so, at this point," Doc answered cheerily. "But Ivan insists on it. The therapy works best when the patient is at ease, so I do as he asks."

"The first couple times, I would have been violent if I wasn't restrained," Shadow muttered. "It's not a risk I'm willing to take."

Doc tossed a smile my way at that. "I take it you've heard this before?"

"A few times," I said with a returned smile.

"Okay, Ivan." Doc reached into his shirt pocket and produced a string tied through a coin with a hole in the center. "Are you ready?"

"Yes."

I folded my arms, leaning against a side table as I watched with fascination. Doc stood off to the side, holding the string in front of Shadow's eyes as he began to swing the coin back and forth like a pendulum.

"Begin to take deep breaths." Doc's voice took on a soothing, even tone. "Match your inhales and exhales with each swing of the pendulum."

Shadow's broad chest rose and fell with each breath, his gaze fixated on the coin.

"Very good. I'm going to start counting backwards from ten. With each number, your eyes are going to get heavier, and your gaze is going to turn inward. Ten…nine…"

Shadow's eyelids drooped, his breaths remaining steady and even while the older man counted. Doc hadn't even reached the number one when he put away the pendulum. Shadow had already reached a hypnotic state. By the time he finished counting, Shadow appeared to be asleep sitting up in the chair, his eyes closed and breaths deep and even.

"Can you tell us where you are, Ivan?" Doc asked after a few silent moments.

"My name is Shadow."

The declaration made me jump. It was still his voice, yet completely different. He sounded younger, more timid.

Doc however, didn't seem fazed. He just smiled. "Alright, Shadow. Can you tell us where you are?"

"I'm in my prison cell." Shadow tipped his head back as if to lean it against the wall behind him.

"The one you grew up in?"

"No, I'm in the mental health unit at the men's prison." A small smile came to Shadow's face. "Jandro just snuck me a flask and I drank it all. I'm numb and it feels good."

I released a tight breath at that. Vaguely, I knew this prison was one of Shadow's better memories. It was where he first met Jandro, where his life improved because he wasn't tortured on a daily basis.

"Mariposa is here," Doc said, keeping that even, calm quality to his voice. "You know who she is, yes?"

"*Yesss…*" Shadow drew the word out like he was experiencing something that felt utterly heavenly. Like a massage or a hot bath. Or…

I bit the inside of my cheek to hide my smile.

"Good. Would you be open to answering some questions from her?"

Shadow's mouth twitched, the smile fading as his

face hardened. I thought he might refuse until another, "Yes," slipped past his lips.

Doc turned to me. "He's aware of everything and knows who you are. Just think of it as his subconscious being in the driver's seat while his conscious mind is taking a step back."

"So he'll remember this?" I asked.

"Yes," Doc nodded. "He remembers everything. Ask him whatever you'd like."

I moved away from the table I was leaning against to stand in front of Shadow. From here I could see that his eyelids weren't fully closed. Even so, his eyes shifted back and forth under his lids as if he were dreaming.

"Hi Shadow," I began.

"Hello Mariposa."

It didn't sound like him, the Shadow I knew, and that was jarring. I just had to remember that I was speaking to an earlier version of him. Hearing him address me in that strange voice seemed to make all the questions in my head vanish.

"You can ask him open-ended questions, but it helps if they are a bit specific," Doc prompted me gently. "Going too broad might pull the thinking mind forward and take him out of the hypnotic state."

I nodded, trying to maintain my focus and come up with something simple first. "Can I ask, when did you first start getting cut?"

"I don't remember." Shadow's voice became flat, monotone. "In my earliest memories, I already had scars and cuts that were freshly bleeding."

I pulled in a breath, fighting the wave of anger, the

hurt on his behalf, to have been abused so young, as a toddler mostly likely. This was what I needed to know, and it was just the beginning.

"Who cut you?" I asked next.

"Everyone," he answered. "Every woman drew blood from me during the days she bled on her monthly cycle. I deserved it. Men had been cruel to women for ages and it was only fair to make me bleed when they did."

A hand came to my shoulder and it took me a moment to realize it was Doc, steadying me as I started to shake. He gave me a knowing, sympathetic look. He'd heard all this before, and from the tightness in his brow, it wasn't any easier to hear the second time around.

"Where were your parents?" It was an impulsive question, a demand through gritted teeth. "How could they let you be treated like this?"

Shadow began to laugh.

Again, the sound was foreign to my ears, like someone else had possessed his body and was laughing through his mouth.

"Loving parents are a myth," he scoffed. "I read about them in books, but they're not real. Do you really want to know where my parents were?"

Doc's hand squeezed my shoulder, a small warning. Even subconsciously, Shadow was trying to deflect. But I had to know. This information was probably the core of everything.

"Yes," I said firmly. "Tell me about your parents."

The strange grin faded from Shadow's face, hardening into a scowl that I knew well.

"My mother became pregnant with me at fourteen years old," he said. "You want to know who my father was? Her grandfather, who raped her."

Air rushed out of my lungs like I had been kicked in the chest. My hand flew to my heart, pounding with a crazy mix of sympathy and fear as Shadow continued on, unprompted.

"He tried to kill her when he found out about the pregnancy, but she escaped and ran away from home." Shadow sounded detached, almost robotic as he spoke. "The Sisters of Bathory found her and took her in. They were a refuge for girls like her, a community that sheltered and protected women from men.

"She was too far into the pregnancy to terminate me, and when I was born, she wanted to kill me the moment she saw that I was male." Shadow's lip curled. Not with a smile, but with disdain. "But the leader of the Sisterhood convinced her not to. She gave my mother a better idea, to let me live so I could suffer." Shadow's eyelids lifted slightly, peering through the thin gaps with an unfocused gaze. "To take the punishment that all men deserved for abusing women."

"Shadow…" My voice escaped in a cracked whisper, all my fiery anger gone and replaced by blank shock. If it wasn't for Doc still gripping my shoulder, I probably wouldn't have been able to stay upright.

"How…" It took a few tries to find my voice again. "How do you know all this?"

"Oh, my mother told me," he answered in that same eerie, flat voice. "Several times. She loved talking about how much she hated me. She hated that I invaded her body and grew inside her, the living result of a man who preyed on a child." Shadow's head tilted to the side. "She both hated me for existing and loved to make me suffer. She cut me the deepest, you know. She blinded me by puncturing my eye and gave me this handsome face."

Shadow's pale eye swiveled under his half-closed lid, the one with the scar cutting through it. A scar that *his mother* gave him. The person who was supposed to love and protect instead delighted in his pain.

"You want to know what her favorite game was?" It was like a dam had burst, and he could no longer hold back everything he'd bottled up.

"What?" I asked with dread.

"She'd leave the door to my cage open. If I tried to escape, she'd come out from a hiding place and whip me with a cat o' nine tails until I collapsed. My back was all scar tissue before I turned twelve years old, by my estimate."

I had to turn away and cover my mouth then, fighting back the bile that rose in my throat.

It wasn't like I didn't know horrible parents existed. In nursing school, I even had a lecture on identifying signs of abuse in children. But this senseless violence went so far beyond child abuse. He was subjected to a lifetime of torture, just for existing.

"The…the other men you've told me about." I turned back to him when I composed myself. "The botanist. The ones who taught you how to read and write. What about them?" Maybe it was a morbid fascination, but I still had to know.

"They were kept with me temporarily and then killed at every full moon," he answered. "A ritualistic sacrifice." Shadow talked over my shocked, gasping breaths this time, the words spilling out of him as if rehearsed. "Only the spilling of a man's blood could slake the thirst of the angry goddess. She demanded vengeance for the harm that had been done to her daughters since the dawn of history."

Shadow's head rolled slowly on his neck, eyeballs still moving actively under his lids. "The sacrificial altar was positioned above my cell. Not that I was ever let out, but I could see a little through the grate in the floor. And I heard *everything*. The chants, the struggles, and the screams. I heard the knife sink into their skin and their last pleas for life. Then I felt their blood."

His head stopped moving, staying upright with his unseeing eyes looking straight at me, and leaned forward as far as his restraints would allow him. "Blood ran over the floor, dripping down through the grate into my cell like rain. Every single month I felt it."

Shadow leaned back. "I used to try stopping them. I used to grow attached to the men who taught me things and told me about the outside world." He pulled in a labored breath. "When that didn't work, I begged the women to sacrifice me. I offered myself freely to their goddess if it would end my miserable existence. But they *refused*."

His voice cracked with clear agony at that final word. "I wasn't even good enough to be sacrificed because I was a product of evil, born of an attack on someone innocent. I was destined to live and suffer."

Shadow's head slumped forward, chin nearly resting on his chest. I couldn't tell if he had fallen asleep or come out of the hypnotic state. All I knew was that I'd heard enough.

"Take him out of it," I said to Doc. "And let's put him in bed to rest."

MARIPOSA

"More?" Doc held the bottle of whiskey over my empty glass, pausing before pouring.

"Yes." I nodded. "Please."

I didn't usually have a taste for whiskey, but nothing was appetizing at the moment. I just wanted to chase away this ache, this awful hole ripped open from what Shadow told me. I wondered if this was how he felt when he tried to drink the nightmares away—chasing sweet, empty numbness.

Doc kept him in the hypnotic state so we wouldn't have to haul him to bed with brute strength. Shadow followed his gentle instructions up to his room, and once settled into bed, Doc talked him out of the trance. I felt awful that Shadow wouldn't let himself fall asleep while I'd been recovering from the gunshot. So I followed Doc back down to the bar, so Shadow could rest up without being put in another straitjacket.

"They called themselves the Sisters of Bathory." At

my confused stare, Doc elaborated. "The cult that kept Iv—Shadow, and sacrificed men."

"You knew about them before meeting him?" I took a sip of whiskey, savoring the fire burning a path down to my belly.

"Rumors, yes, but nothing substantial." Doc stroked his goatee. "You never want to believe stuff like that, you know? You hope, you *pray*, that it's just tall tales." He gave a slight shake of his head and sighed before taking a long drink.

"Is the cult still around?" Panic flashed through me at the thought. What if there were others like Shadow? And more men being kidnapped and sacrificed?

"I don't think so," Doc said. "The rumors stopped roughly ten years ago, about the time Shadow was rescued."

"Rescued?" I repeated. "By who?"

"From what he describes, it sounded like a mercenary army hired by a governor looking to claim the area at the time. They just rolled in, gunning down everyone they saw above ground. Which is damned horrific if you think about it from the army's view—they shot up a remote village full of women and girls."

My stomach dropped at that. "Could they have known it was a cult?"

"I doubt it." Doc gave me a sympathetic look. "Cult leaders kept a tight lid and brainwashed their followers into total obedience. They operated for years under total secrecy. It's not likely anyone spilled."

"So, this Sisterhood built a following out of abused girls? Like the girls' camp runaways?"

Doc nodded gravely. "A girl in Shadow's mother's situation was a typical follower for them, if I were to guess."

I made a sound of disgust as I drained the rest of my whiskey. "I want to hate her but…she was just the victim of one predator and then fell into the hands of another."

"Mm-hm." Doc polished off his whiskey, then quickly refilled it and mine, without asking this time. "It's a shitty situation all around."

I rolled my palms across the glass, thoughts tumbling as I stared blankly at the wall behind the bar. "It's a good thing he came to you," I mused, my eyes flicking to Jen as she swept up shards of glass with a broom and dustpan. We were still finding bits of glass here and there from the shootout with the traffickers. "You seem like you know how to treat people who have been through similar situations."

Doc smiled, looking down into his drink like he was being shy. "All the girls here have faced their own traumas, some brainwashing too. When my license was revoked, I felt lost. Adrift. But this place…" He looked around the dining room with an affectionate gleam in his eye. "It's nice to have a little refuge. And to be able to help people again."

"Okay, now *this* is a story I need to hear." I leaned back in my barstool, turning to face him. "You're a man. How did *you* get your license revoked?"

He shrugged modestly. "Hypnotherapy has always been controversial. The mind, and the subconscious specifically, are so intricate and difficult to study. I used to be a psychiatrist, but..." Doc cleared his throat as though sobering. "Drug manufacturers started offering me and my colleagues *a lot* of money to prescribe their products. The FDA had been completely dismantled by then, so there was no telling what was in these drugs and the effects they would have on our patients. Lots of us suspected politicians were the ones pulling the strings."

"Makes sense," I agreed. "With how the world was going."

"It never sat right with me," Doc said. "Even before, I always had mixed feelings about treating mental illness with drugs. Once those bribes started rolling in I said, 'to hell with it! I'm opening a private hypnotherapy practice.'"

I smiled at him. "Good for you, Doc."

"It was good." He nodded. "For about twenty years, I helped people in a way that didn't conflict with my conscience. I gave them their own tools to face their traumas."

"And then...the Collapse?" I ventured.

"And then the Collapse," he confirmed with a dry laugh. "The first governor that claimed this area sent a notice to my office that said I could go back to prescribing pills at his discretion, or I'd be declared a quack and my hypnotherapy practice deemed illegal."

"Sounds like a typical governor," I remarked, before quickly remembering Vance. For all his imperfections, he was at least fair and wanted to do right by his people. A pang of longing thumped in my chest. I missed Four Corners, my home. And my men.

"Yeah, we've gone through about three governors

since then," Doc said. "The latest one doesn't seem to care about anything except gaining more land. It's not like he protects us, but at least he leaves us alone."

"You might like Four Corners," I offered. "And not just you, but everyone here. It's fair, and relatively safe. I'm sure Dr. Brooks would love to have you practicing."

Doc's smile faltered. "I've heard about this fabled Four Corners, but unfortunately, so have half a dozen governors hungry for territory. I'll be honest, Mari, I'm a little worried for y'all out there." He glanced toward the stairs leading up to Shadow's room. "Everyone's heard about the prosperity out west, the good infrastructure, the citizens with flourishing businesses. It's like a beacon for governors and their generals who want war. A *real* war for a prize worth conquering, not these little border skirmishes."

"I know," I sighed. "We've already been dealing with it. My father-in-law is the general, and my husbands have been supporting his defense effort."

Doc didn't comment on my implication that I have other lovers. "You and Shadow are welcome to stay here until it blows over. I don't expect more traffickers to bother us again." He chuckled. "Or anyone really. They must've heard that gunfight up in Boston."

I gave a regretful shake of my head. "Honestly I'd love to, but they need me out there. They need *us*. Although," I frowned with my next thought, "I wish we could clone you so Shadow can keep receiving his therapy."

"I may have a colleague out that way who can help." Doc winked with a smirk. "But really, I'm confident

Shadow only needs supplemental therapy at this point. He knows how to stay lucid in his memories. He knows how to ground himself and pull himself out if it becomes too much."

"The violent sleepwalking is his biggest concern."

"Ah, right." Doc stroked his goatee. "It's *possible* those episodes may return, the chance of it is greater than zero. But I don't expect it to happen unless he backslides significantly."

"What are the chances of that?" I asked.

"It would have to be quite the traumatic event to trigger such a regression. The sudden death of someone he loves, or being abused again in a similar manner as the cult did." He gave me a warm smile. "Something tells me he feels safest with you, and will go to great lengths to prevent any sudden-death situations."

"I hope he feels that way with me." I spun my glass idly on the bar. "It's the least he deserves after every-thing he's been through."

Doc reached for one of my hands and clasped it with friendly affection. "His mind is stronger than he believes. And with each passing day in a healthy, supportive environment, he heals a little bit more. All he really needs is that constant, gentle reminder that he matters. That he is a person worthy of love and care."

I nodded, returning the squeeze of his hand. "I'll do my best to remind him of that every day."

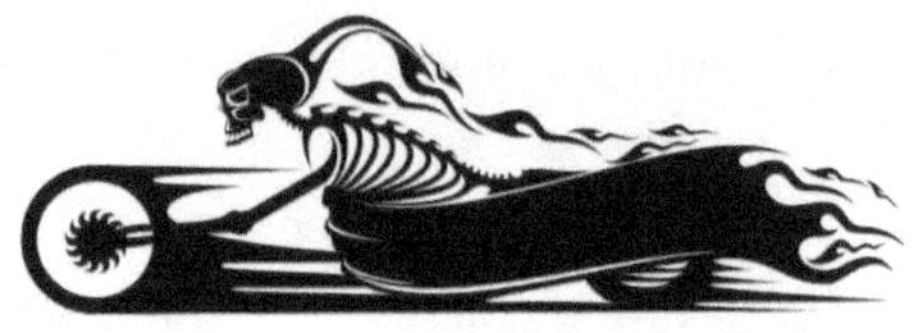

SHADOW

I woke with a start, my legs kicking out with a falling sensation before I jolted upright. My heart pounded as the room snapped into focus. Chairs and furniture remained in their places, nothing broken or scattered on the floor.

Another day of no damage. That was good.

Before I could sag with relief, my eyes landed on Mari sitting at my desk with one of my borrowed library books in her hands.

"Good morning," she greeted me.

"Why are you in here?" I snapped instead of returning her greeting. "I told you it's not safe—"

"Your therapist disagrees," she returned snippily, shutting the book.

"My therapist," I repeated. "You mean Doc?"

"Is there anyone else giving you hypnotherapy sessions?" she teased.

I rubbed my hands down my face with a groan, both

to finish waking up and also to block myself from seeing her. "No, I guess not."

Doc *had* told me the chance of me acting out my dreams again was unlikely. The lingering fear that it still *could* happen never abated, however. Even a one-percent chance felt like too much.

Now that my surroundings and Mari had survived the night without harm, a different fear was riding me hard. For the first time since meeting Mari, I wanted to shrink away, to put as much distance between us as possible. To become small and invisible until she would forget me.

She had been there. She asked me questions, and I answered her. I told her everything and now she knew. She was one of two people alive who knew how I turned out this way, and why.

I was dying to know, and yet terrified to find out what she was thinking, looking at me from across the room like that. Would my worst fear be confirmed, and she was here to tell me we couldn't be together after all? Or was everything she said true—that she loved me before and still did?

I wasn't ready to feel the hurt that would cut through me if it was the former, nor did I dare hope for the latter. So I sat in the middle, caught between the two outcomes that awaited me, until I couldn't stand not knowing anymore.

"Well?" I said, filling the oppressive silence that expanded between us. "You know my past now. Has… has anything changed?"

Mari took a deep, shaky breath, like she was composing herself. I expected that.

I did not expect the tears that followed.

"Shadow…" She hiccuped and sobbed with great gasping breaths and I forgot about everything else.

"Mari." I shoved back the sheets and got out of bed, thankfully still dressed, and went to her. My knees hit the floor in front of her as I took her face in my hands, brushing away her tears with my thumbs. "What's wrong?"

"They…" she breathed shakily, "…*hurt* you."

Her fingers went to my face, shoving back my hair and stroking over my skin like she'd done so many times before. But she was seeing me differently now and it made dread pool in my gut like a well of poison.

"They did this to you," she sniffed, hands moving over me, tracing my scars. "Fuck, you were just a kid. A baby! You should have been loved and all they did was hurt you. Your own mother hurt you…"

I stopped her, taking her hands from me and gently pressing them between my palms. "I'm sorry that I upset you."

"Upset me? No, Shadow." She shook her head and leaned forward until her forehead touched mine. "I just hate that someone I love had to suffer so much."

My breath froze in my chest, rendering me as still as a statue. Did she really just say that? She couldn't have. Not after everything I had told her, everything she now knew about me.

Mari let out a small, sad laugh. "Yes, of course I still love you. I told you I would."

"How?"

The word came out choked, my breath still stuck in my body. My eyes had closed at some point, like I was afraid to see a different reality than what I was hearing. Meanwhile, my hands closed tighter around hers, clinging to the feel of her really being here.

The weight of her forehead lifted away from mine, replaced by the soft touch of her lips. "Because you're still you."

Only then did a rush of breath enter my lungs, filling me up with a hope and relief that I never dared allow myself to feel before.

"I love you, Mariposa." The sentence felt both strange and thrilling to say, a flipping sensation happening in my chest as the words left me. "I love you, and I want this. I want a life with you."

Mari inhaled sharply, still a bit of a sniffle in her nose. I saw a quick flash of her smile before our lips found each other. My hands released hers and fell to her thighs before running up to her waist. She scooted forward in the chair, leaning into my embrace as her arms wrapped around my shoulders.

She was still crying, salty tears coloring the taste of our kisses. I broke away and wiped my thumbs over her cheekbones, desperate to fix whatever was wrong. But she was still smiling, which confused me a little.

"Are you…unhappy?"

"No." She shook her head, then tilted her face to rest her cheek in my palm. "A little overwhelmed, but not unhappy." At my frown, she kissed my palm. "I'm glad you showed me. What happened to you was awful and I hate it that it happened, but I'm glad I know now. I understand better."

She looked at me so sweetly, with the same warmth she always did, and I started to wonder why I never wanted her to know my past in the first place. This was Mari, who never treated me differently, no matter how abnormal I perceived myself to be. My impulse was to open my mouth to warn her, to let her know that I'd still mess things up and not get everything perfect. I would do my best, but she was still the first woman I was ever truly *with*, the first one I loved. I'd fuck something up again. I always did.

Then I realized none of it needed to be said. She knew I wasn't perfect and loved me anyway. This woman never saw me as lesser than her other men, even before we became friends. She forgave me for hurting her even before she knew the whole story. Now she knew all there was to know about me and, like the sun setting every day, she always stayed with me.

Suffering and bleeding were the constants in my life that I never expected to change. I fully expected to be a caged animal until I died. The only other constant I'd experienced was Mari's care and kindness, which grew into a love that strengthened me like nothing else. Because of her, I broke down barriers that I caged myself in. I became more than a broken-down shell that was only useful for its blood.

I became a person, someone with their own wants, dreams, and desires. Someone who wanted to experience what else life had to offer, like loving another person.

"I feel…better, now that you know," I said, still stroking her cheek even though her eyes had dried. "I don't want to keep anything from you anymore."

She nodded her agreement, cupping her hand over mine. "That's the only way this works. Being honest and open about everything." Her eyes darkened as she lowered our clasped hands to her lap. "That's what hurt most about Reaper exiling you. The dishonesty of it."

"Will you forgive him?"

Her gaze flicked from our hands up to my face. "Do you think I should?"

I thought for a moment, curling my fingers around hers and stroking over the small digits with my thumbs. I just loved to touch her and was entranced with the feel of her skin, now that the huge weight of guilt had been lifted away.

"He acted with your best interest in mind," I said. "Not only that, but your physical safety. I can't fault him for that." Mari's eyes narrowed and her lip curled with a cute snarl. It brought a smile to my face, probably my first real one in months. "So yes, I think he's deserving of forgiveness when you feel ready."

She made an even cuter grunting sound, fingers stroking over mine and the simple returned affection brought an elated, weightless feeling to my chest. "I think how he treats *you* when he sees you again will be a determining factor in that."

"Fair enough. When do you want to ride back?" My smile faltered, a quick stab of anxiety hitting me in the chest. "Doc and I meet twice a week. Maybe if we do more sessions—"

"Shadow, he told me he has a colleague near Four Corners who can help." Mari's grin grew wide. "And even then, he said you only need supplemental therapy now. You have all the tools and your mind is strong." She untangled her fingers from mine, wrapping her warm touch around the back of my neck. "And you have me, always."

The anxiety morphed in my chest, becoming a heavy ache, but not one made of fear. It was like a dense brick of emotions wanting to burst from my body, even making my eyes water. Now I understood why she cried even when she wasn't unhappy.

"I would be nothing without you," I said through the tightness in my throat.

"That's not true." Her eyes began to water again too. "You're amazing just as you are."

Our bodies collided with a force that we couldn't have fought even if we wanted to. She crashed against my chest and my hands pressed to her back like we were made to be joined as one. And right then, it was the only thing I needed in the world. More than air, I needed to be inside my woman. I *needed* her lips on my scars and to feel the heat of her skin on mine.

Securing her with my hands on her ass, I rose from the floor and turned us toward the bed. I didn't need to think about kissing her correctly anymore. Even our clumsy, frenzied rush of lips and tongues felt natural and right.

I lowered her back to the mattress, our mouths locked in a tight seal until she clawed at my shirt to pull it over my head. Some part of me wanted to go slowly with undressing her, make it a slow, drawn-out exploration like our first night together, but mostly I just wanted her so fucking badly.

"Tomorrow," Mari said, her touch grazing down my stomach to the button on my jeans.

"What?" I grunted distractedly, revelling in her smooth, unblemished skin as I lifted her shirt away and peeled it off of her arms.

"Let's ride back to Four Corners tomorrow." She had me unbuttoned and unzipped in seconds, shoving my jeans and boxers down my thighs a moment later.

"Okay." I helped her get my pants off and then pressed her shoulders back down on the bed before she got any ideas. My fingers hooked into her waistband and I paused. "How is your leg?"

"Fine, just get those off, please."

Her eagerness was sexy and I felt myself grinning as I leaned over, planting a kiss on her sternum as I worked her pants down her legs, still taking care around the bullet wound wrapped in gauze. Once we were both free of clothing, she hummed and sighed, clamping her thighs around my ribs while her fingers raked over my scalp.

It felt *so* good to be wanted by her. I ran my hands up her sides, palms finding her supple breasts as I dragged my mouth over her belly. I was lost in tasting her skin, kissing her, and feeling her wonderful touch on me. A touch that felt so right, especially after weeks of starving and craving her.

"Come back up here." Her voice was low and husky, fingers running down my arms to squeeze around my hands that were on her breasts.

"Not yet." I kissed the beautiful little scar above her hip, tightening my hands as she prompted until her pert nipples were pinched between my fingers. At her gasping breath I released them, smoothing my touch over her flesh as I brought my mouth lower.

"Shadow…"

"Mari," I answered, utterly in love with the way she said my name, the sight of her back arching off the bed, everything.

Her legs hooked over my shoulders as I kneeled at the edge of the bed. I skimmed one hand down her body, never missing any chance to touch her, bringing it between her legs. She drew in a sharp breath with a moan at the pressure of my hand just stroking her, caressing down the center of her pleasure.

"Shadow, please." She tried to wiggle against my hand to increase the friction. "Seriously, don't tease me too much. I just want you."

My cock was heavy and aching, she was slick and wanting me, but more than anything else, I didn't want to hurt her. I sucked a harder kiss at her hip crease, letting my beard drag over her skin until she shivered. "You know I never tease."

"Liar!" she laughed.

My smile remained until I kissed her pussy, releasing an indulgent moan at her heat—oh fuck, and her *taste*. Was it only three days ago when she rode my face? I felt like an addict needing his fix, my tongue taking long greedy licks through her folds.

Mari started bucking then, and I clamped a hand

around her thigh to hold her in place. I heard her ragged breaths, felt her small fingers curl in my hair, smelled her everywhere, and tasted her sweetness on my tongue. I was torn between eating her until my jaw went numb or pulling away to sink my cock into her.

We have the rest of our lives, a voice reminded me. And it was true. This wasn't like our last time in bed together, when I thought it might've been the last time for good. We weren't saying a desperate, confusing goodbye. This was the beginning of something new for us.

I released her pink lips from a long, sucking kiss and nudged my mouth higher, at the same time moving my fingers in to stroke and test her entrance. Her clit was begging to be kissed itself, so I sealed my lips around that spot as I pressed my first finger through her folds.

"Shadowww!" she cried out, hands tugging in my hair and sending thrilling tingles down my spine.

I moaned against her sex, pressing another finger inside and curling both of them against her slick walls. She pulled harder on my hair and my cock was already dripping. A bit of pain with pleasure, the sensation I couldn't get enough of from only her.

Mari's thighs squeezed around my head, though they barely muffled the beautiful sounds she made as I pleased her. Her breaths came in increasingly short pants, and then seemed to stop altogether as her whole body went rigid, then shook and shuddered in her release.

She squeezed rhythmically around my fingers, hips tilted up to chase more sensation. I kept my mouth glued around her clit until she shoved my head away.

Even then I couldn't back away far, removing my fingers from her channel only to replace them with my tongue so I could taste her again.

"Stop that," she panted, squirming further up the bed. "Come up here."

"Do you need a minute to recover?" I couldn't fight the smug smile as I sat up, wiping my jaw with my hand as I looked at her stretched out on the bed.

"Very funny," she snorted, rolling onto her stomach. "No, what I need is you."

She propped up on her hands and knees, a deep arch in her back and glossy, wet sex on display. I was *almost* put off by the position. It was the same way I'd fucked women other than her, the ones that meant nothing and didn't matter. I didn't want her like that. I loved seeing her face and feeling her skin on mine when we were together.

Mari must have sensed my hesitation because she pressed up to kneeling and leaned back, the tattoo on her back kissing the matching one on my chest as she looked at me over her shoulder.

"You good, love?" She reached an arm up, her small hand coming to my jaw to angle my mouth for a kiss.

"Yes." I pressed into her kiss, answering her sweet tongue flicks with my own. "I was just enjoying the view."

My hands ran up the front of her body, pulling her lightly to me until the full length of her back pressed against my torso. Always, at any given time, I wanted to feel as much of her on me as possible.

"You'd enjoy it a lot more if you were fucking me," she teased, darting her tongue out to the tip of my nose.

I snapped my teeth like I was going to bite her tongue and she laughed, kissing me again. Her legs nudged closer together, hugging my cock in the slickness and heat coating her inner thighs. The groan leaving my chest was a direct result of her smooth flesh gliding over my length, teasing me. I released her from my embrace, my hands finding a hold on her hips as she fell forward to her hands and knees again.

I realized then that this was completely different, even if the position was the same one I'd done with others. My woman lowered her face to the mattress, looking back at me with a plea in her eyes while her ass lifted higher in the air. I'd never had anything like this before. Mari *wanted* me. She *loved* me.

And fuck if I was going to deny her what she wanted.

I splayed one hand on her lower back, using the other to guide my cock to her sex. Her sensitive flesh parted for my blunt head, hugging around it like her mouth had done before. Mari whimpered and tried to rock her hips back toward me, but my hand on her spine kept her place.

"I love that you want me," I said, just staring at where her flesh met mine and fighting the urge to plunge through. "But let me go slow so I don't hurt you."

She let out a cute, frustrated groan. "I know how much I can take."

"I thought I was the dominant one in this position." I gave a playful swat to her ass.

Mari laughed, grinning up at me. "I knew I should have just climbed on top of you."

"You can next time." I pressed forward with a short thrust, watching in fascination at the change on her face. Her mouth fell open, eyelids falling shut as my head nudged inside. I pulled back and it felt like her pussy was trying to suck me back in. When I pressed in a little deeper, my head tipped back with the feeling of her. She was all slippery and hot, delicious pressure on all sides of my cock, with little resistance.

"Oh yes, Shadow…" Mari rocked her hips back and this time I didn't stop her, meeting her in the middle as I pressed forward. She was a sight to behold, arched and stretched out in front of me, the curving lines of her waist and hips more hypnotizing than Doc's pendulum.

And she's mine. She enjoys this. She wants me. The thoughts kept repeating in my head as if to remind me that this was real. I'd never have awkward, transactional sex with a stranger again, but join with the woman I loved because we wanted each other. This was my life now.

Mari reached back, her hands finding my thighs as my short thrusts gradually filled her deeper. I leaned over, my forehead touching the back of her shoulder. The sensation of her wrapped around me and everything she made me feel was dizzying, consuming. Overwhelming in the best way.

"I love you." My arms wrapped around her middle,

mouth brushing her shoulder blade. "Fuck, I love you, Mari."

"I love you, Shadow." She twisted in my arms, angling back to kiss me, I assumed. With my arms around her and not supporting us, the momentum took us sideways and we landed softly on the bed. "Shit! Are you okay?" she laughed breathlessly.

"So much more than that," I promised with a kiss to her neck. I could touch more of her now that we were lying on our sides.

Still inside her, I rolled my hips against her plump ass, making her gasp and arch against me. She moaned when I resumed my thrusts, and my mouth found hers to swallow the beautiful sound.

I like this position much better, I realized. I could play with her clit easily here, tease her nipples, and kiss her. Mari's entire beautiful body was in reach of my touch and I made every effort not to leave any part of her ignored.

My hand ran leisurely down her thigh, and I lifted her leg to see if that would allow me to sink into her any deeper. It did, and judging by her resulting moan and the frantic gripping of whatever she could hold onto, it was very well-received.

"Good?" I checked in with her anyway, my mouth against her ear. Despite her clear body language of wanting me, the lingering fear of hurting her remained.

"More," she begged. "Fuck, please. More."

I rested my head on the mattress, letting her hair tickle my face while I dragged my lips along her neck and upper back. Mari kept her leg lifted while I gripped her waist, holding tight for leverage as I started to fuck her wildly.

Her first scream almost made me stop, but she immediately began crying out *yes* and *more,* and I gave in to the need to rut and fuck *hard.* My hips crashed against the soft flesh of her ass, the slapping sounds and Mari's screams filling the small room. I found a nipple with my free hand, plucking the tight peak to see if I could get any different noises out of her. Mari gasped in response, a strangled moan escaping her like her scream was stuck in her throat.

She was already so snug and tight around my cock, the feel of her squeezing me even tighter just about made me lose my mind with pleasure. I wrapped around her in a tight embrace, my hips driving into her wildly and uncontrollably and my face buried in her neck. Mari grabbed my forearm across her chest and I swore she used the leverage to push back on me as I pressed into her.

"Fuck…" I growled into her neck, squeezing around her tighter with one arm while the other slid down her belly. The reaction when I touched her clit was instant— breathless whimpers and the stuttered rocking of her hips, her pussy closing around me, making me swell and throb.

Her orgasm spurred my own, the grip and slide of her just too fucking good. Sensitivity and aching pleasure raced down my spine, releasing through my cock in a violent rush as I crushed her tight to my chest.

Then I released her, my arms limp and heavy as my pulse thundered and echoed throughout my whole body.

I rolled to my back, sucking in great lungfuls of air as the heady wave of pleasure ebbed away.

Mari curled into my side after we started catching our breath, nudging her head onto my chest. I stroked down her back, nestling my hand into the small dip of her waist. Once the haze of pleasure started to clear, I brushed my lips along her forehead, a question weighing heavily on my mind.

"Would it bother you if I slept in another room tonight?"

She lifted her head, looking up at me with a puzzled frown. "Doc said you don't need to."

"I know." My hand ran along her jaw and I took a fast kiss, her lips still swollen and flushed. "But it still makes me nervous to sleep next to you. And I'm honestly not fond of the straitjacket."

Mari let out a soft laugh, returning her cheek to my chest. "Can't say I blame you." Her hand slid over my body until her fingers clasped with mine. "Would you be willing to get a second opinion from Doc's colleague when we go back to Four Corners?"

"Yes." I brought our conjoined hands up to my lips and kissed her fingers. "It's just hard to break the habit. I don't plan on sleeping away from you forever."

"Better not," she huffed, sliding a leg over mine. "You're such a wonderful cuddler."

"I don't know how that happened," I mused, bringing both hands to her back. "You didn't exactly teach me that."

"You can't really teach cuddling," she laughed,

nuzzling into my neck before kissing me there. "It's just kind of innate, natural."

"Does it always feel this nice?" I murmured, my eyelids already weighing down. Fuck, how amazing would it feel to stay wrapped up in each other all night?

"Hmm, I think it's kind of like sex." Mari placed more kisses along my face and neck. "It's better when there's something more between the people involved."

I hugged tighter around her, catching that sweet, beautiful, luscious mouth in a deep kiss that I never wanted to end. "Then this is the best," I whispered against her mouth.

"It is," Mari agreed, her lips pulled back in a smile.

We kissed and held each other for a time that seemed entirely too short. It felt like a crime to leave her alone in bed for the night, but I would not risk her safety with me again. Not until I was absolutely sure I wouldn't become a danger to her in my sleep.

"I'll be just down the hall in your room," I said, sitting at the edge of the bed as I reluctantly got dressed.

"Okay." Mari had pulled the sheet up to her chest, her hand on my back as sleep pulled down on her eyelids.

I leaned over to kiss her before leaving, fighting every urge to dive back in bed and pull her warm body to me.

"I'll get up early and be here when you wake up," I decided right then, brushing a strand of hair out of her face. "How does that sound?"

A slow, drowsy smile formed on her lips. "That sounds wonderful."

"Good." I cupped her cheek and kissed her again. *This isn't goodbye. Not anymore,* I reminded myself.

"Goodnight, Shadow." Her eyelids finally fell closed, dark lashes sweeping over her cheeks.

"Goodnight." I slowly drew my hand away from her face. "My love."

TWENTY-THREE

MARIPOSA

S hadow made good on his promise.

I roused slowly, stretching and intending to roll over in bed—if it weren't for the long wall of muscle blocking my path.

"Good morning." He sounded amused and at ease. Even happy.

"Morning, handsome," I groaned through my stretch.

Shadow set aside the book he was reading and scooted down in the bed to lie next to me, sliding a large hand over my waist to turn me toward him. He pulled me into a breath-stealing kiss, holding nothing back. It caught me off-guard for a moment, just the unexpected boldness of it. But in the next moment I melted, sinking into his affection and soaking up every morsel until we both came up for air. A woozy smile came to my face when we parted, and I swore right then I'd never take his confidence for granted.

"I don't want to get out of bed now that you're

here," I admitted, curling into him and nuzzling into his neck.

"Don't you miss the others?" It felt like a loaded question, even though I knew he didn't mean it as such.

"I do." I played with the collar of his shirt, dipping my fingers in to touch his bare skin. "But I'd be lying if I said I wasn't worried about how things are now. With all of them." I frowned, stilling my hand. "Things will be different when we get back. I'm just not sure how. I worry that…Reap and Gun might have moved on."

"They would never," Shadow said with a low growl. "They'll be overjoyed to have you back, and eager to make things right."

"Even so," I said hesitantly, running my hand down his chest. "I'm still not sure how eager *I* am to make things right."

"If you can forgive me, you can forgive them." Shadow pressed a soft kiss to the bridge of my nose.

"Apples and oranges," I retorted.

"Are you saying you want breakfast now?"

I laughed, leaning my temple against his shoulder. "It's an expression. It means the two situations are completely different."

"I know. I'm just teasing you." His chest shook with his laugh as he pressed a kiss to my hair.

"From the man that never teases?" I said with fake shock. He just pulled me closer, and I happily snuggled into him for a few blissful moments I wished didn't have to end. "I guess we better start saying goodbyes soon, huh?"

"Yeah." He sounded wistful in his agreement.

I leaned up, kissing under his jaw. "It's okay for you to miss this place. They've taken good care of you here."

"They have," he said, resting his chin on my head. "I'm glad I was able to find this place."

"I am too." So much of my worry before coming out to find Shadow had to do with him having basic necessities like shelter and food, let alone a caring community and a doctor to look after him. It put me at ease that he had all of those things the entire time we'd been apart.

"But it's not home," Shadow added, brushing a strand of hair out of my face with his left hand. The motion drew my eye to the new tattoo inside his forearm, the pin-up that looked remarkably like his drawing of me.

"What made you do this?" I asked, tracing the lines of ink with my fingers.

He sighed, lowering his arm. "Missing you."

"Aww." I took his chin in my hands, kissing him deeply.

Shadow returned my kisses with tooth-aching sweetness before elaborating. "When Reaper told me to pack and leave, the drawing of you was the first thing I grabbed. I looked at it all the time when I first got here." He stroked my cheek, eyes warm and loving. "Then I accidentally ripped the paper and I...couldn't stand the thought of not having something to remember you, so I tattooed myself that same night."

I slid my palms around to the back of his neck, pulling him closer to kiss him more deeply. He followed my momentum, rolling us down until I was on my back and he was on top of me. His hands slid between my back and the bed, holding me against his chest as our tongues surged, trying to taste and feel even more of each other. My legs parted to make room for him between them, but he pulled away on the next breath, slow and reluctant.

"We better get going," he said regretfully. "We have a long week of travel ahead of us."

I nodded and allowed him to lift away from me. Most of my things were still packed from the first time I had planned to leave, so I was pretty much ready after a quick shower and change of clothes. Shadow needed some extra time to pack clothes and tattoo supplies, so I told him I'd wait for him downstairs.

I'd barely hit the bottom step when Jen called out from the bar, "So you're leaving us and taking our hero with you, huh?"

I approached her with a smile, grateful for the spread of breakfast and coffee at the bar. "Word travels fast, I see."

"Doc didn't reveal *too* much, but we were able to read between the lines." She smirked.

"Jen…" I started, but she held a hand up to stop me.

"No, no, none of that. This isn't goodbye, just a 'till next time'. Any time y'all come back this way, make sure to stop here. We'd love to have you."

"I owe you big time." I was trying not to get emotional, but my eyes welled up and my throat was tight anyway. "My history with Shadow is…a lot to explain, but I'm glad you were here for him. All of you. You've all done wonders for him."

"Well he literally saved our lives. You did too." Jen

held up her arms, wrists still bandaged from her rope burns. "I'm a sucker for a good romance, so I'm glad you came out this way and got your man back."

Shadow came quietly down the stairs a few minutes later, dressed in all black like the silent assassin I knew, but also different. There was clear confidence in his steps, his face lighter and less tense than it usually was. He beamed at me, one hand brushing along my back while the other set his duffel bag on the floor.

"Jen, I have a parting gift for you." He unzipped his bag, pulling out a square case slightly bigger than a lunch box.

"Shadow! Whatever it is, you shouldn't have."

It secretly pleased me that she called him by his real name so easily.

"I insist." He set the case on the bar and opened it, revealing a black handgun inside. "It's the one we've practiced with. I left ammo in the safe too, but you'll need to restock eventually." Shadow gave her a hard look. "You're the best shot here. You shouldn't have anyone bothering you anytime soon, but in case someone does, you should be ready."

Jen's smile wobbled a little. "You have too much faith in me. I cowered like a baby and nearly got dragged away last time."

"No, Jen," he told her kindly. "You're brave. I've seen how you protect everyone here. Those assholes won't be coming for you again. Keep working with Doc, you'll be just fine."

She nodded, blinking away tears as they leaned across the bar to hug each other.

"Oh, uh." Shadow dug into his bag when they released each other and pulled out a stack of books. "Can you make sure Telisha gets these back?"

"You can hand them back yourself!" The pretty librarian herself walked through the dining room, a toddler with a curious stare on her hip. "Thanks, Iv—er, Shadow. I'm kinda mad to lose my tattoo artist, but I guess I'll live," she joked.

"Go see Phil, he's just as good as me," Shadow told her. When she pouted and held an arm out for a hug, his eyes slid to me first.

I snorted and helped myself to coffee and breakfast to allow them their parting hugs and words. Doc came down when we were finishing up, taking a hug from me and a handshake from Shadow.

"Just remember what I told you," the older man said, clapping him on the shoulder.

"I know." Shadow nodded. "Thank you Doc, for everything."

Doc just beamed like a doting father. "You did the hard work yourself, son. I'm proud of you." He handed Shadow a small slip of paper. "That's my colleague's information. She's actually a bit northwest of Four Corners in currently neutral territory, but well worth the visit, should you need it."

We ate our fill, packed up Shadow's bike, and said our final goodbyes. Horus screeched from a fence post in the junkyard, where Shadow's growling engine filled the air as we prepared to leave. I watched the bird sail off, becoming smaller as he flew higher. Aside from when I first came upon this service center, I'd barely seen him.

Apparently the sky god was content to be our guide and nothing more.

It was *the right time*, I realized as we began a slow, gentle drive out of the yard. *Just as he said it was.*

I hugged my arms and legs around Shadow, my heart swelling when he released one of the handlebars to rest a gloved hand on my leg. The smile I wore against his back was uncontrollable. For the first time in so long, I felt overcome with happiness. I had Shadow back. Nothing was perfect or completely fixed by any means, but we were on the right track again.

The world flew by us on his motorcycle, the wind whipping as we took winding roads home. We rode hard, but the way back seemed easier than the journey to find him. Maybe I just found comfort in having someone with me, but the long hours in the saddle with Shadow weren't nearly as lonely or painful as being on my little dirt bike. The first couple of days even felt like a vacation. We took scenic roads winding through the southern territories, stopping to sleep at service centers for the night.

Shadow made sure to book us separate rooms to sleep in, but every morning when I started to ask, he told me no. He had the occasional nightmare, but still did not sleepwalk. My hope grew with each passing day, but he wanted a second opinion from Doc's colleague and I'd give him that before broaching the subject again.

The air whipping past us on the bike started to feel different on the fourth day. Humidity turned to dryness. The winter cold hurt more, but didn't seem to cling to me like it did when we were further east. When I saw the faded, discarded Welcome to Texas sign next to the road, the pang of longing and homesickness shocked me. I hadn't considered this place my home in years, or so I thought.

Observant as always, Shadow held me close and squeezed my hand during one of our pit stops. "Do you want to take a detour? Maybe see your old home?" he asked.

I thought about it for a bit, then shook my head. "No. I already know my parents aren't there. There's nothing for me to see here."

"You're sure?" He nudged me and placed a kiss on my temple.

"Yeah, let's keep going."

My parents were out there somewhere, just not here. Absently, I looked to Horus in the sky when we hit the road again, and he spoke to me for the first time in nearly two weeks.

They are not far, daughter. But your instincts are correct.

I swallowed down a hard lump with that knowledge, more questions filling my head. *Does that mean they're together? What instincts, that they're alive?*

Horus didn't provide any more insight, and we rode on like normal. I got nothing from him again until near the end of the day, when we had to be nearly out of Texas and near the Jerriton and New Ireland borders.

I was leaning against the back of Shadow's shoulder, fatigue taking over, when I was suddenly flying over a darkening landscape.

Look, daughter. You must see. Horus' voice in my mind was as clear as my own, as certain as if I had wings outstretched to the sides and eyesight that could spot mice in tall grass.

What am I looking for? It was freaky that Horus just seemed to pull me in whenever he wanted me to see something. Unlike Gunner, who was able to see through him at will.

Look below.

I first saw us—me and Shadow on his bike. Somehow I stayed upright, arms still wrapped around his waist despite no longer being in my own body. Speaking of freaky, watching myself from an outside view had to top the list.

Shadow and I continued to follow the winding road, he seemed none the wiser about my out-of-body experience. My aerial gaze lifted to the horizon ahead of us, where the sun was nearly disappearing behind the mountains.

There.

The shock of it sent me jolting back to my own body, my arms jerking around Shadow as I took a great, gasping breath.

"You okay?" I heard him over the wind whipping past us and felt the squeeze of his hand.

"Stop the bike." I lifted from my seat to yell in his ear, clutching tightly to his leather jacket.

He slowed immediately, pulling us over to the shoulder, then turned around to face me when we stopped. "What's wrong?"

"We have to go a different way," I said, still catching my breath. The ground and sky tilted dangerously in my vision, like the sudden return to land from air had given me vertigo.

Shadow's brow furrowed. "I don't know if there is. We have to go through either New Ireland or Jerriton to reach Four Corners. This road is mostly abandoned—"

"It's not," I insisted. "There's an army a few miles up ahead. I saw them through Horus."

"An army?" Shadow turned more to face me head-on, his face hardening with concern. "How many, could you tell?" It was strangely comforting that he didn't find anything weird about me seeing through the falcon.

"I dunno, thousands." I shook my head. "They stretched all across the landscape as far as Horus could see, forming a long, unbroken line."

"Fuck." Shadow's fist clenched as he realized the severity of this news. "Were they moving? Or camped out?"

"They were moving," I said, my gut churning. "Heading west, toward Four Corners."

TWENTY-FOUR

SHADOW

W e'd be fucked if we got within sight of that army. I cut the engine after pulling over, oppressive silence filling in the space in my head as I tried to think of our next options.

"So we have to head north or south to try to get around them," I mused.

"South wouldn't be good," Mari said. "We'd have to cross into Mexico and could end up captured there too. You never know who border patrol is working for."

"North, then." I stroked my beard, turning my body in that direction. "Into Jerriton."

Mari looked concerned. "How bad do you think it is up there?"

"I'm not sure," I admitted. "The territory only fell under General Tash's control recently, so his hold may not be as well established as New Ireland."

"Sounds like it's our best chance." Mari was looking past me to the horizon, the warm glow of the sunset on her skin slowly fading as dusk approached. "You don't think we're too late, do you?"

"No." I touched her cheek, bringing her attention back to me. "If you saw them only a few miles away, they're not in Four Corners yet. But we have to move fast."

Mari nodded, accepting a quick kiss from me before I turned back around and started the bike up again. *Thank you, Jandro,* I thought to myself as I turned off the interstate, accelerating over the untamed desert wilderness. *You kept my off-road tires on. I owe you, friend.*

The world fell into darkness quickly, with my headlight bouncing over the landscape as the only light source. I had to find a north-bound road at some point to not totally kill my tires, but staying off the road would help us get into Jerriton undetected.

We rode north for a few hours, the cold biting hard at my nose and ears. Mari slid her arms under my shirt for extra warmth, but I could still feel her fingers trembling. As the night wore on, I felt her grip on me loosen from fatigue and knew we had to stop.

She was already nodding off, jerking up when the bike came to a complete stop with nothing but dark desert in all directions.

"Why are we stopping?" Mari mumbled against the back of my shoulder.

"Because you need to rest. I don't need you falling off and becoming roadkill." I swung a leg over to dismount then lifted her out of my seat by her waist. She smiled groggily and I thought back to the moment she told me she liked when I picked her up. "Can you handle unrolling the sleeping bag while I start a fire?"

"Uh-huh," she said with a yawn.

There wasn't much room to lay out anywhere with all the shrubs and rocks surrounding us, but Mari didn't take up much space. Still, she kept shoving rocks and debris out of the way next to the bike to make a bigger sleeping area.

"Are you sure you need that much space?" I teased her, feeding our fire a healthy amount of kindling.

"No, but you do." Finally satisfied, she unfolded my sleeping mat and laid the sleeping bag on top of it.

"Mari." I watched her cautiously. "I'm not sleeping."

"Don't be silly, of course you are." She sat down on top of the sleeping bag and unrolled a blanket, wrapping it around her shoulders. "Come over here and keep me warm."

"Mari, there's no service center around for miles. I can sleep far away, but—"

"And freeze to death? Absolutely not." She stuck a hand out from under the blanket. "Come here."

"You know that's not what I'm worried about." Still, I rose from the fire, now roaring with a healthy blaze as I walked around it to sit next to her.

Mari lifted my arm to snuggle into my side. "How long's it been now?"

"Almost a month, I think?" I let my arm drape over her shoulders as I glanced up, like the glittering night sky would give me answers. "Yeah, about four weeks since I sleepwalked."

The flames danced in Mari's eyes as she looked at me. "And you'd rather risk freezing to death than try *one* night snuggled up with me."

"Yes," I answered quickly. "Because you have much better odds of surviving the night if you sleep alone."

She let out a weary sigh, leaning heavily against my shoulder. "How long, really, until you'll let it happen?"

"I don't know," I admitted, rubbing her arm. Before Doc's therapy, spending a night with her, or any woman, was something I'd never risk again. Now it felt like the final barrier between us, one I was desperate to break through, but not at the risk of her safety. "I think I'll feel better if Doc's colleague tells me the sleepwalking isn't likely to come back."

Mari leaned up, planting a small kiss on my neck. "What's one of your favorite memories from staying at the service center?"

The question wasn't completely out of left-field, but I still gave her a bemused look. She was trying to drum up positive associations to the forefront of my mind, right before sleeping no less. I wondered if this was our new game, instead of saying good morning to each other.

"About a week before you got there, Doc was going to scrap this old Indian motorcycle for parts," I said. "I convinced him not to and was able to get it running."

"You did?"

I nodded. "It was a beautiful little bike by the time I was done restoring it. We were able to trade it for a new chest freezer for the kitchen."

"Look at you." Mari beamed at me with genuine pride. "Jandro will be so happy to hear that."

"Nah. If I tell him details, he'll work himself up over everything I did wrong."

"Oh, whatever." She stretched her legs across my lap and draped the blanket over both of us. "How did it feel to turn that engine and hear it come to life?"

"Amazing." A smile burst onto my face at the memory. I recalled the pulse of elation in my chest when I turned the key and heard the sputter and then the roar, rather than the lifeless clicking sound. "It felt like I brought something back from the dead."

Mari stroked a gentle finger along my jaw, turning my head to bring my mouth to hers. Her lips were cold from the night air and I kissed her deeply, bringing my hand to her cheek to stave off more of the cold.

"How long until we're on the road again?" she asked when one long kiss ended and right before another began.

"Not long." I took another lingering pull from her lips. "It's just a few hours 'til dawn."

Her arms slid under my jacket, pulling her chest flush to mine. "I don't want to sleep alone," she whispered, forehead nudging mine. "We'll be warmer this way too. Do you think you can try tonight? Please?"

"Mari…" I started to shake my head and pull away, but my woman held onto me tightly.

"You trust me?" Her lips skimmed over mine as she spoke.

"You know I do."

"I trust you too, you know." She placed a soft kiss on

the bridge of my nose. "I'd love to see you start trusting yourself."

"It's not about that."

"Yes it is, love." Her mouth skimmed up my face to kiss the scar cutting through my eyelid. "You're more in control than you realize."

It was going to happen sooner or later. This leap of faith, this trust I was putting into myself to not harm the woman I loved. I already had a sneaking suspicion that Doc's colleague would just confirm what he'd already told me. The idea of talking to another doctor was a safety precaution more than anything. I trusted Doc and Mari more than any other medical professional anyway.

Mari believed in me, and she was usually right.

Still, it took a long while and an enormous effort to nod my head and breathe out, "Okay."

Her grin was brighter than the fire and she kissed me again. "Don't worry. Just think about that motorcycle you brought back to life."

"I'm going to think of that and a million other things," I admitted. "Because I won't be able to let myself sleep."

Mari's lips drifted up to my forehead. "Try to get a little rest for me. I need you sharp tomorrow."

"I'll try." My eyelids did feel heavy. Her uncanny ability to calm me, plus the heat from the fire, started lulling me into relaxation.

Without another word, Mari unzipped the sleeping bag and we both slid inside.

———

I WOKE WITH A START, like I always did. The familiar jolt of panic flashed through me as I looked around to assess the damage I'd surely caused in my sleep.

But there was none.

I was still zipped snugly into the sleeping bag, Mari bundled up against me with her face in my chest.

"Good morning," she mumbled, jostled awake by all my moving around.

"Morning, sorry to wake you." I smoothed a hand over her hair, overwhelmed by the sheer relief that she was still here, safe and unharmed. With *me*.

"S'okay. We gotta get moving, right?" Mari yawned and groaned as she stretched within the confines of the sleeping bag. "Do you have coffee?"

She was speaking so casually, but this was huge for me. I tilted her mouth to mine, enamored with the taste of her despite the slight dryness to her lips in that moment.

"I did it," I whispered. "I just…slept. With you right here. Without…*using* anything."

Mari smiled, sleepiness pulling her mouth in an adorable, crooked way. "I knew you would."

My mouth pressed to hers, tongue licking out to seek more of her taste. "You have no idea what this means," I choked out with a laugh. "Fuck, I love you so much."

"I love you so much." Her fingers rubbed over my beard, which was growing coarse and longer than I preferred, but she seemed to enjoy touching it. "And this means you've suffered enough. You've worked your ass off to heal, and now it's paying off."

"And it'll be even better once we're home." I still had

some lingering doubts that all would be well once we stepped into Four Corners, but as long as I had Mari with me, I didn't care what the outcome with the Steel Demons would be.

"Not much longer." Mari started unzipping the sleeping bag as she sat up, the furrow of concern returning to her eyebrows. "Although I guess that depends on what we find in Jerriton today."

"We'll make it through." I rolled up behind her, hooking an arm around her waist and dropping a kiss to her shoulder. "We snuck into Blakeworth, after all."

"Ugh. If one of us has to play slave again, I will scream."

After coffee and a quick breakfast we hit the road again, or the terrain, rather. We didn't find a road until the sun was high, and I think we were both grateful for a smoother ride again.

Horus offered no confirming or dissenting advice about our change in direction, but we could see him soaring high above us as we rode. I could only hope the gods were invested in our wellbeing enough to not lead us straight to our deaths. Freyja certainly seemed to be, but Mari only had the sky god with her on this trip to find me. Last night was the first I'd seen Horus offer his sight to anyone but Gunner. I didn't know it could be done with anyone else, but there was probably plenty I didn't know about our companion gods.

A few miles outside of the last known border, which had been the Colorado state line, I pulled over to the side of the road and turned to Mari in my seat.

"We're a couple miles out of Jerriton. Can you see

anything through the bird?"

"Oh, I don't know." Mari frowned. "I've never tried to see through him. He just kind of pulls me in."

"Can you try?" I gave a light squeeze to her knee. "We'll be going in blind otherwise."

"I don't know how, Shadow."

"Try what Doc did with me," I suggested. "Close off your senses and take some deep breaths. Let your consciousness take a backseat and remember what it felt like to be a bird."

She didn't seem convinced, but gave me a tight nod. "Count me down?"

"Sure." I waited until Mari's eyes closed and she grew eerily still, only her chest moving with steady breaths. "Instead of descending into yourself, you're going to float. Lifting up from your body, higher and higher until you're flying. Ten…nine…eight…"

I counted all the way down to zero and didn't even blink as I watched her. Gunner lost control of his body, twitching and going limp when he went into Horus. Mari's eyeballs moved under closed lids as though she were dreaming, but she held herself upright in the seat, calm and still.

She stayed like that for several minutes and I had no idea if it worked, or if she had just been put in a hypnotic state. How long should I wait until trying to bring her back?

More minutes ticked by and I started growing anxious. I knew Doc's sessions with me lasted roughly a half-hour, but he knew what he was doing. What if this was harmful to Mari's brain?

Just as I was about to touch her, start talking to give her external stimuli to bring her back, her eyes flew open and she drew in a big gasp of air.

"Mari!" My hands shot out to grab her arms and keep her from falling. "Are you okay?"

"Yeah, I'm fine." She brought a hand to her chest, panting like she was out of breath. "I saw, and border security is tight. Their army is well-stocked, just like the one I saw last night."

My chest deflated at that. "So we're dealing with the same thing up here?"

Mari shook her head. "No, not exactly. They're not in a long line." Her breaths slowing, she focused her gaze on me. "I think…I know how we can get in. There's a…can I get something to draw with?"

"Yeah, left saddle bag." I watched her dig to the bottom where my sketchbook was stashed, a strange kind of excitement building in my chest as she flipped to a blank page and started sketching out long lines. "Got a plan in mind?"

"I do, just give me a second." She paused in her diagram, looking up at me with a smile that was both coy and endearing. "Would you be upset if I said it involved helping people?"

"Not at all." I leaned in and pressed a kiss to her forehead. "Are we going to need a lot of guns?"

Mari's grin grew wider. "We probably will."

"Even better."

I hopped out of my seat and went to load my weapons while waiting to hear her plan.

MARIPOSA

"They have these six towers here, and fenced-off, open areas in between." I pointed them out to Shadow using a pencil on my crude drawing. "The fences converge up here, to these buildings."

"Those are prison yards," Shadow mused, his mismatched eyes carefully inspecting my diagram. "So they have a prison complex right at the border."

"That's what I thought it was," I said. "And what are the chances you think the people in those yards are actually criminals?"

"None. Last time we were here, providing protection to Gunner's uncle, we found out that he kept a lot of his citizens in prison. Women, mostly."

Shadow checked the magazine of yet another gun and inserted the weapon into his holster. He may not have had a Steel Demons cut, but was just as intimidating with a tactical vest loaded with weapons and ammo.

And just as hot.

"So you're planning on a prison break?" Shadow asked as he slapped a reloaded magazine into my little .40 caliber pistol and handed it to me.

"Uh, yeah." He must have caught me staring, and grinned while I blushed. "At the very least, we can create a diversion to move through the territory undetected. And then free some people as a bonus."

"Works for me." Shadow seemed calm overall, if even pleased about going to battle again, but right then his face looked grim. "Will we have to separate?"

I looked down at the drawing, chewing my lip as I tried to think like a strategist. Like Gunner, who I missed with a fierce ache at that moment. We were roughly a day's ride away from Four Corners, but crossing through Jerriton was a huge obstacle we could not afford to fuck up.

The last time Gunner and I talked, which felt like centuries ago, he finally seemed to understand where I was coming from, how I wanted everything to be fixed. Maybe it was odd to have hit me right then, bent over a crude diagram and chewing on the end of a pencil, but the realization was crystal clear—I did forgive him.

Now Reaper, I was less sure about.

"At the beginning, I think we have to," I said in answer to Shadow's question. "Once you start shooting the guards in the towers, I'll run in and cut through the fences. I'll deal with anyone on the ground while they scramble to get more people up in the towers. It's the only way they'll be able to see us in the chaos." My forehead met his as I started to look up at him. "What do you think?"

"It's a good plan, probably the best we can do with just the two of us." Shadow grazed the backs of his fingers over my cheek. "I just don't like the thought of my woman in danger."

"Better get used to it," I snickered. "You're fucking with a biker chick, in case you forgot."

"How could I ever?" Shadow's voice was a low rumble as his fingers wrapped around the back of my neck. His grip was strong, but not overly possessive as he pulled me in for a long, deep kiss. Just as swiftly as he planted it on me, he broke away with a growl. "As soon as you see me come back around, you run like hell and get back on, okay?"

"Yes." The word came out more breathless than I intended, my lips tilting up for more.

Shadow chuckled, indulging me with one more kiss before untangling from me and closing up his compartments. "Let's do this so we can go home."

MY FISTS TIGHTENED around Shadow's shirt when the first prison tower came into view. He squeezed one of my hands, a small reassurance before holding his palm out. I handed him the rifle like a Bonnie to her Clyde, and felt grateful for my earplugs when he opened fire.

Shadow was inhumanly accurate with a gun, and it seemed to be thanks to that pale, scarred eye of his. He didn't shoot recklessly, spraying bullets like an action movie hero. He was methodical and precise, firing a single round through the open window of the first tower.

The guard on duty fell out of sight, though I couldn't tell if the shot was lethal or not.

We picked up speed, accelerating toward the towers and barbed-wire topped fencing with a roar. I held on to Shadow with one arm while brandishing my gun with the other. Shadow fired at the next two towers along the fence line before a blaring alarm sounded.

He pulled over at the base of the first tower, coming to an abrupt stop. "Go."

I jumped off and ran toward the fence line, the roar of his bike already growing quiet and distant as Shadow peeled off to take out the other towers. Over the constant blaring of the alarm, a broadcasted message rang out through multiple speakers.

"Inmates, get off the yard and back in the building! Get fucking inside now or get shot!"

"Hey, hey!" I yelled and waved my arms at one group of people getting in line to file into a building. They were all dressed in the same matching gray sweats and seemed to be young adults and teenagers.

A few heads turned in my direction, and I pulled out the bolt cutters that I'd stuck in the back of my pants. My gun returned to my holster for the time being while I started cutting through the links in the fence.

Please, please. I wished I could project my thoughts to them, speak directly into their minds like the gods could. *This is your chance. Fight back and escape.*

A bullet hit the dirt next to me, and I rolled, scrambling for cover behind the guard tower. The memory of getting hit in the leg was still fresh, and even though I healed quickly, that kind of pain was something I never wanted to encounter again.

More shots zipped around me, coming from the yard as they blasted off small chunks of concrete from the edges of the tower. Fear started to overwhelm me as the shots intensified, the shouts of the guards growing louder. *I can't do this.*

I must have overestimated my ability to fight like this. Maybe with more backup I could've handled it, but not with just Shadow and me. I was supposed to be covering him, keeping the guards distracted while he took out the towers, but couldn't bring my shaking hands to raise my gun and turn to face what came for me.

See, daughter.

It was a quick flash, under five seconds, but I was in the sky again. I saw the two guards heading for the tower, for me. They left the prisoners in the yard unguarded and I could count how many steps they'd need to reach me. I saw the angles they were coming at me from, and which parts of their bodies were exposed even with bulletproof vests on.

In the next moment I returned to my own body, and knew exactly what to do. There was no time to think, to hesitate. Only to move.

I spun away from the wall, arms outstretched with my weapon raised and fired before my human eyes even settled on my targets. My shot landed in the neck of the first guard and he went down silently. The other guard ducked and changed direction, running for cover. Now I had time, seconds to set up my next shot, and I took it.

He fell dead a few feet away from his partner, the crowd of prisoners across the yard all staring at what just happened. I ran back to the spot in the fence where I began cutting, holstering my weapon and picking up my bolt cutters again. I had the advantage now, but more guards would come, and I never knew when Horus would give me his eyes again.

"Come on!" I yelled, snapping the tool through the thick wire links. "We're breaking you guys out!"

Finally the prisoners quit staring and started running toward me. I cut a hole roughly my own height, and held it aside for people to come through. A young woman at the front of the group hesitated, eying me suspiciously as she held her arms out to the sides to halt the others. "Who the hell are you?"

"We're just trying to get through the territory to go home," I said. "You guys are kept here on orders from the new governor, right?"

"No, some fucking general who invaded us," the woman snarled.

"Oh, even better." I pulled back harder on the cutaway fence, trying to bend the wires back so the opening would stay. "I can't stick around, but freeing you guys keeps the guards distracted while we ride through."

The woman's expression softened but she still didn't usher everyone through. "What territory you from?"

"Four Corners." I bent the chain links back as far as I could, then picked up my bolt cutters and started jogging toward the next yard. "You're all welcome there if you'd like. Good luck," I called back behind me.

The next yard had already gotten all of its prisoners

inside, but the two guards were racing across the field to man the tower. I shot them both, I was moving quickly so my hits weren't as accurate. They went down clutching their legs and radioing for backup as I cut through the links on that fence too. Hopefully the people inside could break a window or unlock a door to escape.

Our plan was working. The guards scrambled to refill the tower positions to search for us after Shadow had taken care of them, while also keeping inmates contained. I heard over the radio calls that even contained prisoners were fighting back against their guards. The people could hear what was going on before I ever reached them.

By the time I got to the last yard, there were no guards in sight, only people in gray sweats jumping for joy near the fence line. They cheered when I ran up with my bolt cutters and stood back to give me space.

"I dunno who you are, ma'am, but thank you," said an elderly man with tears in his eyes as he leaned heavily on a cane.

"She's an angel, that's who!" called another man in the crowd.

"Just someone trying to help and get back home." I gave him a weary smile. Cutting this fence was going much slower. My hands were cramping and fatigued from the heavy tool and thick chain links.

"Here, allow me." Another man, about Reaper's dad's age, with silver hair, held a rough hand out through the small hole in the fence.

I handed him the bolt cutters without a second thought, grateful for the rest as he easily sliced through the wires that kept them all caged. When the hole was big enough, everyone stood aside while the most frail and elderly men were helped out first.

"Here, I got you." I grabbed the free arm of the first man who spoke to me.

"Thank you, darlin'," he beamed at me. "Never thought I'd live to see freedom and a beautiful woman in the same day."

"I have to go," I said with a returned smile. "Good luck to all of you."

My bolt cutters were returned to me and I took off running along the perimeter, listening intently for the roar of Shadow's bike. The alarms continued to blare in their repetitive, monotonous screeching. Excited voices of freed prisoners shouted over the panicked orders and frantic radio calls of the guards. A motorcycle the size of Shadow's should have drowned them all out, but I heard nothing.

"Fuck, where are you?" I looked around everywhere, even skyward to see if Horus would lend me his view again. My adrenaline was running too high to get into a hypnotic state, plus there was no time. We had to get the hell out.

"Shadow!" It wasn't smart to call out his name, to draw attention to myself, but panic started riding me hard. If he had been captured or shot, this whole plan was for naught. I could not, *would* not, go on to Four Corners without him, even if I managed to slip through the territory undetected. I had come too far, watched him make too much progress to abandon him now.

"Shadow!"

Something slapped over my mouth, a large hand that was also pulling me backward behind a small shack just beyond the fence line. My flight response kicked in, trying to jerk free for a moment before I heard a familiar, "It's me, Mari."

Shadow's hand slid away from my mouth and I took ragged, grateful gulps of air. "Where's your bike?" I demanded in a harsh whisper.

"I stashed it and took the towers out on foot," he whispered back. "It was too loud and they would've heard me coming."

"Guess I should have thought of that," I muttered.

"It was still a good plan." Shadow's gloved fingers ran over my arms and sides. "Are you hurt at all? I heard shots early on."

"I'm good." I smiled back at him. "Some of those were mine."

He squeezed my shoulder affectionately. "That's my girl. Ready to go?"

"Yeah."

Our hands clasped together and I followed as he took off in a run slow enough for me to stay on his heels. His bike was stashed inside another shack just outside of the prison's perimeter—an abandoned pump house by the looks of it. We both jumped into the seat, and Shadow handed me his rifle. I squeezed my thighs around him as we peeled away from the prison, keeping an eye out with the rifle, ready for any guards who spotted us.

No one came after us, the alarms and shouts soon fading into nothing as we made our escape. But we weren't out of the woods yet and I kept my grip tight on Shadow's gun, ever vigilant. We didn't know what else waited for us in this hostile territory.

Only an hour after leaving the prison complex behind did I allow myself to relax a little. This stretch of highway seemed long abandoned—covered in gravel, potholes, and discarded belongings that seemed to have fallen off trucks. Rocky hillsides rose up on either side of the road and I kept my gaze lifted for anyone who might try to snipe us from above.

Shadow must have been thinking similarly because out of nowhere, he braked so hard and suddenly that I crashed against his back. "Fuck!"

I looked ahead of us on the road and cursed out my own agreement. "Fuck."

The wind had blown away some debris lying across the road about twenty feet ahead of us, revealing a spike strip underneath. And roughly fifty feet beyond that, a metal barricade cut across our path. Braced on top of the barricade were long black rifle barrels pointed at us, the shooters crouching on the other side of the wall. Armored trucks took up the road behind the shooters at the barricades, more soldiers in camo uniforms covered behind their vehicles with weapons drawn on us.

Fuck it all, we weren't fast enough. The prison staff must have contacted the nearest army base and told them to be ready for us.

"Shadow…"

"Stay behind me," he instructed under his voice. "Just follow my lead. We'll be okay."

But I heard the apprehension in his voice and it only worried me more.

"Drop all your weapons and get off the motorcycle," one of the soldiers commanded through a megaphone. "We'll let you live as long as you follow orders."

Shadow didn't move right away, and I only tightened my grip on his rifle. A sound behind us had me turning to look—three more armored Jeeps drove up behind us, spreading out across the road to block us in. Soldiers opened the car doors and swarmed out systematically, bracing weapons over doors and across the hoods of their vehicles.

"Shadow?"

"Do as they say, Mari." Shadow slowly removed his two handguns from the holsters at his sides, dropped them on the ground, and raised his hands in the air.

"Shadow, we can't."

"We can't die here either," he replied. "We'll figure something out, but we're not in a good position here."

"They'll throw us in that prison!"

"Then we'll throw riots and rebel until we get out." My big, stoic man even tossed a smile at me over his shoulder. "I know my way around a prison, we'll be okay. We already have supporters on the inside."

"Last warning," the megaphone wielder called. "Drop the weapons and step away from the motorcycle, or we *will* open fire."

I knew that if I dropped that gun, it would be the end. Something twisting and turning in my gut told me there would be no getting out for us. No seeing Four Corners or any of my other men again. I just had to decide if it would be better to die within concrete walls and iron bars, or out here on the road, filled with bullet holes.

At least this way, I had Shadow with me.

"I love you," I whispered. "And I'm so fucking proud of everything you've done."

"Mari," he hissed. "Drop the guns, *now*."

"Duck behind the bike and make a grab for yours," I said in reply.

My decision made, I did step away and into the road as ordered, but I did *not* drop my fucking guns.

"Mari!" Shadow yelled, reaching to pull me back behind him, but stopped when I stretched my arms out to either side of me. One hand wielded his rifle, the other my small handgun, pointing at the soldiers blocking our path both in front and behind us. The rifle was heavy and definitely not meant to be shot one-handed. Good thing I didn't plan on holding it for long.

Time seemed to go still for a single beat, neither Shadow nor our enemies believing what I was doing. Then I squeezed the triggers on both guns, opening fire and letting chaos erupt.

Shadow must have finally ducked for cover behind his bike—I wasn't sure, I couldn't see him. I had tunnel vision, hyper-focused on taking down a few soldiers with me, maybe even clearing a path for Shadow to keep going. They must have returned fire, I didn't know. I stood in the middle of the road shooting forward and backwards, all sound in my ears muted and my mind feeling oddly calm.

I did my part, I thought, watching soldiers duck

behind their barriers in slow motion. *I saved lives. I healed wounds of the heart and body. I loved more deeply than I ever thought possible. I'm ready.*

I saw men aim their guns and shoot back at me, but none seemed to hit. I was still standing in the road, firing so rapidly that my guns burned hot and my hands ached. I felt nothing but my final desire to do my last bit of good in the world—take out some fuckers who would torture and kill me.

Then the ground swung out from under my feet and slapped me in the face. Heat burned my cheek, and the smell of asphalt and gunpowder filled my nose. I could hear everything now, a cacophony of gunshots and shouting voices. A heavy weight pressed down on top of me, smashing my face and chest down into the road.

"Even for an avenging angel, you're pretty damn ballsy," said a voice near my ear.

I twisted my neck to look up, recognizing the silver hair of the man who helped me cut through the fence.

"What...what?" It was all I could stammer out in my disbelief.

"Let's get off this road, darlin'. Your work ain't done."

He lifted up, allowing me to scoot out from underneath him, but kept an arm around my back as we hurried in a low crouch together to the side of the road. The man practically dragged me behind Shadow's bike, where my man gave me a very disapproving look as he reloaded a gun.

"What happened? How...?" I stared at the silver-haired man, who'd escaped the prison complex with a bunch of older men barely an hour ago. "How did you get out here?"

"Stole some wheels and boomsticks of our own." The man grinned, tilting his head upward.

I followed his gaze to the top of the hills running alongside the road. Nothing was there at first, then a few faces—and guns—popped into view. They fired at the soldiers, most of whom were either dead or retreating. More and more freed prisoners looked over the ledge at us, pumping fists and cheering. All I could do was stare with my mouth open—these people lined the hills as far as the eye could see.

I spotted the young woman from the first yard I freed and she waved at us with a smile.

"My daughter up there," the man nodded at her, "told me y'all were heading for Four Corners, so we figured you'd come this way." He looked at me, a bit amused and patronizing. "Didn't know our angel was on a suicide mission, though."

"I wasn't, I…" My gaze fell to my lap, where my sore, bruised hands shook. Shadow grabbed one of them, squeezing gently and rubbing my palm. "I just knew we wouldn't survive if we let them take us."

"Well, maybe y'all got angels watching over you too." The man held a hand out to Shadow, who clasped and shook it gratefully. "I'm Samson."

"Shadow," my man answered, then tilted his head toward me. "This is Mariposa."

"Mari," I told Samson, holding my own hand out to him. "You saved us. All of you."

"Just returning the gesture in kind." Samson helped

us both to our feet with a smile, earning more cheers from the people lining the hills.

Relief swept through me as Shadow and I exchanged a glance, then raised our fists in victory with the crowd.

"There's gonna be more army coming," Samson warned, his expression turning serious. "We'll be happy to escort you out of Jerriton. They won't touch you in neutral territory without orders."

"Come to Four Corners with us," I urged him. "You'll be safe there, everyone will."

"Thank you, but no." The older man shook his head. "Now that we're out, there's more friends and family that need us here."

"Four Corners is yours then," Shadow said. "We're on the brink of war, but will support the people of Jerriton however we can."

"Oh, I'm well aware of the governors playing war games with our lives." Samson crossed his arms. "And let me assure you right now, the people of Jerriton stand with Four Corners."

TWENTY-SIX

GUNNER

"This shit is so ugly," Jandro sighed mournfully at the camouflage painted bikes. "And it's gonna double my workload painting them back to normal after this is all done."

"Oh, we're still planning on being here after *all this* is done?" It was like we didn't want to say what was actually happening—war. Fighting for the simple right to live and exist on our own terms.

I sat on the hood of some rusted out car in Dave's garage, where Jandro had been working out of.

"Yeah, I know." Jandro grinned sheepishly as he wiped his hands on a rag. "Can you imagine it? Getting some time off after saving everyone's lives?"

"Yeah…" I let the word trail off, paying attention to the unease in my gut. Saving Four Corners and everyone within it was a big deal, to be sure. But I couldn't shake the feeling there was something more.

What could be *more* than saving thousands of lives? I didn't know. But plenty of other wars had been fought without gods involved. Without uncanny abilities like fast healing and seeing through eyes other than your own. I'd venture a guess that no gods had appeared during any of the major wars throughout history, so why were they getting involved with a bunch of unimportant bikers?

"I know that look," Jandro called from across the shop. "What are your two brain cells telling you, blondie?"

I ignored his ribbing. "What do you think it means?"

"What what means?"

"Reaper can see through the dead now? I used to see through Horus, but now I can't anymore? Hearing voices and obeying commands?" My hands flailed at my sides. "I mean, we've all been kind of *whatever* about gods coming into our lives over the past few months, but now we're on the brink of war and it's just like, hey we got superhuman abilities, that oughta help!"

"You picked a hell of a time to have an existential crisis," Jandro scoffed.

"Why now?" I continued. "Why us, of all the fucking people who can actually make a difference in the world? Like, I'm starting to wonder if we're being used for something bigger than us."

"Maybe." Jandro shrugged. "But that kind of stuff might be beyond our scope of things, right?"

"They don't want us to lose, but why does that even fucking matter?" I stabbed my fingers through my hair, releasing a frustrated groan. "If they're gods, why the fuck do they care if Tash lays waste to Four Corners? If they're above this petty human shit, why are they even here?"

"Dude." Jandro shook his head. "You need to chill the fuck out. The last thing we need is your head exploding, double-brain-celled as it may be."

"Actually I think it's a perfect time to freak out, I've been fucking chill all this time." I pressed the heels of my palms into my eyes. "To be honest, I don't know how Reaper's seeing through the dead even helps us. It's been over three weeks and there's still no sign of Mari—"

"She'll come back." Jandro's voice dropped to a growl, all humor gone. "She will. She has to."

"After how me and Reap treated her, I don't blame her if she's just gone." I sighed, closing my eyes with my palm against my forehead.

I felt so heavy with regret and guilt over not listening to her. Especially with this foreboding sense that gods were using us for something beyond saving people and ending senseless violence. The outcome of this war was important to them, and fuck me if I could figure out why.

"I'm going for a ride," I muttered, sliding off the car hood and heading for the open bay door.

"Careful out there," Jandro called.

"I know, *Dad.*"

We'd already seen glimpses of scouts creeping in closer from Blakeworth and Jerriton. After Slick and Jandro got ambushed, these fuckers just seemed to get bolder. They stayed in neutral territory for now, but tiptoed closer to our borders with each passing day.

One of General Bray's men even shot down more

drones coming from Tash's direction. They didn't carry weapons or explosives, but the cameras on them had already been wiped by the time we inspected them. They must have programmed to send back any images they captured and then delete the storage.

Shit like that made me feel like we were cavemen, fighting with sticks and spears against guns and bombs. Reaper was optimistic about his newfound ability, but it was still limiting in my view. T-Bone's raven could provide us with an aerial view to a point, but his bird didn't have nearly the eyesight Horus has. We were still limited, disadvantaged.

And war was coming for us within a matter of weeks, if not days.

This leisurely ride around the territory could very well be my last, so I needed to make it count.

My bike was already painted to blend with the landscape, and I physically cringed as I got on. Jandro was right about them being ugly.

I took off with no destination in mind, just following where the road led me. The landscape was beautiful, turning a golden-orange with the late afternoon sun. I wished to be able to enjoy it, but everything just felt fucking wrong.

Mari wasn't here. The absence of her grew vast and overwhelming with every passing day that she wasn't here. How was I supposed to figure out how to win a war without my reason for everything by my side? I hadn't been able to think straight since she came home from the hospital that night, all the hurt and anger on her face upon seeing Shadow's empty room. How I was supposed to strategize and inspire our army to victory when I'd let my own world crumble before my eyes?

The beauty of my surroundings might as well have been an ash-covered wasteland. It was going to become exactly that in a matter of weeks, anyway.

I reached a bend in the road and turned around, heading back to the city. Less than a mile on my way back, the sky began to darken, like night was falling or a storm had started to roll in. But the sky remained clear of clouds and dusk was still hours away. It simply got *dark*.

A chill ran over my skin, all my hair follicles raised at the cold, heavy presence in the air.

"What's happening?" The words were lost, whispered under the roar of my engine, but *something* answered.

AHAHAHAHAHAHAAAA! HAAAA-HAAAHAHAHAHA!

I nearly lost control of the bike with how hard my head rang. It felt like something was loose inside my skull and rattling around. Pain exploded behind my eyes, my temples throbbing like they were being crushed in a vice. The laughter was unhinged, maniacal and wild like the Joker from the old Batman cartoons. And it would not stop.

HAHAHAHAHAHAHAHAAAAAA!

"Stop, stop!" I slapped a hand to the side of my head, the sensation of wetness immediately coating my palm. I pulled my hand away to see the smear of blood that came from my ears.

Gotta get back…warn them. My own thoughts were drowned out by the nonstop, crazed laughing in my head. It felt like someone else had taken up residence in my mind and was shooting up everything with a machine gun, an invader laughing with victory over newly claimed territory.

I pushed the bike hard, accelerating to the machine's limit as I hunched over it and prayed I wouldn't lose control at such high speed.

I'm going to die, I realized as black dots multiplied in my vision. My head hurt so fucking bad, I wanted to smash my forehead between the handlebars for some relief. I couldn't feel my hands or feet, only pins and needles, like they'd fallen asleep. *No, no. They have to know…have to…reach them.*

AWW. ARE YOU DONE ALREADY?! HAAAAAHA-HAHAHAHA!

"Get out." I gritted my teeth with what little of my strength remained. The outskirts of the city were just a few hundred feet away. I could barely see the buildings but I had to keep going, had to get in sight of someone, anyone to call for help.

And do what?

Was it my own voice or the thing inside my head that asked the question so cynically? Did it even matter? I was moments away from death, and if this thing destroying my mind was what was coming for us, then we were all fucked.

Between the numbness and pain shooting off from my skull throughout my whole body, I felt the motorcycle lean dangerously to one side. And I knew I didn't have the strength to pull it back up.

I'm so sorry, Mari. Sorry Shadow, about everything. I wish I got to make it right.

The road hit me with a force that could have turned my skeleton to Jello. And then I felt nothing. No ground, no pain. The laughter was gone, and I both hated and loved how peaceful it felt. I didn't want to open my eyes and face the reality that I was dead.

Look, son.

The voice was masculine, warm and calming like my grandfather's had been. I'd never heard it before, but recognition flooded through me as I dared to open my eyes.

Horus?

I did not abandon you. She just needed to see.

I looked, and the landscape below me was vast. A surge of wind carried me upward, floating northeast over the stretch of road that looked like a thin black stripe from this high up. Gone was the darkness that had fallen when I first heard the laughing—everything looked beautifully normal.

Is Mari okay? Is she coming back? My thoughts raced frantically once I realized that Horus had lent me his eyes again. I felt the tether to my human body like a life-line—going back would be as easy as a simple pull.

Look and see, Horus instructed, sounding oddly amused.

I flew closer, my gaze following the length of the road cutting through the landscape. At first I only saw movement, dark specks like ants from far away, inching closer. They had to be at least five miles out, and Horus beat his wings to fly us closer, as if sensing my urgency.

Is it her? Is it them?

If I hadn't already left my body, I would have once the details came into focus. A single motorcycle with two riders. A big hulk of a man driving, and a woman with long brown hair sitting behind him.

The laughter ringing through my head was my own now, elation and relief filling me up so completely, I didn't care if I was dead. Mari was back, she was safe.

As intense as the euphoria was, the duration was brief. That thing laughing and taunting me in my head was gone for now, but would it come back?

I hovered over Shadow and Mari in Horus's body, not wanting to take my eyes off of them for a single moment. As they got closer, I saw Mari wipe at her ear, blood trailing down her neck. She leaned forward in her seat, inspecting the side of Shadow's head where he too was bleeding.

That was both comforting and completely unnerving.

I waited until they were less than a mile out from Four Corners before making the return back to my own body.

"Owww…"

My head pounded like a drum, but nothing was rattling inside anymore. I blinked several times, focusing my dulled human vision on the clear blue sky above me, where I'd just been a moment ago. After a quick extremities check and finding that my fingers and toes were still attached, I rolled painstakingly up to a seat.

"Fuck, nope. Too fast." The world spun a circle around me and I promptly laid back down. Staying on my back, I gingerly tested bigger movements of my limbs. Ankles, wrists, knees, and elbows were all intact, albeit sore as hell.

A rumbling purr grew louder, that comforting sound spurring movement into my body again. But it was nothing compared to what I heard next.

"Gunner? Fuck, it's Gunner! Stay there, I'm coming!"

The sound of her voice was so fucking sweet, I wanted to cry. It felt like I hadn't spoken to her in years.

"Hey, baby girl," I said to the quickly approaching footsteps, and drew in a sharp breath when Mari's beautiful face hovered over me.

"What happened, did you crash?" She touched a hand to my forehead, the other moving swiftly over my abdomen, then arms and legs.

"Did you hear it too?" I reached up with one hand to touch the drying blood on her ear.

"The laughter? Yeah, that was nuts. But we'll worry about that later, let me make sure you're okay."

"I'm fine," I insisted, hardly daring to blink in the off-chance she was a mirage, or my head trauma making me hallucinate.

Mari looked the same, but something had changed. Maybe her cheekbones were a little more prominent like she'd lost weight. Her mouth seemed to be pressed a little tighter as she examined me for injuries. Her eyes were definitely sharper, harder. More ruthless. I'd find out eventually what happened, but for now, all that mattered was that my girl was back.

"I'm fine, baby girl, really." My fingers rested on her

cheek, thumb trailing over her lips to her chin, turning her face so she'd look at me.

Mari's gaze stole my breath, lower lip wobbling and sharp, ruthless eyes filled with unspilled tears. "Gun…" She reached for my face with a shaking hand, pushing my hair back and touching her fingertips to the trail of blood under my ear.

"Fuck, it's so good to see you." I pressed up, leaning into her without thinking. The moment I remembered and halted, she closed the distance herself, slamming her lips to mine with a ferocity that released just as much pent-up longing as I'd been holding onto for weeks.

More elation and relief filled me as my mouth clumsily, desperately sought out her taste. I'd been starved, wasting away to a husk, and she breathed precious life back into me. I almost thought I was flying again but I was here, right here with her.

"I love you," I said between desperate sips of air. "Fuck, I'm so sorry. About everything."

Mari pulled away slowly, her head turning toward the man behind her. Shadow looked just as I remembered, massive and imposing as he stood guard on the side of the road. With Mari's help, I climbed gingerly to my feet and walked over to him without another word spoken.

Shadow stopped looking down the length of the road and regarded me with a blank expression, like he always did.

"Hey Shadow. I'm sorry." He didn't look eager to shake hands, so I stuck my hands in my cut pockets. "Reaper made the wrong call, and I was wrong to follow his lead. Emotions were running high and we were all panicking, but that's no excuse. You're one of us. You belong with the Steel Demons and we should have treated you fairly, brother."

A sigh deflated my chest. I had imagined what I would say to Shadow if I ever saw him again, but it all went out the window. I could only speak to what I honestly felt.

"We made a bunch of bad decisions that hurt both you and Mari. This whole thing was one-hundred percent our fault. I can't speak for Reaper, but I am so incredibly sorry. If it comes to a vote, you have my word that I will advocate for your return." I swallowed. "If that's what you want."

Shadow's expression didn't change as I spoke, but his eyes flicked to Mari when I was done. I didn't dare peek behind me at what she was doing, but Shadow's hand stretched out in front of us a moment later.

"It's forgiven," he said quietly. "I accept your apology, Gunner."

A breath whooshed out of me as I clapped my hand firmly to his. "Thank you. Welcome back, brother."

TWENTY-SEVEN

MARIPOSA

I almost didn't let Gunner drive himself into town. That crazy laughing, combined with the ear bleeding, meant some serious damage had been done to the inner ear. Shadow and I felt fine, but it could have affected everyone differently. Only when Gunner demonstrated to me that he didn't have vertigo or other symptoms did I allow him to get back on his bike.

"Ride straight to the hospital," I told him, climbing on behind Shadow. "We'll meet you there."

"Damn, I love hearing you boss me around again." Gunner grinned before his lips twitched and went serious again. "Should I let Jandro and Reap know you're back?"

I hesitated before answering, locking my hands together on Shadow's stomach as I rested my head on his back.

"Just head straight to the hospital so we can all get checked out," I repeated. "I'll see them at home."

Gunner jerked his head down in a nod and took off, his engine roaring.

Shadow squeezed my hands once before starting up his bike. "Are you nervous about seeing them?"

I didn't want to be. It didn't seem like there was a reason to be nervous. *Reaper should be nervous to see* me, *for fuck's sake.*

"A little," I admitted, my lips against the back of Shadow's shoulder. "I just…don't know how they're gonna react."

"They'll be happy," he assured me before returning both hands to his grips.

I had hoped seeing familiar faces like Rhonda and Dr. Brooks would ease me into being ready to see Reaper again later. But I had no such luck.

The moment we walked through the hospital front doors, the front desk clerk jerked her head up. "Mari! You're back!"

"Hey Natalie," I greeted as she grabbed her handheld radio—the best way to communicate over distances these days—and reported into it. "Dr. B, we've got Mari and Shadow back, if you can believe it! Same symptoms, blood from the ears."

Dr. Brooks' voice crackled over the speaker a moment later. "Thanks, Nat. Send 'em in."

"Exam room five, Mari," Natalie relayed to me.

I thanked her and led Shadow down the hall that way, noting that it was one of the biggest exam rooms in the hospital. Knocking at the door to announce us, I walked in, unsurprised to see Reaper, Jandro, and

Gunner, all having their ears examined by Dr. Brooks and two medics.

Hades and Freyja were in the room too, sitting calmly against the far wall.

"Mari, welcome back!" Dr. Brooks beamed at me as he pulled the otoscope from Reaper's ear and threw the disposable tip away. "Your sabbatical was enjoyable, I hope?"

"Uh…"

I couldn't pull my gaze away from Reaper, who stared at me wide-eyed, like I was a ghost. The Steel Demons president was still strikingly handsome but looked…awful. His eyes were bloodshot and rimmed with dark circles. His cheeks looked more sunken in, like he'd lost weight. And the smell of his clove cigarettes filled the room.

Jandro unfroze from his stupor first, pulling away from the medic to approach me and wrap me in a crushing hug.

I slid my arms around his broad back, letting myself lean into his strength. "I'm sorry," I whispered, only for him to squeeze me tighter.

"I'm so glad you're back, so glad you're okay," he rapidly muttered, his breaths tight. "Thank the gods, all of them. Jesus, him too."

Jandro's grip finally loosened on me with my tired laugh, and he immediately attacked Shadow with a violent, leaping bear hug that sent Shadow stumbling back a few steps.

"And holy shit it's good to see you again, big guy."

Shadow not only humored him with a returned hug,

but actually lifted Jandro off the floor with a throaty chuckle. "Missed you too, Jandro."

"Okay, now you're just embarrassing me. Put me down, asshole."

Dr. Brooks turned to me with a sheepish grin as Shadow placed Jandro back on the floor. "Should I leave you all alone for a bit?"

"Yeah, if you could, thanks." I pointed to my ear. "I think we're okay, but just to be sure—"

"Haven't found anything alarming yet, but we'll come back when you're ready." The doctor patted my arm and left the room, the medics following after him.

The door clicked softly closed and I was left alone with my men.

All of my men.

Shadow's presence at my back was like a shield, impenetrable and safe, while it was Reaper in front of me who I still felt unsure of. Fortunately for me, he looked just as unsure, and seemed content to hang back and say nothing.

I approached him first, slowly, as I would a cornered wild animal. He remained frozen stiff as I opened my arms to the sides and placed them around him in a loose hug. The contact seemed to shock life into him, a gasping breath leaving his lungs as his hands tentatively rested on my back.

I hugged him a little closer and he returned my gentle squeeze, thankfully not escalating to anything more. I wasn't sure if I could handle a kiss or an ass-grab from him yet. Before Shadow and I walked into this room, I wasn't sure if I still wanted to see him at all.

But the hug felt good, and the ache in my chest loosened. It was a first step I was willing to take, as long as he was respectful of my pace.

Reaper's cheek brushed against mine, seeking permission for a kiss. I took that as a cue to end the hug, stepping off to the side until he and Shadow faced each other head-on.

Reaper didn't look wounded at my rejection and released me without issue. A few tense seconds passed while the two men stared each other down, the Steel Demons president and the man he exiled. This time it was Shadow waiting to see how Reaper would react, the tension palpable on both of them.

Finally Reaper stepped forward, extending his hand. "I owe you one hell of an apology."

Shadow didn't answer, nor did he accept Reaper's hand. His mismatched eyes only flicked to Reaper's hand and then back up to his face as he continued to wait. The room was dead silent, but inside I was cheering. *Don't give him an inch. You deserve more,* I thought.

Reaper blew out a long breath. "I was wrong to exile you without properly considering the situation. We could have come to a different solution, like Mari had suggested at the time." He cocked his head toward me. "I was selfish and short-sighted to ignore you. I made you both suffer, and neither of you have any obligation to forgive me. But I see now how wrong I was and I'm deeply, deeply sorry."

While Shadow considered his words, my fingernails bit into my palms. Part of me wanted to hug him again —properly this time, as my husband. As I watched

Shadow accept his outstretched hand with a curt nod, I almost did. My hands even swung forward a tiny distance, but I drew them back.

The wound he caused was still there, a raw and vulnerable sensation in my body. It was healing, slowly. But these apologies had only slowed the bleeding. The hurt would need diligent, consistent care before it healed. And I still didn't know if he'd be patient enough to stick around long enough for that to happen.

"Thank you," I said softly and then, ready to move on for the moment, opened a cabinet to pull out a pair of gloves. "Now that that's out of the way, did we *all* hear crazy laughter and get bloody ears?"

"Felt like my head was getting bludgeoned from the inside," Jandro offered up.

The others nodded their agreement. "Thought I was a goner for sure," Gunner added softly.

So it was the same for all of us. I too felt that rattling, slamming pain inside my head and wondered if it would be our end right before we reached home. Shadow and I had been riding when it hit us, and he didn't want to stop and risk injuring us further. Somehow we both managed to stay on the bike until it stopped, and soon after that was when we found Gunner.

"And everyone feels okay now?" I took a spare otoscope from its hook on the wall and added a fresh tip to it, receiving nods from everyone in the room. "Did anyone aside from us experience this?"

My gut knew the answer even as the guys looked at each other before answering.

"I was just down the hall from here, visiting Slick," Jandro said. "He and his nurses weren't affected at all."

"Slick?" I repeated, staring at him. "Stephan? What happened to him?"

"Gunshot. He's fine." Jandro rubbed his eyes then pinched the bridge of his nose with a sigh. "It's a long story, *Mariposita*, but he's okay."

"I'll have to visit him later."

Jandro smiled tiredly. "He'd love that."

Reaper cleared his throat. "I was in the conference room with my dad and some lieutenants. I was the only one hearing it and freaking the fuck out."

"So we can safely assume it is just us." I turned around to find the ancient, penetrating stares of Hades and Freyja across the room. "Those of us who've heard the gods."

"Hades." Reaper regarded the dog cautiously, more so than I'd ever noticed before. He seemed almost afraid to touch Hades now. "Is there anything you can tell us about this?"

The time is nearly here.

Everyone in the room heard, as evident from their wide-eyed reactions. The chance of Hades answering a question always seemed slim, but he did not hold back now.

"The time for what?" Reaper asked.

The confrontation that will determine the fall or survival of all. Gods included.

My men and I all looked at each other, disbelief and worry settling over us with a heavy weight.

"That laughing sound, that pain, we all felt like we

were about to die," I lowered to a crouch on the floor, coming to eye level with Hades, "was it another god?"

Freyja stretched, her back arching as her curved claws extended.

It is like us, but different, she answered. *We do not know what name or face it takes, but it is a human concept that has personified and taken form.*

"What is that concept?" Shadow asked the question on everyone's mind.

Chaos. The reply came from Hades. *Senseless violence. And the destruction of everything in existence.*

———

I DID a preliminary check on all the guys' ear canals, then let Dr. Brooks check over them and me more thoroughly. By the time he cleared us, I was more than ready to go home.

Who was I kidding? I'd been ready to go home that first day I followed Horus into the great unknown. But every minute of that journey was worth it to have us all back under one roof. Even Reaper, as shaky as my trust in him still was. His presence too, felt comforting and *right* in our home.

"You probably know we're all dying to hear everything." Jandro cupped my hands as we walked inside, joy and relief washing over me at the sight of the familiar walls and fixtures. "But what do *you* need right now?"

"Hmm, excellent question." I pondered for a moment while letting my gaze bounce all over the familiar touches of our home—things I didn't even know I'd miss, like the bronze sculpture next to the stairs, and the throw pillows on the couch.

"A bath," I decided at last. "And then food, and then cuddles and a long night of sleep."

"You got it." Jandro kissed my forehead. "But tomorrow you and Shadow are telling us everything, deal?"

"Deal," I agreed, tilting my face up for a real kiss. "Fuck, I've missed you *guapito*.."

"*Bonita*, missing doesn't even come close." He wrapped me in a tight hug, kissing me deeply. "Even before you took off, shit wasn't right. It was just…wrong not having all of us here."

Gunner squeezed past us right then, sending back a lighthearted smile. "I'll get the tub filled for you, baby girl."

"Thank you, Gun." A pang cut through my chest. Reaper was usually the one I took baths with. Things still weren't all better, but I hoped they would be soon.

I *did* want Reaper back. I wanted to believe he truly saw how wrong he'd been and felt remorseful. I just… couldn't yet.

He and Shadow did seem to be getting along fine, though. The door leading out to the garage was slightly ajar, and I heard them both tending to the bikes and unpacking supplies.

"You want a different bedroom?" Reaper asked gruffly. "We can trade, if you want."

"I'm okay with keeping it, but maybe ask Mari," Shadow answered. "If she's comfortable being in there,

I can just rearrange the furniture to make it feel different."

"Sure."

Reaper sounded anything but sure about talking to me again, and guilt sliced through me at the uncertainty in his voice. Once so confident and self-assured, the Steel Demons president had nearly lost everything and couldn't seem to find his footing again. With the chaos and senseless violence to come, he *needed* to be able to lead.

I got my towel and headed for the bathroom with the now-filled tub of deliciously hot water, undressing once the door closed.

"He needs *me*," I said aloud as I stepped into the water. "But what about what *I* need?" My chuckle echoed off the bathroom walls at this conversation with myself. Maybe that laughing, chaos god had shaken some things loose up there.

"If he's still the man I fell in love with," I muttered, sliding my legs through the water, "he knows I'll need time to let this go. And he's strong enough to carry us all through whatever comes next."

The longer I soaked in the tub, the smell of spices and marinated meat wafting in from the kitchen became stronger and more decadent. I scrubbed and rinsed off when I couldn't stand it anymore, then quickly toweled off and pulled on a robe to join my men in the kitchen.

"There she is." Jandro beamed from across the counter, steadfastly chopping a head of lettuce. "Hope you're in the mood for tostadas."

"I'm in the mood for anything you serve on a plate."

I ran a hand across the back of Shadow's shoulders, who was already seated and scooping up the remains of his tostada with his tortilla shell. His hair was damp and he smelled freshly showered. I pressed a kiss to the corner of his mouth before moving on to Gunner.

"How was your bath?" My golden, beautiful man leaned back and tilted his lips up, a different question in his sky-blue eyes.

"Wonderful." I planted a chaste kiss on his lips, not wanting to rub our affection in Reaper's face, who appeared hyper-focused on his own food and whiskey in front of him.

"Shadow was just saying he was restoring bikes out at the service center he was at." Jandro waved his chopping knife at him in a mock threat. "Trying to put me out of business, homie?"

"Like you even have a business," Shadow taunted back.

Gunner and I nearly choked on our food laughing, and even Reaper chuckled at Jandro's open-mouthed, exaggerated horror.

"Out!" Jandro pointed the knife out the window to the backyard. "Get out of my house. You're sleeping with the chickens tonight."

"Mari will come out with me. Would you do that to her?"

"Don't drag *me* into this!" I shrieked, swatting Shadow's arm.

The jokes, the food, the stories—all of it was cozy, blissful normalcy for the next hours. Even Reaper was not completely sullen and silent, making playful jabs at

Jandro and laughing occasionally. I couldn't tell if it was intentional on the others' part or it just happened, but as dinner wound down and the guys dispersed, Reaper and I ended up in the kitchen alone together.

"I'll wash those. You should rest." Reaper placed a light touch on my waist, but otherwise gave me space in front of the sink.

"It's okay." I gave him a tight smile over my shoulder, but found myself feeling bashful at how intensely he looked at me. "Gives me something to take my mind off looming chaos and destruction, you know?"

"Right," he said with a forced scoff, but stayed hovering behind me.

I returned my attention to washing the dishes, unsure of what else to do under his heavy gaze. A few agonizingly long seconds passed, and it seemed like neither of us could handle the tension any longer.

"Reaper—" I started to turn to him.

"Mari—" He said my name at the same time, reaching for my hand. "Go ahead," he urged with a small nod of his head.

"No, you." I brushed my hand alongside his, my heartbeat accelerating at the contact. "I'm…not even sure what I want to say."

Reaper pulled in a deep breath, his fingers curling around mine for a loose, gentle hold. "Whatever Shadow needs, I'm willing to help. I'll listen to you, and to him. I know it's not worth much right now, but you have my word." His grip tightened on my hand just slightly. "And I have been taking the consequences to my actions into account since realizing how wrong I was. Not just in personal matters, but everything."

I listened with rapt attention, watching his full lips move and seeing the sincerity in his eyes as he spoke. I swallowed, nodding as my pulse stabilized just slightly.

"Thank you for saying that."

My fingers stretched for release, the heat from him too intense, and he removed his grip quickly. I wrung my hands in front of me instead, dropping my gaze from his.

Who am I? I used to have no problem standing up to him, telling him exactly what I thought with no filter. I didn't recognize this meek, insecure person I turned into, only in front of him.

He hurt me and I'm still licking my wounds.

"Wait," I said just as Reaper was about to turn away.

He spun back around, hope bright in his green eyes. "Yes?"

"I…" My throat clammed up and I forced out breath before trying again. "I…haven't given up…on us. I just—I just need time. I don't want to be angry at you anymore, it's just…"

"It's okay, Mari." He returned to stand directly in front of me, feet nearly touching mine. "This is on me to fix." Reaper reached for one of my hands tentatively again, allowing plenty of slack for me to pull away if I wanted to. "It's on me to earn your trust again. To—" His voice cracked and he swallowed. "To win back your love again."

My next breath released a little more of the painful

ache in my chest, and I lightly squeezed his fingers. "One day at a time, right?"

"Absolutely." Reaper smiled and sent my heart fluttering again. He was always so broody and serious, I forgot how beautiful his genuine smiles were. "For now, I'm just happy you're home safe. And that you're talking to me again."

"Me too."

I kept still as he leaned down slowly, giving me every opportunity to move or stop him. But I had no desire to. I even lifted my chin slightly, so his kiss could land on my forehead.

It wasn't much, and he didn't try for more. But that small, sweet gesture took me one step closer to healing.

To forgiving.

SHADOW

"Come in," I said to the knock at my door, setting down the pieces of my tattoo machine.

The door swung open to show Reaper standing hesitantly in my doorway. "Hey. Mari said she's fine with this room, given that, you know, it changes up a little." His eyes swept over my furniture. "Which I can see you've already done."

"It wasn't difficult," I said, leaning away from my desk. "Jandro and I did it in an afternoon."

The desk had now been pushed against the opposite wall as before, just below the window. It worked out better this way. I liked using natural light when I sketched tattoos. My bed, dresser, and side tables had all been shifted to different walls and configurations too. It felt like a completely different room from before, one that I hoped Mari would feel safe spending time with me in.

"Good. Great." Reaper leaned a forearm against the

door jam. "And we can still trade rooms later, if Mari ever changes her mind."

"Sure." I watched him, his body language curious to me. "I'm sure she knows that."

"Yeah." Reaper hovered in my doorway, not entirely comfortable, but in no rush to leave.

"Was there anything else, president?"

"Oh! Yeah." He snapped his fingers. "I swung by the seamstress today. We got you a cut and she's going to embroider all your patches, matching the original designs. You'll be properly covered by the end of the week."

"Uh, thank you, president." I couldn't hide that I was taken aback. "So, you're not putting it to a church vote?"

"Nah." Reaper shook his head. "It's not club business. It was—" He ran a hand over his jaw, pulling in a deep breath. "It was my foolish and short-sighted actions that led to your exile. The club's got nothing to do with it, this was my error." His hand dropped to his side as he leveled a heavy gaze on me. "I'm just trying to make things right."

"Reaper, you don't have to…" I stood abruptly from my desk, feeling like this conversation needed a better setting than my bedroom. "Is anyone else home?"

He looked over his shoulder, arm still propped up in my doorway. "Don't think so. Why?"

I angled my head toward the kitchen. "Want to have a drink?"

A smirk crossed his face and he thumped the wood of my door frame. "Hell yes I do."

Moments later, we were seated next to each other at the breakfast bar, each with our own glass of whiskey and the bottle between us. The house was quiet, with only the clucking and occasional squawk from Jandro's chickens in the backyard.

"I never blamed you for exiling me," I said to pick up where we left off. "I was never angry at *you*, Reaper."

"Doesn't change that it was wrong." He shifted his glass in a sunbeam on the counter, watching it throw light reflections everywhere. "Mari was pissed at me, and rightfully so."

"I had no idea." I turned my own glass, the amber liquid sliding around. "That everything was so bad here. I thought you would all just…move on like I was never here."

Reaper shook his head, throwing back his whiskey in one gulp before slamming it down and pouring another. "Even before I made you leave, I knew Mari would be pissed for a while. She fought me on it every step of the way. But I just…" His palms flopped to the countertop, staring at his whiskey like it had suddenly become unappetizing. "The truth of it is, I wasn't thinking of anyone but myself. I told myself and anyone who would listen, that it was for her. Her safety and wellbeing, but really, it was just me grasping for control. And you, her, the other guys," he sighed, "you all got caught in the crossfire of my selfishness."

I sipped on my whiskey to let his words sink in. "I appreciate you saying that. It still wasn't wrong for you to be concerned about her safety. If you still are—"

"I'm not." Reaper shook his head, tight-lipped. "Not when it comes to you being with her."

"I still am," I admitted. "I've got a better handle on my sleepwalking now, but the nightmares will probably never fully go away. I want measures in place so she can get away from me if something happens."

"We'll think of something." Reaper rubbed his chin. "Jandro can probably rig a panic button or whatever. You've got us supporting you, man."

"Thank you." I polished off my whiskey, my anxiety releasing its grip on my chest as the liquid heat made its way to my belly. "I mean it, Reaper. Thank you."

The president inclined his head, peering at me with an odd smile. "You know why I trust her with you? The real reason?"

I just stared back at him, unsure of what he was getting at.

Reaper's smile grew, eyes on his whiskey as he swirled it around. "I saw what you did to that guy who shot her."

My eyes narrowed, confused. "You mean…at the service center?"

Reaper nodded, biting his lip like he knew some tantalizing secret. "I saw when he had the gun pointed at her head. And then you ran out there so fucking fast and silent, like a black blur. Well, a shadow." He laughed, bringing the glass of whiskey to his lips. "I saw you turn the guy's head into raw hamburger meat. Skull and brains flying everywhere, it was beautiful."

"How?" I demanded, equally perturbed and fascinated. "Through Horus?"

"No." Reaper downed his glass. "Through the eyes of a dead man on the porch."

"A dead man?" I repeated. Then it hit me. "Hades?"

"Yeah." He scoffed like he couldn't believe it himself. "Seems he was waiting for the perfect moment to show me that little trick."

"You can see through the dead," I said, mostly to cement the reality for myself.

"And what I saw was you," Reaper pointed at me, "unleashing hell to protect the woman you love. Your wife."

My wife. A warmth spread through my belly that had nothing to do with the alcohol.

"I barely remember doing it," I admitted. "I saw he was about to shoot her and it was like instinct took over."

"Even better." Reaper leaned back in his seat. "I'm no scientist, but in my opinion, that means even at the subconscious, cellular level, despite all this other shit you've got going on, you'll do anything to protect Mari." He reached over and slapped my shoulder. "That is why I'm not worried about her safety with you."

"Thanks, Reaper." I understood and appreciated what he meant, but I was still stuck on the whole *seeing through the dead* thing. "Do the others know? About your…sight?"

"Yeah, we were gonna tell you and Mari once you all got settled in." Reaper tilted back on the rear legs of his barstool.

"Have you…used it again?"

He nodded, looking at nothing straight ahead of

him. "Jandro and Slick got ambushed last week and I looked through some of the dead at that scene. Blakeworth guys, not ours." He let out a weary sigh. "It doesn't feel right to look through our own men after they've passed. Like it's invasive and they deserve to rest."

"Who did we lose?"

"Brick, his nephew, couple others." Reaper scrubbed a hand down his face. "Jandro had to leave them to bring Slick back to the hospital. It'll be suicide to get the others' bodies, as much as it sickens me to leave them out there."

"We'll still hold memorials for them. We can do it here at the house."

Reaper nodded. "Governor Vance wants to put a memorial plaque in the City Hall building. Their names and the date and everything."

"That's nice of him to do."

"Yeah, he's a good guy."

Silence hung over us for a few moments, in this rare display of…could this be called friendship?

I didn't know if I'd ever considered Reaper a friend before. In the years I spent in the club, he and I never shared a drink just between us like this. I was his assassin, and he was my president. I knew my role, my usefulness. He had my complete respect and trust as a leader, but it was Jandro who I turned to when ordinary things confused me. Likewise, Reaper treated me with the same cordiality as everyone else in the club, but I wasn't constantly rubbing shoulders with him like Jandro and Gunner.

Now we shared nearly everything. A home, a wife. And now a bottle of whiskey.

"This ability of yours," I said, breaking the silence. "Do you think it'll be useful in…what's coming next?"

Reaper refilled our whiskeys as he answered. "You mean all the fucking enemies surrounding us, or this manifestation of chaos and destruction coming for everyone?"

I shrugged. "Do we know they're completely separate issues?"

"You know." Reaper straightened, his gaze down in his whiskey as he pondered. "They're probably not." He took a quick sip and added, "You know, fuck it. I'll bet you they're not."

"I agree with you." I swirled my own whiskey. "If we have gods working with us, it only makes sense there could be gods working against us."

"Fuck, man," Reaper huffed. "With you, Mari, and Horus back, and now this crazy sight thing, I just…hope we can turn the tide on this war. Because let me tell you, it has been *rough* being without all of you here. These last few weeks have been like we're fighting blind, then our arms are tied up, then our toes get broken, then we catch a cold, and it's just non-fucking-stop."

"We are stronger together," I agreed. "Not just the Steel Demons, but *us*."

"Yeah." He gave a wry smile. "Our little family." His smile faded and his gaze flicked away, as if temporarily in pain.

"She will forgive you," I said. "She's trying."

"I know. It's not even about that, really." Reaper

rubbed his mouth. "Not to make this into a woe-is-me bitch-fest, but with all the gods and the crazy shit we've seen? I wish I could undo it all. Hurting her. Exiling you." He leaned his forehead into his hand. "This is the probably the most valuable lesson I'll ever learn, but fuck, I just wish you two didn't have to suffer for me to learn it."

"It wasn't just you that learned an important lesson," I said. "I wouldn't be sitting here if I was still stuck in my old thinking pattern."

"Oh yeah?" Reaper leaned his temple on his fist to look at me. "What did you learn?"

I sipped my whiskey as I thought of how to sum up all the ways that Doc and Mari had changed me.

"That I'm not everything my past told me I was," I decided. "I'm not inherently evil just because I'm a man. I don't *have* to believe in all of the abuse I internalized. My thoughts about myself aren't always true." My gaze dropped to my whiskey glass, swirling around the last sip. "And I don't have to sabotage happiness for myself. I...have a right to be happy."

"Damn right you do." Reaper slapped my shoulder again. "Shit, I know a few people who could afford to learn that." His face was flushed from alcohol, his voice growing louder and more boisterous as it often did when he drank. But then he lowered his voice again, his face serious. "I never did say thank you, Shadow."

"For what?"

"Just," he flung his hands up, "for being you. For being there for Mari, being someone she needed. For loving her when she couldn't rely on me."

"Reap—"

"Don't fight me on this. Just, thank you, Shadow."

The front door lock turned right then and opened, Mari and Jandro's voices floating across the house a moment later.

"Where have you two been?" Reaper nearly stumbled sliding off his stool but quickly saved himself.

"Shopping." Jandro dumped four large bags of groceries on the counter. "Now that we're feeding two-and-half more people again," he added with a wink at me.

"You talking about that spare tire you're growing?" I jabbed a hand out to slap his stomach, earning a glare in return.

"No, I'm talking about you, Hulk-Smash! And it's still winter, okay? My fluff adds a protective layer of warmth."

"Shadow!" Mari came in with the rest of the bags, digging into the bottom of one with a determined grin on her face. "Have you ever had goat cheese?"

"No." I leaned across the counter to kiss her. "Is it much different from regular cheese?"

She groaned into my kiss, taking a small bite of my lip. "It is a whole other *level* of cheese! Hey, why do you taste like whiskey?"

"We've been catching up," Reaper said, hovering nearby. He relaxed when Mari turned to squeeze him in a brief hug.

"Is Gunner still at City Hall?" Mari asked. Her arms loosened around Reaper, but didn't entirely let go.

"Think so." Reaper draped an arm around her shoulders, his gaze at her full of longing. "Why?"

She looked back at me. "Did you tell him while you were catching up?"

"Not yet," I said. "I wanted to wait until we were all together."

"Tell me what?" Reaper's eyes flicked up to me.

"Go ahead, Mari." I started digging through one grocery bag to help with the unloading, curious about this goat cheese she was so wild about.

Mari pulled away from Reaper and made sure Jandro was listening too. "I know the oncoming war is going to be rough, but we *do* have allies out there. They helped Shadow and I break through Tash's army on our ride back."

"Well shit, don't leave us in suspense now." Jandro made a valiant attempt at juggling bell peppers and promptly dropped all of them.

"Jerriton," Mari said.

Reaper looked confused. "I thought the territory was under Tash's control."

"It is, but the *people* of Jerriton don't support him. Why would they? Gunner's uncle mistreated them, and a bunch of them were in prison under Tash's rule."

"We broke them out," I added. "At first only to create a distraction, but they overwhelmed the border patrol and allowed us to escape the territory."

"They escorted us all the way to neutral territory," Mari said. "They're wanted fugitives in Jerriton now, but they're crafty, and there are a *lot* of them."

"Damn," Jandro muttered.

"Fuck," Reaper agreed. "This…could be huge. We gotta tell Dad and Gunner."

Mari squeezed another hug around him. "We can win this, guys. Whatever happens, we're strongest together."

Reaper rested his chin on her head, soaking up and returning the embrace. "I do believe that now, more than ever."

Epilogue

HADES

Horus's presence was frazzled, energy coming off of him in harsh waves of tension as we watched over the humans. The falcon body he inhabited couldn't sleep, its feathers puffed out and eyes still alert, despite the darkness of night. Freyja noticed it too.

"What's troubling you?" she asked him.

"We've reached that point," he answered. "It's a black wall from here. Not even we can see what happens next. Without our foresight, I'm concerned about the humans."

Gods existed outside of the bounds of time. Since our inception, we had seen all that occurred up to this point. But from now in the present, we could look back, but see no further ahead.

Whatever happened next would depend on them, these humans we had formed bonds with.

"They will prevail," Freyja said. "They have each other. They have love."

She reached out toward the sleeping humans. We

didn't have bodies, or forms in the physical sense, but her presence drifted over the three people in the bed. As if prompted by Freyja, the two men, Jandro and Gunner, scooted closer to Mariposa, wrapping tighter around her with their limbs. Freyja's cat form purred contently at the foot of the bed.

"It doesn't matter what happens next," I said. "All that is meant to happen will happen. They will prevail, or this will be the beginning of human extinction. And ours."

Gods didn't die. We either existed, sustained by human belief, or we faded into obscurity. Sometimes gods were renewed, rediscovered long after their followers' devotion faded into nothing. But if there were no humans left at all, we were done for.

No god had a chance of re-emerging from nothing. We arose from thoughts and ideas. Our inception began when humans took a sharp evolutionary path away from the other animals. When they began learning, conceptualizing, and scheming.

"Come now, Hades," Freyja chided me. "It's alright for you to admit you've grown attached to them. Even your reaper, as bullheaded as he is."

I did not answer, merely observed the humans in their sleep state. Many thousands of generations ago, Reaper's ancestors invoked me into existence. They entrusted me with their dead, and gave me the purpose of shepherding souls into a final resting place. To ensure the balance, I entrusted human reapers to take lives as needed. This one, supposedly the last one I would need to carry out my hand, was one of the worst I encountered.

Historically, humans had been honored to carry out my commands. The balance of survival was so delicate—billions of threads intertwining into a rich, complex fabric. Plucking the wrong one could send the whole thing crashing down, plunging all beings into nonexistence. Reaper's stubbornness almost did that, more than once. For all their innovation and brilliance, human beings were just as remarkably good at destroying themselves.

And in spite of it, I did grow attached to him and the humans he surrounded himself with. I wanted these people to survive, to leave their mark on history and carry their species into a new age. Not only because their survival preserved the existence of gods, but because these five infernal, short-sighted, ridiculous creatures were willing to fight for it.

I recognized devotion when I saw it. The devotion of these humans to each other and to their cause was awe-inspiring, even to us gods. It was no fault of theirs that the whole of human existence rested on them. The balance had been sliding toward chaos for generations, and the tipping point just happened to be in their lifetime.

"We have done all we can for them," I ultimately said in response to Freyja's remark. "We have put them through trials, and all have emerged victorious. They have our eyes, our wings, and our hearts. Now the choice is theirs—to fight for humanity, or submit to the chaos."

Just at the fringes of my perception, I felt the ghostly echo of wild, uncontrollable laughter creeping in.

TO BE CONTINUED IN RUTHLESS - STEEL DEMONS MC BOOK 8

PRE-ORDER RUTHLESS HERE

Acknowledgments

Another Steel Demons MC book, another wrenching of my soul through my fingertips. Thank you reader, for journeying through Shadow's backstory and his return to his place at Mari's side! There is still healing to be done and a war to fight, so I hope you'll hang in with me. We have two more books to go and I still have a little left to throw at these characters…

For regular updates, exclusive teasers, and excerpts, join my reader group, Crystal's Coven. We're a friendly bunch, and I'm always posting in the Coven first before anywhere else online.

A special thank you to my pack--Kathryn, Aleera, and Lana for listening to my whining and keeping me accountable. I love you babes.

Telisha, Janet, and Izzy, thank you for being such amazing cheerleaders, friends, and confidants throughout the evolution of this series. You all help me write the best books I possibly can!

I rarely thank my husband in these parts (oops!) but he deserves a shoutout for his endless patience and support.

It's not easy dealing with a writer spouse, so thank you, Mr. Ash for allowing me to sometimes neglect you for my fictional characters. You're my favorite happily-ever-after and I love you.

See you all in the next book!

-Crystal

About the Author

Crystal Ash is a USA Today Bestselling Author from California. She loves writing steamy, heart-wrenching romance with tortured heroes, especially if they're in a reverse harem. Crystal's other loves include animals, mythology, and well-crafted alcohol, most of which can also be found in her stories.

When she's not writing, she's probably drinking craft beer with her husband or trying to coax her feral cat into accepting affection.

crystalashbooks.com

facebook.com/Crystal.Ash.Romance

instagram.com/crystalashbooks

amazon.com/author/crystalash

bookbub.com/profile/crystal-ash